The Bridge to Home

A.F. JORDAN

The Bridge to Home
A.F. Jordan© 2016

All rights reserved. No portion of this book may be reproduced, stored in a retrieval system, or transmitted in any form or by any means—electronic, mechanical, photocopy, recording, scanning, or other—except for brief quotations in critical reviews or articles, without the prior written permission of the publisher.

Publisher's note: This novel is a work of fiction. Names, characters, places, and incidents are either products of the author's imagination or used fictitiously. All characters are fictional, and any similarity to people, living or dead, is purely coincidental.

Cover design by Astute Communications at www.astute.co
Interior design by Renee Evans at www.eneeevansdesign.com

ISBN-13: 978-1-4245-5137-8

Printed in the United States of America

For My Tribe

The Eastern Mountain Lion, *Puma concolor couguar*, is known by many names: cougar, catamount, puma, panther, or painter as the mountain folk say. Some call it ghost cat. Once the most widely distributed land mammal in the Western Hemisphere, cougars have been eliminated in most of their native habitat. The United States Fish and Wildlife Service considers them to have been extinct in the Appalachians since early in the 20th century. The people who live in the mountains tell a different story, however, and unsubstantiated sightings continue to be reported. . . .

PART 1

THE MAIDEN

Shaggy winter ponies toss their manes in the icy wind, running the ridge line of a jagged mountain. A young girl, clad in skins, hunched against the cold sky, watches hungrily from the low-hanging branch of a tree. If she could jump a ride on one of them, she might make it home before she froze to death. She'd seen others do it in the summer, waiting quietly until the wild horses passed under and then dropping lightly onto their backs and grabbing hold of their tangled manes as they tore away. She didn't know if it would work now, when the ponies were so cold and her fingers were so numb, but it was her only hope. It was almost dark and she had nothing with which to make fire. She'd seen what happened when people froze to death and she was afraid. The stiff, hollow-eyed corpses of shepherds, hoarfrost clinging to their hair, their skin blue and translucent, were sometimes dragged into the village in spring, after they failed to return with their flocks.

Before the shudder from that horrid remembrance had rippled through her small body, a beautiful white pony was almost beneath her and running at a fast trot, tossing his head from side to side. "Andraste! Help me!" She whispered as she dropped onto his back, startling the pony and causing him to buck and then break into a run. The girl's body slid to the side and she almost lost her grip on the shaggy mane, but in her panic she found her power. "No," she shouted emphatically as she pulled herself up onto the back of the frightened animal. The pony was running at a full gallop now, toward a grove of giant hemlocks. The little one leaned down and gripped his strong neck with both her hands and began to sing into his fur. Her voice, tremulous and keening at first, settled into a melody. As her own panic quieted, so did the pony's. Just as they entered the grove, the animal slowed to a trot and then a walk. "There now, that's a good one, it is," she crooned into his velvet ear and turned him gently around and headed in the direction of her village.

"Gael!"

She could hear frantic voices screaming in the cold night under bobbing torchlight, as she and the pony topped the last hill and her village came into view below.

"Gael! Where are you?" The little one threw her head back and laughed with delight and relief. She wouldn't die tonight after all and they had missed her.

Digging her heels in, she whispered to her savior, "Come Gruffyn, take me home."

The child came thundering into the village, clutching the long ropey mane of a snow white pony. Her mother, who had passed through hysteria into catatonia since the child had gone missing hours ago, rose from her stupor and pushed her way through the throng of villagers, who were shouting with jubilation. Little Gael sat her pony triumphantly, amidst her neighbors, a broad gap-toothed smile lighting up her small face. In the torchlight, she was radiant, a little queen.

Her mother stumbled through the crowd and gathered her daughter into her arms, roughly pulling the child from the animal and making her cry out.

"Hush," she said into Gael's auburn hair. "Hush now, you're home."

"Mama, you're squeezing me," came the child's muffled response. And then, "Wait! We can't leave Gruffyn. He saved me!" The pony had already been secured and was being led away for the night, munching contentedly on a handful of hay.

"We'll see him in the morning, my bad, bad girl."

Gael gave way to tears then, seeing how she'd frightened her mother... how close she'd come to losing her.

Years went by and Gael grew into a beautiful and sturdy young woman whose headstrong ways often piqued her mother.

"Mama," she said one day, out of the blue, "I'm going on a quest."

"What are you talking about, Gael?"

"I'm taking Gruffyn and we're going to see the wide world."

"In the name of Brighde child! You're not yet grown yourself and that poor pony is an old man."

"Mama, I am so grown. I'm fourteen. And Gruffyn is stalwart, you know that. He proves his mettle every day."

"So, just where will you be going on this quest of yours?"

"Don't know. Wherever the wind blows us."

"Sometimes I think the wind blows right through your empty head," muttered her mother. "Will you kindly bring in the water before you go."

"Of course," As she stood in the doorway she looked back and said, "I love you, Mama. Don't forget that."

Her mama shook her head and laughed. "What a strange girl you are."

Later that night, after her mother was asleep and the village was quiet, after the silver moon was hung round and full in the clear sky, Gael climbed down from her sleeping loft, retrieved her burlap sack from its hiding place under the covers, and with a fond glance toward her mother, slipped off into the night, leading Gruffyn quietly with a hand on his neck, never dreaming that this would be the last she'd ever see of her home, her mama or her beloved village. She was off to claim her place in the wide world. Off on a quest.

Chapter 1

Jane May Gideon was haggard and heartbroken and nearly fifty with a faint smell of burning bridges streaming behind her like tattered ribbons when she pulled into the town of Gideon, North Carolina. The first rays of dawn crept over the peaks of the Blue Ridge Mountains. Leaving everything she had ever known behind her, and driving all night, she might have been more depressed than she actually was. No one could blame her if she had been, but the thing about Jane May Gideon was that, in spite of everything, she was an optimist. Though this infernal optimism didn't always suit her, it seemed to be permanently entangled in her nature.

Jane May Gideon was no Pollyanna. This was not blind, youthful optimism. This was not *look on the sunny side* gratuitous gaiety. She was not concerned with silver linings or any of that nonsense. No, Jane could be as curmudgeonly negative as the next tired, slightly overweight, middle-aged divorcee. She could slide down into the abyss of existential anguish with the best of them. She just couldn't stay there. She was buoyant, dammit. Like Virginia Woolf, she would fill her pockets with stones of sorrow and loss and wade out into the water to drown and she would go under just like anyone would with pockets full of despair. She just couldn't stay under. Infuriatingly, as if she had polka-dotted, air-filled floaties sewn into her damn clothes, she would pop up out of the depths, and with a sigh, she would drag herself out of the water, shake off and get on with it.

The problem with maintaining a crushing sense of doom on *this* morning was Spring. It was late April and these mountains were so alive! The tender green woods were dappled with dogwood blossoms and blushing redbud trees. Jonquils bobbed their heads on the roadside. Trees quivered and sang, sap rising, branches stretching and reaching for the sun. Birds chattered as they scooped up worms for breakfast. The soft morning sun glinted off water in ponds and tumbling creeks, and those mountains! Rising up, ridge after ridge, scalloped blue and hazy, the ancient peaks abiding, as they had for tens of thousands of years, resplendent in the morning light. Jane May's eyes were wide with wonder at the glory of this brand new day.

But wouldn't someplace flat and dusty and hot have better suited her state of mind? With swarms of mosquitos and the occasional lonely tumbleweed stumbling by? Hadn't that been her plan? To go west? How in the world had Jane May arrived in this holy hell of a paradise?

What could she have been thinking three days ago when she had angrily announced, to no one in particular, at the coffee shop down the street from her apartment, "Tell you what I'd do, I'd get out of this podunk town and go see the wide world." She had looked around, embarrassed, to see if anyone had heard her. She couldn't be sure. Actually she couldn't be sure of anything anymore, but it seemed that the man in the corner, sipping a cappuccino, had dived a little deeper into his newspaper and the two young mothers, wearily comparing cute toddler tales, had definitely looked a tiny bit askance at her for not quite keeping up appearances in public. People whose lives were the most haphazardly held together seemed the quickest to pass judgement on others when the facade of wellbeing began to crack. As if Jane May's falling apart could start a chain reaction, putting their own carefully constructed reality in jeopardy, the two young women sprang into action, forming a water brigade of disapproving looks to wet down their own roofs before the flames could reach them.

That was what it was like when you lived in the same small southern town where you were born and raised and your house caught fire. All the neighbors showed up to gawk. Sure some of them would wrap you in a blanket and give you a hug, maybe bring a pot of soup, but they'd soon be calling each other and reveling in the review of your behavior during the crisis. Jane May longed to burn in anonymous obscurity.

"Yes," she heard herself say on that fateful morning, to no one in particular, "it's time to go." Maybe she was trying to prove to herself that she had a plan. Of course she had no plan, but she did have pride, and now, having voiced her intention aloud and in front of people, she had singlehandedly driven herself into a corner. There was nothing to do now but pull up and go. So after throwing everything she could think that she might need for who knows how long into her car, and opening the atlas at random to North Carolina and having Gideon just jump off the page at her

... *That's my name. Well, his name* ... here she was, two days later, on the edge of the Smoky Mountains, on a beautiful spring morning, exhausted, disoriented and gnawed to the bone.

And free. Jane May Gideon had never felt freer than she did at this moment.

Or more alone.

The parking lot was gravel and overhung with blooming apple tree branches. Clumps of soft clover sprouted here and there. The sign on the highway had said:

Old Mountain Inn
Come Home to the Land of Blue Smoke
Clean. Cheap. No Phones.

Jane May's weary soul longed for home. *Home*. She had loved to roll the roundness of it around in her mouth like a fat, ripe grape, anticipating the sweet release of juice. Now the word caught in her throat.

Jane May Gideon had come from a place of sturdy ancient oaks and mild sea breezes. Snowy egrets, gulls and pelicans patrolled blue skies, billowy with clouds, floating above Spanish moss-draped mysteries. A place where roots ran deep and home was where you were born and where you died. Where elegant antebellum houses stood like proud southern ladies in susurrating hoop skirts, hiding secrets under secrets, under secrets. Shhh.

Jane May Gideon had done that which simply wasn't done in her world. She'd pulled up roots. And she felt those ragged fibers now like raw nerves, for the first time exposed to air.

The low slung weathered log buildings with green shutters and trim were comforting, the faded red Adirondack chairs lined up across the front porch were friendly and hopeful.

"You lookin' for Mai Zinni?"

Jane May bumped her head on the doorframe of her car as she was getting out. She hadn't noticed anyone outside when she pulled in. Looking around, she couldn't immediately tell where the disembodied voice had come from.

"She's gone off," came from the shadows near the front door where an old man sat on a fat slice of a tree, carving something small with a pocketknife. Curly, white shavings lay all around him in the grass.

"I'd like to rent a room," she said, thinking that the man seemed a little off. What was he talking about anyway? She was too tired to wonder at this point.

"For how long?" The bent over man had neither looked up nor stopped peeling off wood.

The question threw Jane. She had no idea . . . . All she wanted was to sleep.

"Maybe a day or two."

"Only rent by the week," still not looking at her, "hunnert and fifty."

"A week?

"Yep."

"All right, fine. Do you have internet?"

"No'm." A man of few words, this one seemed, but then he added, "Mai Zinni'll be back in a day or so. She'll see you then."

"I'm sorry, what's that?" Irritation rose in Jane May's throat and prickled the hair on her forearms. "I have no idea who you're talking about."

"Oh, well." Infuriatingly, the old man was smiling. "I thought you was looking for her."

"Why would I be looking for someone I've never heard of?" She snapped at the poor man before she could stop herself. After a deep steadying breath she said, "I'm sorry," carefully modulating her voice and hoping at least to appear calm. "I'm very tired and I just need some sleep and I don't know who you're talking about."

The man didn't elaborate and Jane May didn't care much by now, so a deal was struck, a key handed over, and out of nowhere a small, brown-skinned boy appeared and carried her luggage around the front building, past three others, and down a path into a hollow with a clear running stream at the bottom. They crossed a wooden footbridge that spanned the stream and there, nestled into the trees, was a squat little stone cottage that might have come right out of the pages of a fairy tale. In spite of herself, Jane gasped in delight, spreading her arms and turning slowly to take it all in.

The cottage was made of smooth stones and wood with an arched front door of heavy oak that was almost hidden off to one side of the small porch. Overhanging vines and a small round window completed the enchanting tableau. Moving her purse to the other shoulder and balancing a box of provisions on her hip, Jane fumbled in her pocket for the key the old man had given her.

"It ain't locked," said the boy, stepping around her, shouldering the door open and setting her two bags down on the floor next to a stone fireplace. Diffuse green light crept in through various windows, including the round porthole by the front door, giving a sense that the room was under water. Jane May Gideon giggled with delight as she sucked her cheeks in and opened and closed her lips, presenting to the boy a tired, middle-aged woman, imitating a fish. He smiled and responded in kind, getting the joke. After handing the boy a couple of crumpled dollar bills from her pocket, Jane May closed the door, opened the two casement windows over the well-worn sea-green sofa, and set sail to the sound of rushing water for the land of nod.

The moon hung full and round and golden-orange. Under it, a hill with the flickering glow of firelight behind, creating a halo effect. She walked barefoot, the grass beneath her feet cool, soft, and springy. When she topped the hill she saw the fire—a large bonfire with the logs laid tepee style. As she came closer, sparks, no, fireflies emanated from the blaze, making a sound like bzzz-pop. As they popped, they took off, wheeling up, up, up in the sky toward the huge ball of the moon.

Jane May awoke with a start, the word *Rise* hanging in the air, as if someone had spoken sharply in her ear. She was wide awake, but unsure, for a few seconds, of where she was. Images tumbled around her, flashing, and then rolling out of sight . . . a large cat, amber eyes piercing, someone dancing in the firelight, bending low and muttering . . . something?

Shaking off the dream, Jane May Gideon sat up, stretched, and began, for the first time in several hours, to assess her situation.

Forty-nine years old, married more than twenty-five years, suddenly, against her will, single again. The last time she'd been a single woman she was barely even a woman, more of a child, at the tender age of twenty-four. She'd been snared and tamed before she was even aware of her own wild nature. So here she sat, in a strange little house, behind a rundown inn, somewhere in the mountains of North Carolina, far from her home and the only life she'd ever known. Alone, her luggage at her feet, hot tears sliding down her face, Jane May Gideon struggled to find her bearings in the watery green light.

She'd paid for a week so it was settled then, she'd stay for a week. "Might as well make yourself at home," she said aloud, standing and brushing away the tears.

The little house was small, but snug. It almost seemed to embrace her. There was a good energy here. Lately, since she'd been on her own, she'd begun to feel her intuition returning. She knew it had always been there, but she had stopped listening long ago. When? She could not even remember, but it was coming back now and she welcomed it like a long lost friend. That voice deep inside her that knew things. Knew, for instance, that this stone cottage in the woods, in the mountains, was a safe, sweet place to be until she could somehow find some ground under her feet again.

Chapter 2

John Hawkes pushed the buttons on his cell phone, wondering why in tarnation they had to be so small. How was a full-grown man supposed to manage this little thing? Everything, it seemed lately, rubbed him wrong, like a tomcat being brushed all cattywompus.

He needed the revenue, but this fractious woman arriving unannounced first thing in the morning and wanting a room had thrown him off his game a little. It had been weeks since the last guest had checked out, and he'd gotten used to the routine. Nanette came down every morning and swept and ran the vacuum. She'd run a rag over all the surfaces and maybe clean the bathrooms once a week. Little Charlie ran through like a whirlwind and that did the old man's heart good.

John had gotten used to the quiet and the freedom to take off for days at a time if he felt like it, which he often did. It had been a long, hard winter and business had all but come to a standstill. At first he was panicked about it. How would he keep things going? But eventually he realized that they'd be fine. They always had been. The whole enterprise was pretty low-key and the property had long ago been paid off, so the bills were minimal. Nanette had side jobs, so she'd be okay. People always found the inn in the high season, usually just from the one sign on the highway. He wondered if he might ought to think about replacing that sometime. It was getting old and faded now, but it seemed to do the trick. One citified guest had told him that it was the "retro-vintage" sign that drew them in.

Anyway, this woman, Jane May Gideon she called herself, there was something about her. Something that captivated and irritated him at the same time. She was unkempt, rumpled, and irritable, which may have just been from traveling, but it seemed like it might be part of who she was. A frumpy thing, but with a kind of light in her eyes. A liveliness, which he'd seen in another woman, a long time ago. A determination that she wasn't going to give up. John Hawkes didn't believe in coincidence and he didn't believe that this woman had randomly popped in here. Probably had something to do with Mai.

For the third time, he punched in the numbers to Mac's cell phone. His big old fingers had so much trouble with these little buttons. Mac Harkness was John's oldest and one of his only friends. He could talk things over with Mac and get a balanced point of view without Mac needing to spread his business all around town. It was ringing. Good. He was about ready to forget the whole thing and just sit here whittling all day long.

"John!" Mac beamed into the phone. "What is the marvelous reason for my good fortune today?"

"Oh hush. You know several more fortunate things than me calling has already happened to you today. I just wanted to see if you'd mind some comp'ny this morning."

"Of course! I'm always happy to see you. Things are slow this morning. Come on down, I'll put the kettle on."

"Be there inna few then." John clicked off and wrote a note to Nanette, telling her about the woman in the cottage. The place was clean. Nanette kept it and all the rooms ready for unexpected guests, but now she'd need to keep a supply of towels coming and get in there to clean every day. He would pay her a little more, so it would be good for her and Lord knows that girl wasn't afraid of work. Between the inn and the running around that Mai had her do and her part-timing at Alice's bakery in town, and the little bit of extra that John gave her when he could, she managed to keep Charlie fed and clothed and shod. He was a happy little fellow, he was, and a light in John's life, but it just seemed like nothing was enough anymore. Or everything was too much, that was more like it. Everything just pushed him to the edge these days.

John opened the door to *The Light Within* and wondered how many times he'd heard the little tinkling bell as he walked through this door. A thousand? Ten thousand? If he'd come in here three or four times a week, every week for fifty years, give or take a few for when he'd been gone—oh never mind. His old brain was too tired for figuring.

"John! Welcome!" Mac came rushing, like a tornado, out from behind the brocade curtain at the back of his shop. Even his beloved old friend wore John slap out these days. After enduring the inevitable embrace, John took his place at the massive old round table behind the curtain. How many times had he sat at this table, drinking tea, and sometimes, especially in their younger days, whiskey? Sighing, he shook his head free of arithmetic again and accepted the hot cup of fragrant tea that Mac placed before him.

"How have you been?" Mac started in with the small talk, an irritant, like sand to an oyster, except that it never produced a pearl.

"Fine. I didn't come to talk about my current state of health."

"I know, I know," said Mac fondly, "I could tell when you called that you had something on your mind. Tell me."

"Well not much. A lady checked into the inn early this morning."

"Oh? Where was she from?"

"Dunno. Somewhere south, I'd say, by her accent."

"Does she seem nice?" John was becoming irritated by the placating tones that Mac was using to tease information out of him. Sometimes this man man could be so dang patronizing. He was trying to tell a story here and Mac just kept interrupting him.

"Hell, I don't know! Nice. What does that mean?" John shifted in his chair. His bones hurt now, all the time.

"Well, was there anything remarkable about her?"

"Yeah."

Both men became aware of the ticking of the old clock on the wall as minutes wore on. Over the years, Mac had become somewhat adept at John's pithy conversational style. He could wait. And he did. Birds twittered and sang. A garbage truck rumbled down the street, punctuated by the shouts of men throwing refuse into the back of the truck. In the far distance, a train whistle.

"I don't know, see? I don't know what it is about her. I feel like somehow she's connected to Zee, you know?"

"Ah," Mac rubbed his chin. "Do you think she could be the one?"

"Now, how in the world would I know that? I'm just saying, it looks like maybe she's got some business with Mai Zinni."

"Did this woman say something about Mai?"

"No, in fact, she don't seem to know who she is. It's just a hunch, you know? Just a feeling I got."

"Okay." Mac was still for a few moments. He respected John's intuition. Everyone who knew Mai Zinni knew that she was waiting for someone to whom she would pass down the knowledge and lore that she had been given by her own mother and grandmother. The knowledge had, in fact, been handed down from mother to daughter in Mai Zinni's family for as long as anyone could remember. Mai felt strongly that it wasn't meant to end with her, but she had no idea how that would work. She waited patiently, going about her business and growing older, knowing that somehow, someone would materialize and that she would recognize her when she came. Could this woman be that one? John and Mac wondered in silence as they sipped their tea.

Presently John pushed his chair back and rose creakily to his feet. "Well, time will tell, I reckon," was all he said. "How's the fish been biting?"

"Haven't had a chance to get out yet this year," answered Mac. "Don't be such a stranger, John."

"Aw, you know me," he muttered as he lifted the brocade curtain and let himself through.

Mac smiled as his friend's heavy footsteps signaled his retreat. The bell tinkled as the shop door closed behind him. "Yes, yes I do," he murmured, with great fondness. "I do know you John."

Chapter 3

The day before Jane May Gideon pulled up stakes, packed her car, and left the town that had been her home for all of her life, she took her dog, Shiloh, to her ex-husband's house in the country. This had been her home for most of their time together, which was all of her adult life. They had bought it in their second year of marriage, when Lenny had been asked to join the law firm where her father was a partner, and they'd begun to feel flush with new wealth and possibility. The country place was beautiful, with a mix of open fields and woods, which hung heavy with Spanish moss. A large pond graced the pasture in front of the house and it was one of the sweet pleasures of Jane's life to watch the sun come up over that pond from the front porch of the house, a cup of coffee in her hands, a notebook by her side on the glider. She had treasured those hours when the world still slept and she felt like the only one alive, sustained by the stillness that filled her. It was hard to come back here, but she knew she had done the right thing in leaving and letting Lenny have the house. There were too many memories. And besides, what would she do with a big house like that?

This felt the same, this leaving the town where she'd been born and had lived all of her life. It was as if she were being led by some unseen force and there was nothing to do but follow. It was hard to explain and mostly Jane May didn't care to explain it, not to herself or to anyone else. Most especially she had not cared to try to explain it to Lenny. She hated to leave the dog with him, but it wasn't practical to take her and she figured it was the least Lenny could do. After all, the border collie mix had grown up there. There were the other dogs, the pond, the twenty acres. He had wanted to know where she was going, what her plan was, when she'd return and on and on and on.

"None of your business!" She had told him.

"Jane, don't be crazy," he'd said, with infuriating calm, "you can't just run off without a plan."

Really? He had said this to her? It was outrageous considering that they were officially divorced now and especially considering what he had done. Had he had a plan? As out of line as this tack he was taking was, he had raised doubts. She'd faltered briefly, thinking, *Well, what am I doing? Shouldn't I stay put and formulate a plan for recovery? How will I get my life back on track? I should create a spreadsheet and put things in folders—wait just a minute! Whose voice is this? His or mine?*

She had buried her face in Shiloh's fur and whispered in her ear, "I love you and I thank you for your sweet presence. Be happy." The dog responded by licking her face and trying to get in the car with her. She cried all the way home. Another in a litany of losses.

Jane May Gideon was learning to hear her inner voice again and she would fight to stay tuned in to it. That night, fueled by her newfound resolve, Jane had written a letter to Lenny. On her way out of town the next morning, she dropped it in the mail. With a half-smile of satisfaction she'd rolled down the windows, pushed a CD into the slot and stepped on the gas. The lyrics told her to get her motor running and head out on the highway. And so she did.

Dear Lenny,

This is goodbye. Goodbye to the dream of us forever. The dream that we were different, special, destined to be together. Once, you said that we were more and better than our parents, that we were here to break the chain of dysfunctional, unhealthy relationships. Well, goodbye to that. We are part of that chain. Maybe Isabelle will be better, maybe her children will be better still. This is goodbye to always hearing your voice in my head and wondering if this is the way you'd want me to do it, if you would approve, if you would be angry or think me silly. Goodbye to that and hello to answering only to myself. This is goodbye to always trying to cover for you and manipulate my own thoughts to fit with whatever muddy thinking you were doing. This is goodbye to trying to present a united front for our daughter. She will have to sort it out for herself now. This is goodbye to letting you have any say in my spending, my eating, my dressing, my decorating, my reading, my thinking, my cooking, my record-keeping, my organizing (or not), my gardening, my traveling, my coming, my going, my vision, my thinking, and my being. Goodbye to mind-numbing loneliness within our home and marriage and hello to the spacious loneliness of solitude. This is the end of silencing my own voice, of diminishing and belittling what I know to be true. From here on out I listen to me. I am not crazy. I am not silly. If I am a jealous woman, as you say, you made me so and goodbye to that too. There is no need for jealousy anymore. It was only some kind of desperate attempt to save us when intuition had been silenced. So inferior, jealousy to intuition. Now that I am free to hear myself, I have no more need for gut-twisting doubt. This is goodbye. Goodbye to comforting each other. Goodbye to caring for each other. You will have to count out your own vitamins now or let that go. You will have to feed yourself with care or not, it's up to you. You will have to bounce your thoughts off of someone else, or let them swirl around inside your head, picking up steam, and never seeing the clear light of day. You've always mostly done that anyway. Goodbye to blind trust. That can never exist when intuition is strong. Goodbye to the dream of safety and protection. It was never anything more than a dream, anyway. I'll protect myself now, as far as I am able. Goodbye to our history together. We can't agree on what it was, so let's just wrap it up in something soft and put it away. Goodbye to hopes for something better. It was what it was and that's all it will ever be. Goodbye to growing old together. You never wanted to grow old or see me grow old anyway. It seemed to frighten you so. Now we'll grow old apart. If we're lucky. Goodbye to the sweetness of sharing at the end of the day. Goodbye also to the good sex that we enjoyed. (At least I did). I'm pretty sure that's not possible without the years and years of discovering everything about another person and we don't have that many functional years left. Maybe the kind of exciting new love that you discovered is compensation, and maybe I'll find that someday, but I damn sure won't destroy anyone else to have it. I wish you well and that is true. J.

Chapter 4

Jane May picked up the box of fruit and snack food that she had brought with her and headed up the three wooden steps, past a round table and four chairs, to the kitchen. It was a small galley-type room with an old porcelain sink and two casement windows overlooking the rushing creek. An apartment-sized gas stove and ancient refrigerator with rounded edges must have been original to the house. The floor was flagstone, and the cabinets on bottom were pine with a red linoleum countertop and open shelves above, stacked with white plates, hanging mugs, and glasses in two sizes. Jane May opened the windows and a breeze rustled the softly-worn white curtains. Leaf shadows danced across the room. Next to the stove a stoneware jar bristled with a wondrous assortment of wooden implements: spoons, tongs, spatulas, forks, and even a long back-scratcher. Hanging above were patinated pots and pans, and in the corner was a broom with a gnarly handle made from a tree branch. Jane May took a bowl from the shelf and filled it with the fruit she had brought and put the other things away in a pantry cabinet. She stood for a moment in the middle of the little kitchen and took it all in. She smiled. This felt right. It was good.

Nature dictated her next move and she was delighted to find an old claw foot tub dominating the bathroom. A good soak might be just what she needed. The room was small, but clean and cozy. White bead board paneling stood, like a garden fence, around the bottom third of the walls, with pale blue plaster above. Opposite the door was a small leaded glass window. Jane May began to feel as if a strong but tender hand were smoothing her hair and whispering in her ear, *there now, just rest.* Tears welled up again and she sat her tired, heartsick self down on the edge of the old bathtub and let herself cry until she had no more tears. And then she turned on the tap, stripped herself naked in the forest light and with leaf shadows dancing on her soft body, she lowered herself into the hot water with a deep sigh. The dream she'd had on the sofa came flooding back to her.

There was drumming. It was soft and slow, like a heartbeat, at first, but as she had approached the hill it had gotten louder and faster and when she'd crested the hill the drumming had reached a fever pitch. She couldn't see the drummers—there seemed to be more than one. Nor could she see the mountain lions that formed a semicircle at the edge of the firelight, but she saw their flashing yellow eyes, and she felt their presence. She was cautious, wary of them, but she was not afraid. She was aware of herself, standing firmly, almost defiantly, as if daring anyone to question her right to be there. A beautiful woman danced near the fire. Her body was long and willowy, her skin a golden brown in the glow of the fire. Strong, slender bare feet flitted and stomped, arms forming arches and swirls in the air, her torso bowing and lifting, lifting and bowing. Reaching for the moon and then inviting the earth to rise with her in homage to its celestial sister. There was singing too. Or something that undulated between chant and song. Jane May could not make out the words. They may have been a foreign language, but she felt that this was a song to the moon and the fire and the earth. A life affirming song. The lions, who had been watching silently from the shadows, began to step into the firelight and the woman's dancing slowed and slowed some more until she stood, feet planted, arms lifted to the sky, breathing hard with seven mountain lions arrayed around her. On her left side, a pure white one and on her right, pure black. Behind her, on the far side of the fire, five golden panthers fanned out, gazing into the shadows as if standing watch over this ritual. And inside Jane May Gideon's head, the word *Rise*.

And so she did. She rose from the bath, which by now had lost its comforting heat. She found a threadbare towel that had once been white, and stepped into the shadows of mid-afternoon. Deep in the woods as the little house was, it seemed later than it must be.

In her haste to slip away into the warmth of water, Jane May had not even carried her bags to the bedroom and so had to return to the main room. Nothing but the threadbare towel stood between her and utter nakedness. She thought that quickly would be the best way to go, since the shutters were all open and she would be exposed to anyone who might be lurking outside. She grasped the insufficient bath towel to her breasts as best she could and, because it didn't come all the way together, she danced sideways onto the stage of the living room toward her bags, and bent to pick one up. Having to free one hand, the towel slipped from her fingers and fell. Lurching for it she looked up toward the large casement windows over the couch where she'd napped and saw movement across the creek, in the shadows. Or she thought she did. *What was that?* But there was nothing. She recovered, snatched the towel around herself, picked up her bag and retreated to the bedroom.

Twenty minutes later, Jane May Gideon stepped out the front door of the cottage in the woods and headed back up the path the way she'd come this morning, and there she met the small boy named Charlie. He appeared on the path just as she crossed the creek and stepped off of the footbridge.

"Where ya goin' lady?"

"Well, hi Charlie," she said, brushing aside her surprise.

"Hi. Where ya *goin'*?"

"To get some things from my car, want to help me?" Jane May figured he wanted some more of her raggedy dollar bills and she was happy to oblige him. He was charming in a mischievous, impish way and she sensed a kind of kinship between them already.

"Can't. My ma'll whip me if I ain't home soon." On the last word, he broke into a run, kicking up dust.

Jane sputtered, waving her arms around. "Bye, then," she said as the dust settled. When she reached the top of the rise and saw the low brown buildings hunkered down as if whispering to each other, he was gone and there was nothing to indicate that he'd been there moments before. The soft light of late afternoon smoothed everything over. All was still except for the thrumming of hundreds of tiny bees' wings and, as she stepped from the dirt path onto the parking lot, the crunch of gravel beneath her shoes.

"Fine day."

The disembodied voice startled Jane May again, as it had when she'd arrived this morning. She wheeled and looked toward the spot by the front door, where the old man had been before, but she couldn't catch sight of him there. She turned in a slow circle, looking for a body to hitch the voice to.

"Oh, there you are." He was farther down on the long porch this time, in one of the Adirondack chairs, in a nest of curly wood shavings, still carving, still not looking up. She approached and took in the sharp smell of the wood—cedar, and the *shoop, shoop, shoop* of the knife, releasing thin layers to float to the ground. Now she could see the thing taking shape in his twisted but still deft brown fingers ... a cat, standing, front feet planted, ears alert. Jane May felt a prickling on the nape of her neck, which rose up the back of her head. Mountain Lion. It was clearly a mountain lion emerging from the chunk of wood at the coaxing of the old man's knife.

"That's beautiful," she said. "May I sit?"

"Course. Ever'thing suit you?"

He looked up for the first time and she saw what she'd somehow missed when he had signed her in this morning: his eyes. One was deeply dark chocolate brown with only the slightest hint of a pupil. And the other was a clear blue with darker flecks radiating from the center. These were finely set in the leathery brown face like twin pools in a topography of grooves and crags. They gave the strange impression that he was looking inward and outward at the same time.

Jane May was momentarily mesmerized, until he said, "Is there a problem?"

"I'm sorry," she said, flustered.

"With the cabin," the old man returned to his carving.

"Oh. Oh yes, I mean no, it's lovely and very snug and comfortable. Just what I need right now." Jane May looked away as tears welled up, again, unexpectedly. *What in the world?* There was a deep well of sorrow inside her and she kept stumbling upon it and falling in. Brushing the one escaped tear off her cheek and inhaling, she turned back to her companion, who seemed to her something of a stone in the middle of a rushing stream. At first she had thought him frail and bent, but she realized now that he was solid. Steady. She felt anchored here next to him. Protected, somehow. "May I ask your name?"

"John," he said, without looking up.

"John then," she lowered her gaze, feeling suddenly shy. "Did you see Charlie come this way?"

"He's a slippery one, that boy."

"Yes, he certainly is. I was going to have him help me finish unloading my car, but he said he had to get home."

"You can drive around," said John, nodding toward an opening at the far end of the parking lot. Jane May hadn't noticed this before, but now she could see the dirt drive winding off into the trees. It must skirt around the compound and come up behind her cottage.

"It ain't paved, but it's smooth enough. You can make it," he said, glancing at her car.

"Well, thank you," said Jane, rising to go and extending her hand to the old man. "It's so nice to meet you." He set the tiny cat figure down on the arm of his chair and took her extended hand in his. Instead of shaking it, he turned it over in his own and passed his fingers slowly over the small wart on the outside of her index finger.

"Mai Zinni'll take care of that." This was the second time since she had gotten here that he had mentioned this strange name.

"I'm sorry, who is this Mai Zinni?"

"Old Deborah woman lives over yonder a ways."

The skin prickled again on the back of Jane May's neck. She had heard of the Deborean Clan. Way back in the late 18th century, when the Celts had first come to these mountains from Ireland, Scotland and Wales, some of them had married into the Cherokee clans who were settled here. Legend had it they had preserved and melded practices from the two ancient cultures and become a powerful but secretive clan of shamans and medicine women and men. Sometime during the heyday of the flower children, seeking answers anywhere they could find them, some young people had pushed their way into a tradition that had historically been passed down through generations, father to son, mother to daughter. Outsiders had stormed the gates and thrown open the doors. Now there were covens that met and communicated online. People paid a lot of money to be initiated by high priestesses into offshoots of the Clan. But could there be descendants of original Deboreans still in these mountains? Was that even what he had meant? *Old Deborah woman*, Jane thought she had heard.

The old man released her hand and returned with the greatest economy of movement to his carving. Without looking at her, he said, "She'll be back soon. Be patient."

Well for heaven's sake, thought Jane May, *I'm not waiting on this woman. I don't even know who she is. All I want is some peace so I can figure out what to do next.* Irritated with the old man again, Jane May turned her back on him and walked to her car without looking back. Did she hear him chuckle? *Good Grief! I don't need this.* She backed the car out and entered the tree lined drive.

Chapter 5

John opened his one blue eye on the graying dawn. Birdsong filled the air like evanescent bubbles rising to the surface. His consciousness rose too, from the dreamworld. Where had he been? It always felt so strange, this returning. Or was this the leaving? More and more, he wasn't sure. The lines were blurring, the veil thinning. He hovered here between the solid screened in porch and the ethereal images, trying to remember. Grasping in vain at the dream, which disappeared like smoke.

Finally, it was as if someone kicked him in the rear end and the dreamworld door slammed shut and his surroundings came into sharp focus. He had slept on the narrow bed on the porch, lulled by the night sounds and the stars overhead in the inky sky. He often did this when the weather was pleasant. It reminded him of a time long past. He had gone out west for a few years and during that time it had been his habit to go, for weeks at a time, into the desert seeking peace and solitude. He never found peace, but solitude was so deeply rooted inside him that he was never far from it no matter where he was. What he had found in the desert had been a surprise and he wished that, just one more time, he could get back there. Just one night alone, under that vast empty sky. Alone, but not alone. That voice. How he longed to hear it one more time. And since he had only heard it there, he assumed it lived there.

He would never forget the desert voice that had spoken to him all those years ago when he couldn't think of any reason to go on with this charade of a life. He'd been in Chaco Canyon in northern New Mexico for two weeks. He hadn't seen another human being in all that time. He'd gone there to get away, to try and sort some things out. And there was another thought in his mind too. A thought that he hadn't acknowledged for the first week that he'd been there, but the vastness, the quiet and rocky finality of the place had finally forced the thought to the surface. He couldn't see a way to keep living in this world. He'd tried to picture it and it just wouldn't come clear. Goddamn it! What was the purpose of his life? All there was anymore was misery and loss and shame. How could his abiding possibly serve anyone, much less be bearable for himself?

He had wandered in circles for days with these thoughts, mimicking the flight pattern of the spiraling birds of prey. Finally, burnt by the sun, exhausted by his despair, he had lain down under a rock overhang and made a silent offering of himself to the wildlife of the canyon. He didn't, couldn't, believe in a God beyond this world, so he offered his bones to the birds, the coyotes and bobcats, the foxes that he'd heard calling to each other from the borderlands between night and day. And he fell into a deep sleep.

From the depths of the dream state he heard the word, *Rise*, and he did. He rose and emerged from his shelter. He stood in the chilly night air, reeling under the starstruck sky and waited. And waited. And waited. And then he began to scream, "What the fuck? What the fuck were you thinking!" His voice boomeranged off the surrounding rock formations, bouncing back and forth, *what the fuck, the fuck, what the fuck!* "Who are we to you, anyway!" No answer came, only his own voice, thrown back at him, hollow, merciless. After a while, spent, he sank to the ground trembling under the weight of the vacant heavens.

Resolved, he rose again and retrieved his backpack. He unbuckled the straps, felt for his knife and pulled it from its sheath. He would have to be brave and swift and precise. Relief flooded his body as he anticipated the end of his suffering. He thought of them then, he did, his family, his few friends, but he was beyond compassion, wild with his own pain, unable to think clearly, he told himself that they would be better off this way. Everyone would.

And then, from somewhere behind and just above him, a voice, as clear as the desert sky, "My son, you have to stand it." He ignored the voice and positioned the knife against the radial artery of his left wrist and readied himself for the opening. He imagined the blood, bright in this muted landscape, the slow draining away of his vitality.

"That's the only way you'll ever understand," came the voice again. Louder. "Death is nothing but a change of location. Know what you know. And get up and stand it." The voice, melodic and gentle, melted into a wind that rose and shook the stunted trees and whistled round the rocks, spawning dust devils and sending John scurrying back under the overhang, and ultimately back to his life.

Suddenly an overwhelming need to pee cut rudely into his nostalgia. He yanked the covers off himself and rose, too quickly, only to be thrown back onto the bed in a swoon. "Dammit all to hell!" He lay back down on his side, fighting for equilibrium as his bladder let go, wrapping his lower body in an exquisite warmth. No use in fighting it now, he exhaled deeply and allowed himself to sink.

And there at the bottom of the well was an open doorway with sunlight spilling through. Drawn by the light, he stepped over the threshold and into the meadow. Their meadow. It was, as always, awash in honeyed light, the air filled with the buzzing of bees and the busy twittering of birds. The soft breeze that tickled the back of his neck bespoke the coming summer. He looked up and there she was. Her dark hair hid her face as she bent over, picking blue flowers. But he saw her. He saw right through her as if she were made of glass. She was part of him. He was flooded with light. Infused with warmth.

And then like a window shattering, the whole scene shook and cracked and shards flew out in every direction.

He gasped as he felt himself thrust through a wormhole into his tiny outdoor bed, now cold and clammy and humiliating.

"Shit!" John Hawkes muttered angrily. "This ain't no goddamn way to live."

Slowly this time, so as not to be overcome by dizziness, he eased himself into a sitting position, dangling his legs over the side of the mattress, and rested for an agonizing moment as fear and shame seeped through his cells. He rose and stripped himself and then the bed.

He was walking with his bundle of disgrace to the laundry house a half-hour later when he heard her.

"John."

Turning, he spat on the ground and said nothing.

"I'm back, John."

"So I see."

"I just wanted to let you know."

"And ya did."

She looked tired to John, as if she were deciding whether to go on or not.

"How's everything?"

"Ever'thing's fine."

"Well, okay then," she paused. "You all right?"

"Yep."

"Want me to help you with that laundry?"

"For the love of Pete, woman!" His strange eyes penetrated her for just a moment, his heart breaking all over again, and then he turned and resumed his stiff walk to the laundry house.

Feeling her turn to go, he said over his shoulder, "there's a lady lookin' for ya. She's in the cottage." With that he disappeared around a bend in the path as Mai Zinni got into her old blue pick-up and headed for home.

Chapter 6

Waking from a dream, Jane May didn't immediately remember where she was. There had been a woman. She was talking, teaching.

The woman squatted on her haunches, before a fire. She was outdoors, in a clearing in a forest. She poked at the fire with a long stick. She was beautiful. She could have been young or as old as the constellations overhead. Her long hair was every color caught in the light from the flames. Jane May could not see her eyes, but she could hear her voice. The woman was giving a teaching on something. Jane May awoke in her dream and tried to listen, sensing that something important was being handed her, but she couldn't make out the words. She became increasingly aware of the sound of drumming. Jane moved closer in an effort to hear the woman's words, but the drums were too loud.

"Wha . . .?" she gasped as she sat up, startled into forgetfulness. Had she heard something? Jane May shook her head and rubbed her eyes and swung her feet to the floor, remembering the drive yesterday and the little boy, Charlie, and the old man with the strange eyes, but not the dream.

Shuffling to the bathroom, she stopped and stood, slatted by shafts of sunlight through the shutters in the living room. *It must be late,* she thought to herself. *How long have I slept?* Inexplicably, she thought of Jack. She blushed as memory rushed in. Jack feeding her mangoes. She was wearing only a thin cotton slip. He lifted her up onto the kitchen counter. It was July and hot as blazes outside. It hadn't rained in forty-nine days—a record.

Holding her gaze, Jack had picked up a perfectly ripe mango and offered it for her inspection. The late afternoon sun pushing roughly through the window illuminated the rosy fruit and made her feel like First Woman.

He began slowly to peel the fruit, glancing at her with a sweet, shy tilt of his head. They had spent most of the afternoon in bed. The peach red peel spiraled, blushing, to the floor in one piece and he left it there. Slicing off a bit of the orange flesh and pushing it between her lips, he groaned softly.

    She held it in her mouth. It tasted like desire. Sweet juice dripped from her chin and he licked it off as the room grew suddenly shrouded and the first clap of thunder shook the house and the heavens opened up and drenched the dry earth with torrents of fresh, clean rain. She'd jumped from the counter and, holding hands, they'd run into the yard, laughing, arms flung open, until a flash of lightning, so close and so brilliant, had sent them hurrying inside and back to bed, where they collided with each other, laughing and kissing, and there they'd spent the rest of that day and night, raising the furies and reveling in each other. Each clap of thunder had taken them higher and higher. Each flash of lightning illuminated them to each other for a surreal instant, their faces contorted in ecstasy.

    Jane May shuddered, engulfed in a heady brew of embarrassment and arousal. She'd only been divorced for a little over a year when she and Jack had met. She was not ready. She had given too much, too soon. Hell she had given everything immediately. And predictably, Jack had run as far and as fast as he could after only a couple of months. And Jane May was bereft and felt more alone than she had in the months after her long marriage had ended. This ending somehow more final, more painful . . . this hurt manifesting all the other hurts and rolling them into one wound so deep that she thought it would never close. But eventually it had, its thin covering pink and tender. She'd wrapped her heart in another layer of thick wool, a weak attempt at protection.

She was flooded with other memories now. Going much further back. Her grandfather's place in the country. It had been a small farmstead with a little white house and a garden out back, and on the long approach to the house, a peach orchard. Jane May had loved to go to Grandma and Grandpa's house. Her mother's father had a wise and gentle way about him that spoke to something deep in Jane May's solitary little soul. And in the early spring, the peach trees, lined up in frothy pink rows, were cloudy with bombinating bees. And then June. Sweet June when the days began at dawn and fuzzy peaches covered every surface in her grandmother's kitchen and even the back porch, which groaned under the weight of baskets full of ripe fruit. The smell of peach cobbler in the oven and preserves bubbling away on the stove filled little Jane with happiness, and sometimes in the late afternoons, her grandfather would call her to the front porch to crank the old wooden ice cream maker. Scout, her grandpa's giant white dog, would lie on the porch watching as she turned and turned the crank until her arm ached and her mouth watered in anticipation of the cold, sweet cream studded with ambrosial chunks of frozen peaches. Those summer days were light and soft now in her memory. Time had done some burnishing, buffing the rough edges here and there, so that she barely remembered her grandpa's occasional bursts of anger, or the way her grandma would get very quiet then and tell Jane to do the same. "Shhh, hush now child. Don't aggravate him. He's tired and just needs some peace. Go out and play quiet for a while." He could be so gentle, so kind, so comforting to a lonely little girl, but his mood sometimes turned on a dime. She never understood what brought the change on, but knowing that it could happen colored her whole world in ways that seemed small, but perhaps were large. She was a little less exuberant. She learned to keep a watchful inner eye on her childish joy, lest it bubble over and irritate him. She became what the grown-ups called, admiringly, a quiet child. "What a good little girl you are," they would say. "So respectful, so obedient. You always mind and you never act ugly."

Jane May remembered playing in the yard with Scout. The large white creature was probably the closest friend Jane May had for most of her childhood. They were constant companions whenever she visited the peach farm. Scout stayed protectively by her side and seemed to listen as she told him all of her secrets. This day, she was throwing a ball for him and he was dutifully bringing it back again and again, when Grandpa came out onto the porch and told her to go inside and take the dog. She and Scout filed past him and as they did, she noticed that he had a pistol in his hand. She knew that Grandpa sometimes hunted squirrel and deer, but she had never actually seen him shoot anything. He would leave and then come home later with some dead thing slung over his shoulder or lying in the back of his pick-up.

She watched in fascination from the front window, her arm around her large furry friend, as her grandfather walked between the rows of peach trees, shooting one bullet into each tree at point blank range. Was he mad at the trees? Was he killing them? The only thing he said when he came back in was, "Maybe we'll get one more crop out of them."

Many years later Jane May learned that this was folk wisdom. Country folk believed that shooting old fruit or nut trees would shock them into producing again, thereby putting off for at least one more season their inevitable decline.

This memory, so long forgotten, and the one before it, more recent, more raw, produced in her now, a longing, a soul disturbance. Like the fragments of some half-remembered dream that she was only now waking up from. When Jack had come along, she had been like those old peach trees, shocked into waking up in one last valiant attempt at life. Sap rising, unexpectedly greening, she had been surprised to find herself ripe, juicy, ready for one more harvest season. And what a glorious season it had been. He had given her back her joy, a long forgotten part of herself. She would treasure the memory forever, but that was over now. Surely it was.

Chapter 7

Startled one morning by an insistent knocking, Jane May fumbled for her glasses and tiptoed to the door, peering around the window to see who was on her porch at this hour. She opened the door and there stood Charlie, the cowlick at his forehead sticking straight up, and a lovely young woman with long dark hair gathered into a braid at the back of her neck. "I am so sorry to bother you, Ma'am. I'm Nanette and this is my son, Charlie. I believe you've met him already?"

"Yes. Good morning, Charlie!" The little boy's head was hanging down and he mumbled something under his breath. So different from the confident swagger he'd had when she first met him.

"Speak up, boy!" The young woman had Charlie by the collar.

"I'm sorry I took your dollars lady." Charlie's contrition was genuine, but Jane was confused.

"Well, but you helped me with my bags. That was a tip I gave you. You earned it."

"He most certainly did not!" The young woman snapped. "We don't take charity and Charlie is not employed by this establishment. Period." With that she thrust the still crumpled bills into Jane's hand.

Jane May didn't know what to say, but before she could think, the woman snatched the boy up by his arm and turned on her heel, tossing her head like a proud filly and flinging words over her shoulder, "My boy won't bother you again, Ma'am. If he does, he'll be sorry." With that they were gone, the mother stomping off, the boy's feet barely touching the ground as he was swept along in her angry wake.

Jane stood on the porch for a long moment, her mouth open, as if she expected to find the words she wanted any minute. She'd not gotten a chance to get a thought in edgewise since the whole exchange began. *What an angry unpleasant young woman,* she thought now. *And, poor Charlie....*

Jane was out of breath as she stomped up the hill toward the main building an hour later. She was indignant and wanted some answers. "John, I need to talk to you about Nanette."

Sighing, John leaned the ladder he was carrying against the laundry house and motioned for Jane to join him in the Adirondack chairs at the front of the building.

"Well, I reckon I was 'bout ready for a rest, anyway. What's on your mind?"

"This Nanette woman showed up at my door at the crack of dawn and she was mad as a wet hen and dragging poor little Charlie by the scruff of his neck. All because I tipped him a couple of dollars for helping me with my bags. She was rude to me and almost abusive to the boy. I wonder if she needs to be reported to the authorities." Jane had launched into her tirade without even sitting down. The two of them stood toe to toe.

"Hold on now!" John's hand was in front of Jane's face. "I won't have that kind of talk about the girl. She's a good mother. She may be prouder'n she needs to be, but she loves the boy and is doing all she can to raise him up to be a good man. You need to simmer down, 'cause you don't know what you're talking about."

Suitably chagrined and stepping back, Jane May shut her mouth and sat down in the nearest chair. Taking a deep breath, she began again, "I'm sorry, John. Truly I am. You're right. I just got here and I don't know what I'm talking about and I don't even know why it made me so mad. I just really like that little boy, you know. We connected somehow when we first met and I hated to see him like that this morning. Ashamed, beaten down."

"Aw hell, he ain't beaten down." John took the seat next to Jane May and fished his whittling knife and the little mountain lion figure out of his pocket. He sucked in a breath and took up his carving, apparently done with talking.

Jane waited. She breathed in the lovely spring morning and felt a tentative calm returning. After a while she hazarded a question vaguely in John's direction, "So what's the story with this Nanette?"

"The story?"

"Yes. Should I stay away from Charlie if I see him again? Obviously I'm not to give him any money for helping me. Does she live near here or what?"

"Aw, Nanette, she blusters and blows, but she don't mean nothing. She's just got her pride. She don't trust strangers, I guess, so until she knows you, she may be a bit stiff. She works for me, keeping the inn clean and such. Lives in the holler over yonder way." He jutted his chin out in a general direction.

"Stiff? Hmph."

"Once she's comfortable with you, she'll be as nice as can be. I'm betting you two will be good friends."

"Well, okay. I guess I'll just lay low and wait for her to be nice. As for the two of us becoming friends, well that's hard to imagine."

After a bit of a pause, the silence broken only by the shoop, shoop of the wood shavings falling to the ground, John smiled to himself and muttered, "Yeah, lay low. Hunh. Now there's something hard to imagine."

Chapter 8

This was going to be a long day. Nanette had a list of things to get done if she was going to have to keep the cottage clean and supplied for at least a week. Hopefully that woman would be leaving soon. She knew they needed the business, but she didn't like this lady from the get-go. Who did she think she was buddying up to Charlie and giving him money. Rich people just set her teeth on edge, feeling like they had some kind of right to try and save everybody else. This woman didn't know her or her boy and she just needed to move on or go back to where she came from, Nanette really didn't care which. When she'd taken Charlie to her cottage yesterday to give back the money, the poor lady just stood there like some kind of befuddled cow.

She didn't have time to think about it today. There was too much to be done. *Everybody just needs to mind their own business, and leave me to mine.*

She did all of John's grocery shopping when she shopped for herself and Charlie and that needed to happen today. She'd also drop in on Alice at the bakery and see if she could alter her schedule a bit to leave more time for the inn. Charlie needed some things for school and she had promised Mai Zinni that she'd gather some of the tender new fiddleheads that grew in the woods down behind the cottage and take them to her. Mai Zinni would have a tea party prepared and she would expect Nanette to sit and visit. It was Nanette's pleasure to do that, but she would be pressed, if she was going to be on time to pick Charlie up from school.

She was thorough, but quick, about tidying up John's living quarters. She moved through his rooms, dusting his few possessions. Here were his books, old and worn, always shuffled on the shelf as if he took them out often. She picked one up off the table where he'd left it and looked at the cover. The Mists of Avalon, which showed a lady riding a white horse on its cover. She set it back down just so and returned to her dusting. On the window sill, a heavy river stone and the skull of some poor animal. Beside his bed, a framed photo of him as a young man holding a child. The little girl laughing, John smiling. Handsome and strong he was. Nanette loved the old man he had become.

He had probably literally saved her life and Charlie's when her no-good ex-husband, Ricky had beaten her that last time. She was almost nine months pregnant and still that lout couldn't keep his hands off her. The pregnancy had been hard. She had a lot of pain in her back and she was so tired all the time. In spite of all of it, she had kept working at the local library right up until the end. She was the children's librarian and she had loved that job. She initiated story time and it was quite popular. She would have guest readers sometimes but often she would dress up in costumes and read to them herself. That was the best. It was one of those days that Ricky had come to the library and made a scene. Since she was huge and round, and also because it was almost Halloween, she had dressed as a pumpkin to read a seasonal story. She had all the children gathered around, enthralled by her reading and enchanted by her costumery. The up-stairs librarians and several of the patrons had come downstairs and stood on the periphery as she entertained the children. All of a sudden, here he comes, Mr. Got To Have My Way, busting up the party, insisting that she come with him right then. She didn't want to alarm the kids any more, and she knew from experience that there would be no placating him, so she allowed him to drag her by the arm, berating her and calling her names that should never be spoken aloud in a library, not to mention in front of children.

He dragged her out the back door and tried to shove her in his truck, but the pumpkin suit had a metal frame and she couldn't fit in there, so he started ripping it apart in the parking lot. He was getting angrier and angrier but she didn't have anything on except underwear under the damn thing, and when he got down to that, his whole mood changed. Nanette was always surprised by Ricky's desire for her even as she got bigger and bigger. Sometimes he was rough and she was afraid that he would hurt the baby, but this day, something was stuck in his craw and she was really frightened. He mauled her right there in the parking lot in her underwear, grabbing at her breasts and her bottom, as she tried to squirm away. Library patrons were coming and going and none of them could decide whether or not it was their place to interfere, so they all looked down at their shoes or up at the sky.

One man did say, from a safe distance, "Hey, Buddy. Leave her alone." But his voice was drowned out by Ricky's yelling.

Ricky tried to wrestle her into the truck and he was breathing all hot and heavy and saying what he was going to do to her and how he would hurt her if she didn't let him. She thought that her best bet, even though she was practically naked, was to try and stay in the parking lot, where maybe somebody would help her or call the police or something.

He took his first swing, which caught her square in the jaw, just as John pulled his old pick-up into the parking lot. He was old and creaky, but it didn't stop him from flying from the truck and pulling Ricky off of her and punching him right in the nose. Ricky lost his nerve as soon as he hit the pavement. Apparently his tough bravado stopped at nearly naked pregnant ladies. He was no match for John and he whimpered and whined as he begged for mercy.

John gave him one parting kick in the ribs before he wrapped his arms gently around her and walked her to his truck. He retrieved a blanket from behind the seat and wrapped her up in it, just as her water broke in the parking lot. After helping her into the cab and assuring her that she was safe now and everything would be okay, he turned to the small gawking crowd that had gathered and simply said, "God help you." Then he spit on the ground and climbed into the driver's seat and sped away toward the hospital.

Nanette was bound to him from that moment on. Even if he hadn't gotten her to the hospital. Even if he hadn't stayed in the delivery room with her until Charlie made his triumphant entrance into the world. And even if he hadn't given her a home and a job and a new life away from Ricky, those few moments in the parking lot of the library on a chilly, golden day in October had bound her to him forever.

The library didn't require her services after that. They'd been very understanding and accommodating of her, but they couldn't risk the children's safety any longer, the head librarian had told her sadly when she came to visit and see the baby a few days later.

Nanette finished straightening up John's rooms, ran the vacuum over the rugs, and as an afterthought, she went outside and picked a handful of the daffodils blooming around the steps and put them into a mason jar and set them on his kitchen table next to the book. It was a small thing, but she hoped that it would give him a little joy.

Chapter 9

The next morning Jane May awoke again to a pounding on the door of the stone cottage. This had seemed, at first, like a peaceful place to rest, but that was not turning out to be the case. She stumbled out of bed with dream fragments, like cobwebs, clinging to her hair and her skin. Brushing the last of them from her eyelashes, she opened the door a crack and saw no one there. Dropping her gaze, she found the open face of Charlie.

"Mornin'. Mai Zinni said give you this." He thrust a folded piece of paper through the door. "She's ready's to see you now." With that he scampered off down the path, as if the scene yesterday with Nanette had never happened.

"Well for heaven's sake," Jane muttered under her breath, "Who the hell is this person anyway? She's ready to see me? What nerve."

The note contained an address, nothing more, and Jane May dropped it emphatically onto the round dining table as she headed for the kitchen and coffee.

Later, showered and dressed and having drunk her fill of coffee and fortified herself with toast and fruit, Jane May prepared to leave the cottage for a few hours. She didn't take the paper with the address on it. Of course she didn't. She certainly wasn't going to go looking for some arrogant, presumptuous (and likely crazy) woman whom she'd never met before. No. But since she was here for at least a week, she might as well get a feel for the place and begin to settle in.

Keys, purse, bottle of water, and just in case, the GPS device. That should do it. She didn't plan on getting lost. No one ever does.

As she strapped herself into the car, she took a deep breath and offered up a prayer for protection and guidance. In spite of the pain and confusion that swirled in Jane May these days, she knew, on some very deep level, that healing was inevitable, and she fervently hoped that she was not really alone although it certainly felt that way most of the time now. "Everything's okay and I am fine," she repeated over and over to herself, a mantra. She couldn't remember exactly when the door to the spirit world had closed with a definitive click. She'd grown up seeing more than most people apparently did, or at least more than most people admitted to. She always sensed beings around her and felt watched over and safe because of it. When her grandfather died she was in junior high. He'd come and sat on her bed every night for weeks, talking companionably to her about the other side. It had always been this way. It had been first or second grade before she realized that this was not the way most people experienced the world. Some children saw her on the playground talking to one of her childhood friends, Willie Peaches. Jane couldn't remember a time when Willy wasn't with her. Her parents couldn't see him, but they never seemed bothered by his presence. In fact, they asked about him and included him often in conversations. But when she explained to the children at school that she was talking to an invisible friend who went everywhere with her, they laughed and snorted and forever after called her *Ghost Girl*. She had learned then to keep certain things to herself, but she had never stopped seeing or hearing. Until recently. It was so lonely without them. Why now, she wondered, when she needed them the most? This was a bitter loss to Jane May. But still, she knew that she was healing. Sometimes she experienced this as a comfort and sometimes not. For what would be left if she let go of her grief and her pain? They had become her companions, she realized this now with a jolt, but despair was a country that she could not reside in forever.

 She could almost feel the pieces of herself being knit back together even as she still ached from the rending. Driving away from her hometown had been the best thing she'd done for herself in a long, long time. And the most painful. Prying those deep roots up from the ground, dirt still clinging to the hairs, exposed and wondering where her nourishment would come from now. What would sustain her if not that ground, that place, those people?

 It was a gorgeous morning, Jane noticed, as she put the car into gear. When Charlie had awakened her, a grey mist was rising from the creek and drifting ghostly through the trees. Now the mist had lifted and sunlight filtered down, throwing sparks over the water, illuminating patches of moss, and catching on spider webs that swagged the trees like strands of diamonds. The way the world had of going right on, stunning you with its beauty and breaking your heart at the same time, was enough to send Jane May back to the warm comfort of her bed, but no. No. She wouldn't give into that urge this morning.

As she left the parking lot of the inn, Jane May glanced into her rearview mirror and caught a glimpse of Nanette, with a stack of towels, going into the front door. *Hmph! I guess I'll be seeing a lot of her.* Jane May sighed and pulled onto the highway, vowing not to think of the sour woman right now. She was off to explore and she didn't want the bad taste of yesterday's encounter to color her view of Gideon.

She pulled the car into a parking space in front of a row of shops on Gideon's quaint and colorful main street. Trees, punctuated with street lamps, lined both sides of the street. From the lamps hung wire baskets, boisterous with cascades of vibrant flowers. There was a cheerful bakery with a large plate glass window shaded by a sky blue awning with fluffy clouds. Jane's mouth began to water as she looked inside at the cases full of delicious treats. A warm, sugary fragrance wafted out the open front door, and a happy painting of a pie with a bluebird pie vent emitting spirals of steam that spelled out *Alice's Pie in the Sky* graced the window. A woman, (could it be Alice?), scurried among the tables, happily pouring coffee and handing out treats on white china plates. She looked so nice in her blue apron, wisps of grey hair escaping from a french twist, that Jane May longed to go in and sample all the sweetness. But the shop next door, which featured a painted wooden sign that read, *The Light Within—Esoterica for the Modern Pilgrim*, caught her attention and drew her to it. Regarding the colorful sign and the wood door with a lace curtain scrimming the glass, Jane May had the strange sensation that she had been here before.

In a way, Jane May Gideon was like a newborn baby these days. Squinty-eyed and wrinkled, disoriented by the unfamiliar surroundings in which she found herself. She felt raw and new and completely vulnerable. Her inner bone structure, soft and malleable. A primal cry on the verge of bursting forth from her lungs. And yet, she felt strangely at home in this place that she had never been. Deep inside herself some yearning stirred.

Standing on the threshold of a new life, she could become anyone now. Anyone. Maybe even herself.

Between the two shops, Jane stopped to read a sandwich sign on the sidewalk. It announced an upcoming street party. There would be music and dancing and food after the stores closed on Friday night. Maybe she would go.

She pushed open the door and stepped over the threshold and into *The Light Within*. The moment carried more weight than Jane May could have imagined, but was marked only by the tinkling of a bell.

Coming in from the sunlit street, the interior was dark and smelled of dust and incense and mystery. It took a long moment for her eyes to adjust to the dim light, but when they did she saw nooks and crannies stuffed with objects, shelves crammed with books, CDs, strange figures of people and animals, bowls and bells. The space was diffused with a soft golden light emanating from flickering candles and strings of tiny white bulbs. Some objects were beautiful and some were disturbing, but the whole was strangely compelling. All manner of things dangled from the ceiling: bells, exotic looking kites that resembled dragons and huge moths, strange wooden beings with painted wings and eyes that watched silently. Jane May turned slowly round, trying to take it all in. In the turning, she saw a small man behind a heavily carved wooden counter and just as she spotted him, the man spoke.

"Greetings. And welcome. You've found us!" he exclaimed happily, as if he'd been expecting her. His hair formed a thick white fringe, a monk's tonsure, around the back of his head and curled over his ears. His blue eyes, set into a round face, were small and sparkly, heavily lined in the corners. His mouth seemed to be permanently pulled up into a half-smile.

"Well, yes." She fumbled for words. "I'm new in town and I'm out for a day of sightseeing."

"Yes, of course. Well, you'll want to see the waterfall. Have you seen the waterfall?"

"No, I've just arrived and . . . ."

"You'll want to see that," he interrupted. "When you leave here, drive up the highway for about five miles," he pointed the direction, "then take the first left past the second stone tunnel. Drive until you come to an old wooden bridge. Cross the bridge and park just past it on the left shoulder.

You'll see a path running up through a rhododendron thicket. Follow the path to the waterfall."

"Now wait." Jane May had gotten confused in the flurry of his words. "Did you say the first left?"

"Don't worry. You'll find it. Now look around the shop and enjoy yourself and let me know if I can be of any assistance to you." With that he turned his attention to a large ledger book spread open on the counter in front of him.

Understanding that she'd been dismissed, Jane May did as she was told. She enjoyed herself. The little shop was fascinating. There were beautiful stones and statues of deities, many of which she didn't recognize. There were three floor-to-ceiling shelves stuffed with books. There were tarot cards of every description, ancient Tibetan singing bowls squatting on embroidered silk cushions, small velvet bags, and carved wooden boxes, and among all these things, the candles. Candles, flickering softly and casting shadows on the walls and ceiling. Jane May was enchanted. She picked up a small statue of some kind of goddess, carved from bone. The smooth surface and sinuous lines of the little woman made her smile, but the carving was also disturbing and lewd. The tiny woman was squatting and holding her vulva open. Good Lord! As she studied the small carving in her hand, her face grew hot and blushing with embarrassment, she set the little woman back down on the shelf and turned away from the man who was grinning although he hadn't looked up from his ledger.

Next she stood over a display of tarot cards laid out on a long table which was covered with a beautiful embroidered scarf. There was a deck fanned out on the table and some other cards laid out roughly in the shape of a cross. Off to one side was a pyramidal stack of boxes showing cards of different designs. She knew nothing about reading tarot cards, but she'd been to a woman once, while on vacation in New Orleans, who had used them to tell her things about herself that no one could have known. Things that she didn't even fully know herself. Secret things that resided in the innermost rooms of her heart and had never seen the light of day. "The magic is over with the man. It's run its course. He's turned to someone else." Jane May had been shocked. Shocked. By then her marriage was strained, yes, but she was by no means ready to give up on it. This woman was adamant and Jane May had become angry, throwing the money they'd agreed upon down on the table and storming out. But she knew, even then she must have known that it was true. It would be several years before she was able to admit it to herself, though.

Today, standing in this shop, she felt so drawn to these cards, with their strange images. What could they tell her now? She'd let her hands linger over the display, and finally picking up a deck, had turned over the top card. The High Priestess, the card read at the bottom. At the top was a roman numeral two. A beautiful, dark-haired woman, robed in blue with a strange headpiece. She sat on a throne with a crescent moon at her feet, and a backdrop of broken open pomegranates. Flanked by two columns, one black, the other white, in her hand, a scroll, with letters on it. Jane May felt as if she recognized this woman. She was studying the card when the little man said, "The Lady. She's telling you to pay attention to your dreams and intuition."

A piloerection of goosebumps sprang up on her forearms. Her dreams. Her intuition.

Suddenly ready to be alone in the sanctuary of her car, she scooped up the salacious little goddess and a deck of cards, took them to the counter, and reached into her purse for cash.

"Ah, Sheela na Gig! Now she's a wild one, she is," said the man with a slightly suggestive tone. Jane May was embarrassed by this wee wanton woman and her own desire to own her and she wished that the shop owner would stop talking, but alas, no such luck. "The Mother Goddess, the crone aspect. She is found on old churches across the British Isles. She's usually above a window or door." He laughed heartily at this. "Everyone argues about the meaning, but a little woman brazenly showing her genitalia is a strange thing to find in a church, no?"

Jane May was now blushing furiously and only wanted to exit the premises if he would just hand over the bag containing her purchases, which he had purloined behind the counter.

Leaning in close, the little man spoke in a conspiratorial whisper, "Go to the waterfall. Most folks won't ever go there. It's only for those with eyes to see." Drawing back, he gave her a wink and then, dropping his gaze to her hand resting on the counter, he offered, "Mai Zinni'll fix that."

Embarrassed and flustered, Jane May covered the small wart with her other hand and turned to go.

"Wait! You're forgetting your cards and your Sheela," he called happily.

Snatching the proffered bag from his outstretched hand and avoiding his smiling eyes, she said, "Thank you," as she reached for the door. "I've enjoyed your shop. It's fascinating."

"Come back soon," he said, more of a command than an invitation. "Next time I'll read your cards. Enjoy your drive."

Jane May drove, in a state of agitation, back to the cottage on the creek and shut herself inside to ponder the events of the morning.

Chapter 10

Mai Zinni had been hearing rumblings about this woman who'd blown into town and she had to admit she was curious. A little anyway. She'd sent for her this morning and now she would wait. So when Mac came to her cottage, capering this way and that and rubbing his pudgy hands together, she invited him in and let him talk.

"She picked up the High Priestess, Mai. Right out of the blue! And she bought the little bone Sheela na Gig from Scotland. She's staying out at John's. Why do you think, of all the places in the world, she's landed right here in our backyard?"

"Well now, let's just simmer down, Mac. Could be any number of reasons why she's here. Why don't we just wait and see."

"I've just got a feeling, that's all. You know, Mai? A strong feeling."

"Sit down and I'll fix us some tea." She was intrigued. When Mac got a strong feeling, she listened. He knew her better than anybody, except maybe John. Mac had known her almost all of her life and he knew that she had been waiting for someone. Had been ever since her Little Star had run off, taking so many of Mai's hopes and dreams with her. She had long ago given up hope that Little Star would come back home, but she knew that someone would come. The knowledge that had been passed down for as long as anyone could remember was surely not meant to die with her. What sense would that make, and Mai Zinni, unlike John, did believe that there was some sense to be made of the world. They may not understand it, but the whole thing had to rest on something that made sense. And what made sense to her was that someone would come along to whom she could pass on what she knew.

"Mai, she's lost. You can tell, and I don't think she has any idea why she's here, but there's something about her. I'm dying for you to meet her," Mac said.

"And I will if it's meant to be." She wasn't going to tell Mac that she'd already sent for the woman. "Now drink your tea and hush up about it, please."

Mac and Mai went way back. He remembered her mama and her grandmama. He'd been there through all the ups and downs of her life, and likewise she had shared his and treasured his friendship. But she wasn't ready to talk about this woman until she had at least met her, so she steered the conversation in another direction.

"Have you seen John lately?"

"Sure. I was out at the inn a few days ago. We had a drink together. And he came in the shop yesterday for a visit. He seems fine. He wanted to tell me about the woman, Jane. She'd just checked into the inn. He has the same feeling that I got from her, Mai."

"Good. I been worried about him lately."

"Why?"

"Can't say, really. Just a vague feeling. Nothing, I s'pose. Glad you check on him."

"I do, Mai. I care about John, you know that."

"I do. Um hmm. And I'm grateful for it."

They sat in silence for a bit longer, sipping their tea, and then Mac stood up. "I should get back to the shop. Need anything?"

"No dear. I'm fine. Thank you for coming. It's always good to sit with you for awhile."

Mac hesitated and then embraced her for a long moment. When he left he did not look back.

Chapter 11

Glistening with sweat, and a little out of breath, Jane May began to get the feeling that she was circling.

She had found the path to which the little man had directed her with no trouble. She'd parked and pushed her purse up under the front seat out of sight, grabbed her water bottle, locked up, pocketed her keys, and ducked into the dense tunnel formed by twisted rhododendron branches reaching toward each other with their waxy green leaves. It was cooler in the tunnel and the ground was soft. Jane May could just barely stand up straight and the branches gently brushed her graying head as she made her way down the dirt path. In another month or two this tunnel would be resplendent with pink blossoms. Jane May wondered if maybe she would still be here then.

She felt giddy, alone in these unfamiliar woods. An adventure—tinged with a bit of fear. What might she encounter here? Were there bears? Snakes? She'd lost track of time in the rhododendron thicket, enchanted by the cool dappled shade and the busy chatter of birds. At last she emerged into a clearing, guarded by huge and ancient trees, cloaked in green moss. Large stones lounged about on the forest floor like great reclining beasts. Some of these also wore thick coats of wooly emerald moss, studded with white blooming stonecrop.

Jane May paused and inhaled deeply, closing her eyes. She felt the forest through her skin, cool and dense and primordial. Her nostrils flared with delight, breathing in the clean smell of the deep decay of leaves and insects and fallen trees and the rebirth of mushrooms and moss and tiny saplings. The entire life cycle was being played out right here, right now! Her ear canals widened and expanded to take in the cacophony of sound: sweet birdsong and leaf rustle, insects chirping, frogs calling, water drip, drip, dripping, the wind dancing through the branches in the canopy high overhead. Roots extended down from the arches of her feet deep into the ground and spread in all directions, like tributaries, or veins. She felt her hands unclenching and her heart opening like a flower.

Something shifted inside her like the tumblers of a lock, falling perfectly into place. When she opened her eyes, the scene before her had also changed, even as it endured. Beams of sunlight had threaded themselves through openings in the heavy branches high overhead and dust motes and tiny silver winged creatures rode them playfully to the forest floor, and when they met and bounced off the bits of mica scattered there, sparks of gold flew up and danced in the air.

Behind all the music in this rarified atmosphere, Jane May thought she heard laughter. Straining her ears, she realized the rippling sound was coming from her own throat. How long had it been since she had laughed? Now that it had begun, she wanted more. Throwing her head back and spreading her arms wide, Jane May Gideon laughed and laughed.

Meandering through this enchanted forest of dappled light and glitter, she followed the glad sound of tumbling water until she came to a wide rock-strewn stream. The sound of water increased until it became a roar. The waterfall. "Only for those with eyes to see. Most folks won't ever find it," the little man in the shop in town had told her.

As the roaring grew louder and louder, Jane May went faster and faster, scrambling over fallen logs and tree roots as big as her thighs. The path rose steeper and steeper, until all at once, there it was. She shaded her eyes and looked up to the top. It must have been sixty or seventy feet high. Rainbows arced above the mist rising from the falls. The thundering sound of the water threatened to shatter the tiny bones of Jane May's middle ear. At the bottom, near where she stood, there was a blue-green pool, with a rock ledge that embraced the back half of the pool like a lover's protective arm. It looked like you could stand behind the falling water on that ledge and Jane wanted to do that. Quickly, before she could stop herself, the frumpy middle-aged woman kicked off her shoes, shimmied out of her blue jeans, flung off her blouse, peeled off her panties and bra, and with a yelp, dove headfirst into the pool.

The water was shockingly cold, but it was just what she wanted. With her eyes wide open, she sliced her way down through the depths. Sunlight filtered in mosaic shafts and Jane May swam like a mermaid who was completely at home. The water was crystal clear and she could see the rocky bottom, but couldn't begin to reach it. Her cheeks bursting, she surfaced and made for the farthest end of the ledge. She swam along the edge of the pool toward the thundering falls. As she approached, she saw that the space behind actually did open into a cave of sorts. Curious, she darted under the water and came up into the cool dampness of the overhang. The sound was deafening. She pulled herself out of the pool and scrambled onto the slippery rocks. As her eyes adjusted to the dimness of the place, she began to pick out details: small ferns growing from the walls, bits of crystals glinting now and then, and against the back wall, a large stone, flat on top or nearly so, indented a bit near one end. Jane May felt like a child in a cathedral. Hushed and awestruck, she minced along carefully and made her way to the big stone. The roar of the water had become almost like silence, so rhythmic that it flowed uninterrupted over her mind, smoothing her edges like a river rock. Climbing onto the large stone, she found that the natural indentation on the top of it formed a Jane May shaped seat, with a slight back rest, and she sat cross legged as she had learned to do in the yoga classes that she'd taken in that other life, which now seemed so far away and removed that surely it was someone else's. She breathed in slowly, savoring the damp smell of the place, the negative ions of the waterfall infiltrating her body and rearranging her cells. She sat like this, on the rock in the cave, behind the waterfall, naked as a brand new day, breathing slowly and deeply, while time passed or stopped or did somersaults over itself.

Unconcerned with the antics of time, when it felt right, she rose and walked under the waterfall and back into the light, and dove again into the deep pool.

Jane May floated on her back, letting the sun warm her face, enjoying the feel of her hair fanned out around her head and undulating like seaweed on the surface. She rolled over and floated on her belly to feel the warmth on her back. Far below a trout darted by, catching the coppery light on its scales and flashing it back to the surface.

A large, sun-warmed stone lay on the edge of the bank, beckoning, and emerging from the water, she shook off like a jubilant dog, and laid her body out along the hard length of it. Her skin gratefully soaked up the warmth of the sun and the rock. Red light danced on her closed eyelids and she surrendered to the heat and the light and the roaring of the waterfall.

Her eyes flew open. Had someone spoken? The word *Rise* seemed to hang in the air, and like Eve in the garden, Jane May realized that she was naked. She scrambled to her feet and began gathering her clothes. What had she been thinking, lying naked on a rock, drowsy as a snake on a summer afternoon? She struggled into her panties and jeans. Fastened her bra and buttoned her blouse woppyjog. Had someone spoken? Danced on one foot, as she pulled on a shoe. *Rise* fluttered in her head like a bird that had, hapless, flown in through an open window. The other shoe now. *Rise!*

A flash of blue. She jumped up and followed, without wondering why. Crashing down the path, breathless, catching blue glimpses now and then. Jane May began to feel that she was circling, being led around and around by this flash of blue. She couldn't seem to catch up.

Finally, sweat-slicked and laboring to catch her breath, Jane May was spit out of the path and into the tiny front yard of a little house. She stood panting at a waist-high hedge that surrounded the cottage. Neat but weathered, the foundation of the house was rounded river stones while the main construction was wood, shiplapped and stripped of its paint by the working together of the elements and the passage of time. Once a dark, forest-service green, the paint had faded, causing the cottage to almost disappear in the wooded grove in which it squatted. In a minute, Jane May's eyes adjusted to the deep shade thrown by the tall black walnut trees, the poplars and the metallic birches, and she made out the small figure of an old woman rocking in a chair on the tiny front porch. The woman wore a faded blue skirt, leather boots, and a thin, brown, moth-eaten sweater. In her lap was a black cat. Jane May was startled by this visual cliche' of a fairytale witch. The old woman rocked on. Unruffled by her disheveled, out-of-breath visitor, she simply said, "Hello," as if she had been expecting a caller.

"Oh!" Jane May began to stutter, "I'm sorry. I was out for a walk and I . . . I . . . ."

"Come inside and let's get you dry."

"I, uh . . . ." Jane looked down at her now clammy and soiled blue jeans, and erstwhile white cotton blouse.

"There's the gate to your left."

Jane May's gaze slid to her left, across the green hedge and she found the old wooden gate, set back into the shrubbery as if it had also grown there. She lifted the latch and stepped into the little yard.

She was aware that this whole thing was odd. The house in the deep woods—was there a road somewhere? Yet she felt somehow that she had no choice but to see it through. So she climbed the steps to the porch, reached out her hand and said, "Jane May Gideon."

"Yes," said the old woman, as if she already knew. "I'm Mai Zinni Trew."

Suddenly Jane May was dizzied by the rotation of the planets and their hurtling through space, as the dream world and the waking world collided. She had not set out to find this woman, in fact had adamantly not wanted to find her, had left the paper with her address that Charlie had delivered yesterday morning, back in the cottage, and yet, here she was on Mai Zinni's porch. Why? How had this happened?

She had come too far to turn back now, so she followed the old woman and the cat into the dimly lit house.

How much time had passed? She'd been drinking tea by the fire in the little house in the woods for what seemed like hours. A pleasant drowsiness had come over her, dulling her senses. The cat, whose name was Period, reclined in her lap, purring.

Attempting to gather her wits, Jane May rattled her teacup and knocked her chair over in her scramble to get up.

"I'm so sorry," she mumbled, righting the chair and shushing the cup in its saucer.

"I've lost all track of time! I'd better get back to my car before dark. Thank you so much for everything. I hope I haven't inconvenienced you too much," she babbled.

"Nonsense. We've had a nice visit." The old woman took Jane May's right hand in both of her own and held her gaze silently for what turned into an awkward interval. Retrieving her hand, Jane asked to use the bathroom before she left. When she emerged, the old woman was standing by the back door. "I imagine I'll see you again," she said decisively, as she opened the door. "Main road's right up that path."

Jane May stepped uncertainly out onto a small stoop. "How can that be?" She shook her head, confused, but turning around, saw that the old woman had already closed the door.

Confused, she went down the stone steps and paused, trying to find her bearings. It had been a very long walk from her car to here and she'd arrived in the front yard. Oh well, clearly there was a shorter way. She started down the path, nice and wide and winding gently through tall hardwood trees, punctuated with pointed evergreens, and was surprised, after only fifty yards or so, to come out on the road in the precise spot where she'd left her car earlier today. It certainly seemed strange, but here was her car, right where she'd left it, with no sign of another path, and the sun was dropping in the western sky and she felt something like a small animal gnawing at her insides as she remembered she hadn't eaten a bite since breakfast. So chalking up her confusion to being directionally challenged—hadn't Lenny chided her about this many times—she cranked her car and back tracked to the inn.

It was only after she'd soaked in the huge old bathtub and gotten into bed later that night that she realized the little wart on her right hand was gone without a trace. Her breath caught and her mind rooted around looking for a sensible explanation, but exhaustion won out. Jane May quickly slipped under the surface of consciousness and let sleep carry her away.

Chapter 12

Nanette spun around, loaded for bear, as John pulled the plug on the vacuum she was using to clean the threadbare carpet in the reception area of the inn's main building. "What the . . . ?"

"Sorry. You was lost in your head, girl. I been trying to get your attention for a while now."

"I'm sorry, John." Nanette softened, as she always did in his presence.

"It's okay. Can you take a break for a minute? Sit with me for a bit?"

"Of course. What's on your mind? Is everything okay?"

"Ever' thing's fine. Let's sit outside. It's a beautiful day." And it was. A day like only these mountains could offer up. Soft, warm, fragrant, with a hint of a breeze that kept everything in dreamy motion. "Ms. Gideon down in the stream cottage said you were harsh with Charlie."

"What? If she has a problem with me, she should come to me!" Nanette's normally liquid brown eyes hardened.

"Don't sound like you give her much chance for that." John's voice was gentle. His eyes betrayed his deep affection for this young woman.

Nanette hung her head. "Maybe I was a little hard on him, but he doesn't work here and I don't want him taking money from strangers."

"Well seems like to me, if he helps, taking money ain't a bad thing. Teach him that he's got to earn what he gets. The value of a dollar, you know. He may not work here, he's only a kid, but he does live here and he can help out and he ought to be able to take a tip when he does."

"I guess you're right, John. It's just . . . I mean . . . who is she anyway?"

"She's a paying customer, I reckon. A guest at this inn. Why does she bother you so?"

"I don't know. Mai Zinni's been asking about her. Had Charlie go over and give her Mai's address."

"And?" John waited while Nanette struggled to know her own mind on the subject. She spoke so softly that he couldn't hear. "Sorry. What was that?"

"I said, you know that I wanted to be Mai's apprentice. I wanted her to pass down the knowledge to me and it should be me!" Nanette was getting worked up now and John let her go for a while, knowing that she needed to get this out. "I'm from here, John. I know the old ways. I know the plants. My granny taught me. I'm not from Mai's lineage, but neither is this woman!" Her voice had crescendoed and raised in pitch and now she was whining.

"Now Nanny, you know that there ain't no accounting for that woman's thinking. And you know there's no chance of changing her mind. It's not about you, girl. It's about following some inner knowing that she's got. Something she's got to follow. Ain't nothing can be done about that. You just have to learn to accept it."

"I know. I've tried. You know I have. I thought I *had* accepted it until that woman showed up here. Seems like she's working her way into every corner of my world, too. I even saw her coming out of Mac's store yesterday. Now what business do you think she has with him, for God's sake?"

"Don't reckon it's none of our business, but she's probably just getting to know her way around town."

"I suppose you're right and that is infuriating, you old bear." Nanette rose and kissed John on the top of his head. "I'd better get back to work, so my boss doesn't fire me."

"You'll go easy on the boy, then?" John didn't look up from the block of wood and the knife he'd fished from his pocket while they were talking.

"I'll think about it." She flipped her long black ponytail as she disappeared into the lodge.

Shoop, shoop, shoop. John smiled to himself as fragrant curls of wood fell to the ground around his feet.

An hour later, John had dozed off in the warm sunlight. Charlie took the opportunity to sneak up behind the old man's chair and clap his dirty little hands over John's eyes. "Guess who?" he squealed as John jumped.

"Damnation boy! You'll give an old man a heart attack." He reached around and batted at the boy who swung around the other side of the chair and planted himself directly in front of John.

"Guess what I found?" The boy was about to burst, he was so full of himself.

"How do I know." John had picked up his knife and the little unfinished carving and resumed rhythmically shaving away the parts that weren't mountain lion.

"Guess."

"Your manners?"

"No, Uncle John!" Charlie danced from one foot to the other with uncontainable excitement.

John laughed and looked up from his carving. "I knew it wasn't them you'd found. What in the Sam Hill is it?"

"Who's Sam Hill?" Temporarily distracted, Charlie stopped fidgeting and looked expectantly at John.

"A man who thought crazy thoughts and cussed all the time."

"Bet his mama whipped him a lot!"

"I bet she at least wanted to. Now what is it you found?"

"Close your eyes. Go on, close 'em."

John opened one eye in time to see Charlie scamper to the edge of the parking lot and squat down on his haunches. The boy began to make soft clicking noises with his mouth and he held out his hands and waited. He was whispering urgently into the brush.

John closed his eyes tight again as Charlie stood and turned, slump-shouldered.

"You can open 'em now," the boy said, defeated. "He ain't here. I thought he would stay."

"Who, son?"

"Punkin. I found him in the woods, he was just crouching around trying to catch a mouse. I kept him from eating the mouse and gave him some of my sandwich instead. He liked it. I named him Punkin 'cause he's yellow and he looks kinda like one. But he's spottier than a punkin and his feet are so big! I wanted to show you and Mama."

"Well, what was he?"

"A cat. A real big one, too, but nice. I could barely hold him, he was so big."

"Charlie, what are you talking about?"

"Uhn, Uncle John, listen!" The boy was becoming frustrated. "I'm telling you. I found a cat and he's my friend and I named him Punkin. He followed me back here, but then, just now, when I looked in the bushes, he was gone. I don't know why." Charlie's voice trailed off then and he returned to the edge of the woods and began to call, "Punkin? Punkin, come back!"

John rose and went to stand behind the boy. "He must have needed to go back home to his mama, don't you think?" Charlie had a fine imagination and John appreciated it, but sometimes you couldn't tell where his fanciful wanderings left off and the real world took over. This time he figured it must be all imagining. The boy couldn't have found a wildcat, could he? Probably just an old stray.

"I need to tell Mama. I know he'll come back and I want to be sure she don't make him go away. He's mine."

"Hold on there, Pal!" John didn't think Nanette was quite ready to hear about her little man toting bobcats around in the woods. And he needed a minute to think.

Could this indeed have been a bobcat kit or could it be . . . John knew that some people thought cougars were extinct in these mountains. They had been officially declared so in the 1920s, but there were many who disagreed. Mai Zinni had always been among them. She claimed to hear them sometimes in the forest and to have been visited in her grove on more than one occasion, but there had never been any witnesses other than her and sometimes her *visions* got mixed up with reality in her mind. Wait a minute. This was crazy thinking. Wasn't it? The boy did have a way with animals—always had, ever since he was a baby. But this? Nah, couldn't be. Nanette needed to find some friends for this boy. He was spending too much time alone.

"He liked it when I scratched him 'tween the ears, like this." Charlie reached up and scratched his own head, then closed his eyes and mimicked a cat enjoying a head rub. "His fur was spotted, like a baby deer. He was so cute, Uncle John. Would you help me look for him?"

"Charlie, this kit's a wild thing and his mama would be mighty worried about him if he disappeared."

"Oh, I don't think he has a mama," the boy said hopefully, "he don't."

"And how do you know that?"

"'cause where was she? A mama wouldn't leave her baby alone in the woods."

"Well, maybe she's trying to teach him. You know, you got to give 'em a little leeway, so's they can learn how to take care of themselves."

"No." Charlie was getting uncomfortable with this line of thinking. "He's mine. I'm gonna find him again and I'm gonna keep him." Charlie was backing away from John as he spoke and they both looked toward the door when Nanette stepped out onto the front porch.

"There you are, Rascal. Did you finish your chores?" Nanette stepped toward Charlie and, sensing that he had an ally in her, he regained his earlier enthusiasm.

"Mama! I found this cat in the woods and his name is Punkin and he's mine. Can I keep him? Please Mama. He needs me. I'll do all the work. You won't have to do nothing."

"Goodness Charlie, hold on. Where is this cat?" She looked at John and raised an eyebrow. He responded with a slight smile that said, *Don't worry. The boy's off in his head again.*

"Down in the woods, by that lady's house. Can I keep him, Mama? Can I?"

"I don't know, Charlie,"

"Can I go look for him? Please?"

Nanette sank down into the chair next to John, laughed and said, "Sure, Sweetie, go look for your kitty cat. I'm tired. My boss works me half to death. I'll just sit here and wait for you to get back. Don't be too long, you hear?" Then to John she said, shaking her head, "That boy of mine."

"Yep. He's got quite the imagination."

"Do you think there was a real cat?"

"Well, can't be sure, but he said it was big. It just might be a painter cub."

"What? There are no panthers in these mountains. Haven't been for years." Her momentary alarm gave way as she noticed John smiling.

"Maybe not."

"He can't keep it, whatever it is." Nanette sounded sure of herself, but she looked at John in a way that said, *He can't can he?*

"Well, let's don't go borrowin' trouble. We ain't seen a cat, now have we?"

"I've been so hard on him lately. I wish he had some friends."

"Aw, he'll be fine. Imagination is a good thing. Don't ever'body have it. Just the lucky ones." John pushed himself up out of the chair he'd been sitting in.

"John?" He turned toward her. "Do you really think Charlie might have found a panther cub?"

"Naw, probably just some old stray." the old man smiled and patted Nanette's shoulder.

"John?"

"Yes?"

"Thank you. Thank you for being such a good friend to Charlie."

"He'll be okay," John turned away quickly and went inside, the screen door slamming behind him.

He stood in the kitchen and sniffed angrily. He swiped at his eyes and, taking a glass from the cupboard, filled it from the tap. *Hell!* he thought, *that kid'll wear you out with his tales!*

Charlie did have a way with animals. It had been evident since he was a tiny thing, barely even walking. The birds would come and sit on his shoulders and eat seeds out of his pudgy little hand. Coons and foxes and squirrels never seemed afraid around him at all.

John could envision Charlie as a young man, a muscled cougar walking by his side down a forest path. He held the vision close to his heart for a long moment before shaking it off.

Later that afternoon, after Nanette had collected Charlie and gone into town, John took a little walk into the woods.

It was an unusually warm day and the afternoon light made it even warmer. John's old bandana was put to good use. Mopping sweat from his neck, his brow, he forged ahead deeper into the woods. He well knew the Safe Range that had been established for Charlie and he walked the perimeter of that and then spiraled back and covered the interior as well. He'd also been a boy himself so he ventured a little bit out of the Safe Range. He'd brought an old knap-sack and into it he put wild mushrooms when he found them. Might as well get some supper out of this mission. He was good at finding hickory chickens—the morels that grew around old apple trees and other nutrient rich places. They only grew for a little while in the spring and they were hard to find, blending into the leaves and roots as they did. They were worth looking for, though. He would cut them length-wise, soak them in milk, fry them up and have a delicious dinner. His mouth watered in anticipation.

Having found no sign of Charlie's cat John headed back to the inn. He was well within the Safe Range and walking along the side of a shallow muddy creek bed when he stopped to examine a pink lady slipper bloom. The sight of them always took him aback. A large showy flower, the single swollen bloom had a sexual quality about it that made John blush with long ago memories whenever he came across one.

As he stood now, a depression in the mud of the creek bed caught his eye. Squatting again for a closer look, he sucked his breath in. He put his big hand down in the mud next to the print for comparison and saw that it was big. He searched through the files in his brain. But he knew what he was seeing. Didn't he? This was the print of a big cat. A really big cat. Four toes, retractable claws not visible in the print. This thing was three and a half, maybe four inches across! He could only find the one print and it wasn't fresh, and so he couldn't be sure, but the hair on the back of his neck prickled and he wished he'd asked Charlie if the cat had a bob tail or a long one.

Chapter 13

The tiny bell tinkled as Jane pushed open the heavy wood door the next afternoon. She slipped from the sunlight into the rarified interior of *The Light Within*. She breathed heavily, trying to steady herself. She felt as if years had passed since the last time she'd crossed this threshold.

"You've come back." There was such pleasure and warmth in the little man's voice that, in spite of herself, Jane stepped forward toward the voice. She searched and found him in the shadows, by the heavy brocade curtain. The slight swaying of the fabric told her that he had been in the back when she'd come in. She wondered just what was back there. Her mind began to conjure seances, strange rituals and bitter aromas, when he spoke again, bringing her out of her revery. "Did you find the waterfall?"

"Yes. And Mai Zinni Trew, the woman who everyone seemed to think I needed to meet." She heard the questioning in her own voice.

"Good! I am Mac, by the way, Mac Harkness. I'm the owner of this strange little place."

"Nice to meet you, Mr. Harkness."

"Oh please, we're going to be friends. Call me Mac."

Wariness and enchantment vied for Jane's attention. Enchantment won. "All right, Mac. When I was in before, you said you'd read my cards?"

"Of course! Follow me." And, with that, he disappeared behind the curtain. She was being admitted to the inner sanctum.

Once the curtain was pulled back and she'd stepped through, it wasn't all that mysterious, but it was a warm and inviting space, and not without its exotic touches. The centerpiece of the area was a large round oaken table. Seances! Maybe she'd been right about that part. There was a small kitchen area across from the curtain, a little nook bumping out, dormer style, from the rest of the room. It had an arched window with a sink and counter set beneath it. On the counter was a hot plate with a kettle atop it. Below the sink, concealing the pipes, hung a curtain, predominately red, with a swirling purple design woven in. On one side of the sink were hooks, holding earthenware mugs, and on the other, two shelves with teas in boxes and jars, lined up. This is where Mac stood now, selecting mugs and choosing a tea. He turned and invited her to sit at the table and she did. While he prepared the tea, she looked around the room. There were two large windows hung with ancient lace curtains flanking the kitchen area, and two more on the wall to the left of it. The afternoon sunlight created intricate shadow patterns on the walls and on the worn surface of the table. The windows were open on this mild day and a light breeze lifted the curtains and made the shadows dance. Jane May quickly became entranced by this dance. When her focus returned, she found Mac studying her and humming a low and hypnotic tune. As soon as he realized she was aware again, he stopped singing and quickly turned back to the tea.

"Well then," he said, setting the mugs down on the table, "shall we get started?"

Mac produced a deck of cards from the pocket of his tapestry vest and begun shuffling adroitly. He had her cut the cards three times and, fanning them all out on the table face down, he asked her to quickly, without thinking, choose one card. She chose one from the middle and he turned it over. The Hanged Man. Mac didn't seem surprised and quickly slipped the card back into the deck and reshuffled. He asked her to cut again.

The cards were like birds in his hands. Inky blue birds with colorful underbellies, flashing as he shuffled. He began laying cards face down on the table between himself and Jane May. First one card with a second one lying crossways on top of it, then another above and one below. He continued with one card to the left of the initial four and then one to the right, one below and to the right of that and three more above it, until he had a pattern of cards on the table that resembled a cross. He seemed satisfied and sat back in his chair, closed his eyes and sighed. Jane looked from the blank, inky cards to the man and back. And she waited, as dust motes rode the shafts of sunlight and somewhere a clock ticked out the minutes.

Finally Mac opened his eyes. He took a deep breath and looking directly into her eyes and extending both of his hands, palms up, he asked, "Are you ready?"

The question seemed weighty, but Jane had no idea what to make of it, and so she simply said, "Yes."

"Place your hands in mind, please." She did so and was surprised by the warmth radiating from his palms. They sat like this for a moment. Mac's eyes were closed and so Jane May closed hers, too. The little man's lips moved, but she couldn't hear what he was saying. Finally, he withdrew his hands and Jane opened her eyes.

Slowly and with great care, Mac began to turn the cards over, beginning with the first one he'd laid down. The Hanged Man. Jane gasped. She'd watched him return the card to the deck and shuffle and shuffle and shuffle. She'd cut them herself. How could this be?

On the card, a person hanging upside down, tied by one foot. In spite of the uncomfortable position, this person seemed perfectly at ease, with both arms folded behind his back and his hair aflame. "What does it mean?" she asked. Mac hesitated slightly and she thought she detected a trace of a smile.

"This card is you, Jane. You've received a call, yes? A call to a more spiritual life. A more authentic life. It's why you're here. You are prepared to make the necessary sacrifices to follow this calling."

Sacrifices?

Now he revealed the second card. "This represents the obstacles standing in your way." Five of Swords. A figure in a green tunic, standing on the shore, holding three swords. Two more were lying on the beach with a pair of figures looking across the water. There were mountains on the far shore. One of the figures had an aspect of grief or defeat, hunched shoulders, head hanging down.

"You've been hurt. Betrayed. You've suffered loss." Tears sprang to Jane's eyes as Mac spoke and she brushed them away. "You're learning to adjust. To accept what's happened. Uncomfortable, but necessary. The past and what's happened to you is still holding you back and you've got to move on now. Do you understand?"

Yes, she understood. But was she ready, really ready, to move on? Her whole life seemed like an erratic dance of one step forward and two steps back.

Mac reached for the next card. When he had all the cards turned face up, Jane May was looking at a riot of colorful scenes. Women draped in saffron and cinnamon robes, holding golden cups aloft. A woman in white, with garlands of fruit draping her head and her tunic, was petting a lion. White horses outfitted in festival regalia, with proud or aggressive riders.

Pensive youths and royals wearing golden crowns and perched on ornate thrones. There were deep blue skies and mountains and seashores, lush fruits and ornately carved animal heads. The cards laid out on the old table held stories and Jane May wanted to unlock them. She let her eyes go soft and the images began to run together. Faintly she heard the pounding of hooves and felt a warm breeze, lifting her hair . . . .

Mac's voice brought Jane back to the room. "You have all that you need already in place, my dear. I see a kind and maternal female who will help you in your quest."

Quest? Am I on a quest? Jane wondered. *I thought I'd just run away from home.*

"You'll meet opposition, but you will overcome it and transform the opposer into an ally. You are surrounded and upheld by a pervasive and gentle but fierce feminine energy. This manifests both outwardly, in actual women, but also from inside yourself. This feminine energy is balanced by masculine influences as well. In the past, the strong men in your life have been both brave and false, treacherous and clever. These influences will give way to wisdom. Men who understand and embody authentic power, compassion, protection. Power that comes from within, not in dominating another. Your struggle is largely inside yourself. It's a matter of learning to trust your inner voice and your guides."

Jane was fighting back tears as Mac spoke, his words resonating deeply within her tired and wounded heart.

"I'd like to draw your attention to this card." Mac pointed to the woman, dressed in white, caressing the head of a lion. At the top of the card, a roman numeral eight. At the bottom, the word Strength.

Jane inhaled sharply, as the image of the lion fully hit her. The mountain lion that John was carving, the animals she'd thought she'd seen in the woods around her cottage, and in her dreams.

"This is your house dear, your environment. You stand on a foundation of strength. Your strong will is a fine asset which will serve you well. The beast within you can be tamed. You are exactly where you need to be. You will grow beyond your imagining and you will be successful. But, and I must caution you, happiness is not guaranteed. Happiness does not come with success. Happiness comes from within you and must be carefully and intentionally cultivated. Do you understand?"

She didn't. Not fully anyway, but she was so overwhelmed that all she wanted to do was be alone to process what she'd heard, so she said, "Yes. I understand. And thank you, Mac. Thank you for your time. This has been invaluable. How much do I owe you?"

"Oh, Pet, this one is on the house. And don't you hesitate to come back with any questions you may have after you've had time to take all this in. It's a lot, I know. Just remember that you're exactly where you're supposed to be right now." With that, Mac stood up and began to put away the cards and the tea things.

Jane slung her purse over her shoulder, thanked him again, and as she pulled back the curtain, Mac said, "I hope you'll come to the street dance on Friday. The whole town turns out. It's quite lovely."

"I saw the signs for it. It sounds like fun. Maybe I will. Thank you."

The interior of the car was hot from sitting in the sun, so she lowered all the windows and sat, stunned, for a few moments, eyes closed, hands on the steering wheel. Jane's need to be alone was strong now. She turned the key and the engine rumbled to life. *I have everything I need. I'm right where I'm supposed to be.* She smiled to herself as she backed out and headed for the inn and her safe little cottage.

She hadn't meant to come here. She was going home to shut herself up inside her cottage and think about the reading. But somehow, on the way, she had turned the car around and headed for the rhododendron tunnel and the waterfall. She didn't want to see the old woman again. Not today anyway. She had had enough intensity for now, but she was drawn, ineluctably, to the forest. She had felt such peace yesterday in this place. She wanted to feel that again. But it was not to be. Today was a day to be shaken up. Hung upside down. Hair aflame.

Jane May parked where she had parked her car before. She could even see the grooves left by her tires in the gravel pull-out. But she couldn't find the path that she'd taken. Where was the rhododendron tunnel with its twisted branches arching overhead? How could she not see it? She tried again and again to penetrate the underbrush, knowing that the path must be there. But again and again she was met only with brambles, which tore at her clothes and her skin and allowed no entry into the forest. She could plainly see the short path to Mai Zinni's house.

I suppose I could go that way and just hurry past her house into the forest. Maybe she's not even at home. I think I can back track the way I came yesterday and find the waterfall again. She made sure that her car was locked and headed down the path. As she came around the last bend and was in sight of Mai Zinni's little house in the clearing, she stopped dead in her tracks. Nanette was coming out the back door carrying a large basket, with Mai Zinni right behind her. Jane May prickled with irritation. *Why am I seeing this angry woman everywhere?* The two women made eye contact and held it until Mai Zinni's voice broke the spell.

"Jane," she said simply, "have you met Nanette?"

"Oh yes. We've met."

Perhaps Mai Zinni sensed the animosity between the two, but she didn't let on. "Come in then. Nanette, stay. We'll have tea. I wanted you two to meet anyway. This is perfect."

Just perfect, thought Jane.

Jane tried to protest, but the old woman would have nothing but that the two women entered her house and sat at her table after Period was shooed from his cozy nest on one of the chairs. They were served a simple, delicious spread of hard cheese, tea, and the most delicate little sweet cakes Jane had ever seen.

Nanette sunk down at the table with an exaggerated sigh. Jane did the same. The two women sat sullen as little girls, forced from their play and made to sit like ladies. Neither initiated conversation, so Mai Zinni carried it for them.

"Nanette works at the inn where you're staying, Jane, but I s'pose you knew that already. She's been such a help to John. There's no way he could have managed things himself these last years. And he's been a regular savior to her as well. When little Charlie was born and Nanette was all alone, John took her in, gave her a home and a job and a father figure for the boy."

Nanette squirmed as her personal life was hung out like laundry on a line for Jane May to examine. Feeling almost sorry for the younger woman, Jane May tried to change the subject by asking what was in the basket that Nanette had been carrying. It was a large, beautifully made basket with a twisted vine for a handle and an intricate pattern woven into a border around the rim. A bundle of feathers had been attached where the handle joined the basket on one side. A muslin cloth covered the contents.

"Oh, Nanette's picking up sweets to take to the bakery for me," Mai Zinni answered, before Nanette could get her mouth opened. The younger woman was looking more and more peeved and she took this opportunity to take her leave.

"And I need to get them there before I have to pick Charlie up. Thank you for the tea, Mai." Ducking her head, she added, mumbling, "Ms. Gideon." She scooped up the basket and was gone in a flash.

"Call me Jane," Jane said, but Nanette was out of earshot.

Mai Zinni chuckled. "Ooowee! She don't like you."

"Well, for heaven's sake!" Jane was really flustered now. "I barely even know the woman and I haven't done one thing to make her dislike me except to tip Charlie when he helped me with my bags. She's the one with the problem."

"Simmer down, now." Mai Zinni was still smiling. "She don't mean nothing. She's a proud one, that's all. You'll be friends before it's all over, I'm betting."

"Hmph! That's what John said. I don't need any friends and certainly not friends like that. Thank you for the tea. I'd better get back to the inn now."

"Did you find what you came for?"

"What?"

"What you came here for today, Child. Did you find it?"

"Well, I . . . I mean . . . I wasn't really coming here. I was trying to get to the waterfall that I found yesterday and I couldn't find it, so no."

"Oh. Well, maybe next time." The old woman turned away and busied herself at the sink.

Jane sensed that she was being dismissed and again anger rose in her throat. *The nerve of this old woman. I just want peace. I just want to be left alone. I came here to get away from people. To have some time to myself, for Pete's sake!*

Jane May slammed the kitchen door and stomped up the path to her car. Only when she got there did she wonder why she hadn't seen Nanette's car when she drove up. How had she gotten herself to the old witch's house. *Oh well, what do I care?* Gravel flew like shrapnel as she spun out of the parking area and onto the road.

Chapter 14

Mai Zinni awoke early, as she always did. There was nothing but a lace panel covering her bedroom window. She liked waking to the sun, lying down as the moon rose, dreaming under the stars. When the weather was warm, she mostly lived outside. When it was cold, she built a fire in her iron pot outside or she stayed in, preparing salves and ointments with the dried and infused flowers and plant materials she'd gathered in the spring and summer, or dreamed, or sewed, which was getting harder all the time. This past winter she had sewn a quilt. This might be her last. Her fingers weren't as nimble as they used to be and her eyes could barely see to get the needle threaded. She took pleasure, though, in sitting by the firelight, the quilt spread out over her lap, Period curled into a punctuation mark, nestled beneath it warming her legs. What pleasure to while away a winter's evening creating something new and beautiful. It took her back to her childhood when she'd sit at Granny Street's feet, playing with a corn dolly or homemade wooden blocks, while Granny sewed her colorful quilts. Her grandmother had been known across these mountains for the quality of her hand-sewn creations. Her stitches were straight and tiny and her color combinations exquisite. She created intricate patterns with tiny pieces of fabric, cut from her own worn out dresses and those of her daughter and her granddaughter, Mai Zinni. Her quilts, along with her canned jams and sourwood honey, kept them in shoes, while Mai Zinni's mama worked cleaning houses and gathering galax leaves to sell to the local florists. They had a simple life, but a good one and Mai Zinni never went without. She smiled now to recall those long ago years.

 The quilt that she'd pieced this last winter was made of fabrics she'd gleaned from the Goodwill and also things that people brought her. As she'd sat by the fire piecing the bits together, she had mused about the lives of the people who'd worn the clothes . . . the thread she used tied all those people and their stories together. *What a mistake people make thinking that there is any separation between us,* she thought. *Really, if you could get up very high, into space, or heaven, you'd be able to see that we're all part of one organism. Everyone connected. Everyone's actions affecting everyone else in small ways and big ones, too.* Sewing these quilts out of the cast-off detritus of stranger's lives—tablecloths, work pants, handkerchiefs—gave Mai Zinni a feeling of connection.

Granny Street's quilts hung in museums and private collections, still, to this day. Mai Zinni's creations would never be as fine as that, but they had warmed people she loved on cold nights, and that was good enough for her. Little Star had lain with her mama and daddy outside on summer evenings, star-gazing, on one of those quilts. They had tucked her into bed under another. Mai's quilts had been used as picnic blankets, tablecloths, and one of them had served as a pall on Granny Street's coffin when she was buried. All these patches, all these stitches forming kaleidoscopic patterns which connected Mai Zinni with all of her ancestors, backward and forward, too, as surely some of her quilts would survive to warm others.

This new quilt would go in the hutch where she kept them all. She didn't have anyone in particular in mind when she was working on it, just sewing for the pleasure of it. Sometimes, if she knew she was making one for someone in particular, a new baby, or an old friend, she would remember stories about them as she sewed or put prayers and hopes for their health and happiness into the cloth as she stitched. Mai Zinni believed that part of her went into anything she created. Some energetic halo imbuing the object, giving it life. If she was sad, say, while sewing a quilt, the recipient might experience sorrowful dreams. If she sewed a quilt for someone just married, she always tried to get a happily married couple to sleep under it at least once to put that steady, happy feeling in. They were not so easy to find though.

This particular quilt contained the glow of firelight and the memories of a woman who had lived and loved, laughed and shed tears aplenty. She hoped that whoever sat wrapped in it someday might feel a contentment. And also a longing for the people they had loved and lost. These are the things she had felt as she sat, sewing, through the winter.

Unbidden, a picture arose in her mind. The new woman, Jane May Gideon, wrapped in the quilt, her face illuminated by firelight.

Mai Zinni had been surprised by her arrival. And at the same time, not. She'd been expecting her for such a long time that when she finally arrived, it was almost anticlimactic. She just simply drove up to the inn one day. Shouldn't there have been a shooting star heralding her coming? An earthquake? Some sign?

Mai Zinni had lived her life by signs. So had her mother and her grandmother and her grandmother's mother before her. She didn't know any other way and couldn't imagine how people got by without guidance and markers to show them that they were on the right path. And so she was a bit reluctant. There hadn't been any sign. Or maybe she had missed it. Sometimes that happened and when she looked back she would remember—oh yes, there was a big storm the day before and I found a feather. Or deer came into the yard . . . or I had that dream . . . always something. But with this one, nothing. Still, she felt sure that Jane was the one she'd waited for. The one to whom she was to impart the knowledge. Maybe she needed to believe it.

Jane May didn't know it yet. Of course not. But that was okay. Mai Zinni was nothing if not patient. She'd waited a long time already and she was in no hurry to push things now. She would wait for Jane to get comfortable.

Meanwhile, a beautiful day was dawning and Mai dressed quickly and left her cottage, lifting her gathering basket as she went out the door. She loved to be in the forest just as it was waking up in the morning. Fog drifted among the trees and a chill permeated the air. She was wrapped in a heavy woolen sweater even though it was Spring. She moved carefully among the large stones and the fallen logs, picking her way through the shadows. As she moved, spears of sunlight began to find their way through the canopy, lighting a patch of bloodroot here, a mushroom there. Mai Zinni deftly picked and dropped things into her basket, murmuring thanks as she went.

She considered the plants of the forest to be her kindred. Allies. Helpers. She loved them and had tremendous respect for them. She knew which ones to harvest and when and which to leave alone. She never took more than she needed for herself and her potions. She always asked the plants silently before she picked and thanked them afterward. She brought an offering whenever she gathered. Her grandmother had taught her that. Today, it was bits of bread that she'd baked yesterday. She broke off pieces and left them along the trail, a gift to the dwellers of the forest, in thanksgiving, and also that she might always be welcomed here and allowed to partake of the bounty.

When her basket was nearly filled with mushrooms, bloodroot, violet leaves and flowers, and the roots, flowers, and leaves of dandelion, she sat down on a fallen log cushioned with moss and broke out a thermos of coffee from a deep pocket in her skirt. *Ahhhh*, she breathed, as her hands cupped the hot metal cap, and she drank the warm, viscous liquid with delight. *My life has been so rich.* The privilege of living her whole life in a place as botanically diverse and beautiful as this was almost more than she could believe. Her ancestors, farther back than she remembered, had loved this very land upon which she sat having her cup of coffee. Her feet rested on dirt that their feet had touched for thousands of years. Their blood, their tears had watered this ground, their bodies had fertilized it, as hers would one day. Mai Zinni's eyes filled with tears thinking of this long line of ancestors stretching out behind her. She loved them so and she was grateful to them for all the gifts that they had imparted to her, all the memories, all the help and guidance that they provided still. She was never alone. So surrounded was she by the kindred and the ancestors, not to mention the human beings that she'd been blessed with. John and Mac, Nanette and Charlie, and this new one, Jane May. Mai Zinni missed her Little Star and that baby that she had never known. She missed her grandmother and her mother, but they weren't gone, not really. She felt them all near and she was grateful and empowered by them.

She remembered a dream that she'd had the night before.

She was young and strong. Powerful, but humble and kind. She was in her forest, but the trees were bigger than she had ever seen them. Huge behemoths, they were. She was clothed in skins of some sort. As she walked along a trail that snaked among the giant trees, she became aware of the presence of another. Looking behind her, she was surprised, but not frightened, to see a lion, tawny and regal, keeping pace with her. She stopped and turned and the lion spoke in a voice deep and rich, "There is a plan, my dear one, and it is going well."

She opened her mouth to question the lion, but it had vanished into the mist, which now permeated the forest. She turned to continue on the path and saw, in front of her, a tree, larger than any of the others, and beneath it an opening in the roots nearly large enough for her to stand upright in. She entered it, bending only slightly to do so, and was in a large hollow space with roots for a roof and a moss floor. Light filtered in from a source which she could not see. An amber light infused the space with warmth. She felt so at home here that she lay down on the moss and fell immediately to sleep and into a dream.

In the dream within a dream, she rose out of her self, sleeping in the root house, and walked out into the forest again. She ambled down a path, carpeted with thick leaf mould, until she came to a clearing. In the clearing was a large bonfire and around the bonfire were people dancing. Many people, and she seemed to know them all, and she moved closer and began to sway to the sound of drums and her swaying soon gave way to a frenzy of movement and that soon gave way to flight and she was flying over the scene of the people dancing round the fire and...then she woke up.

Bones creaking, for she was no longer young and strong, Mai Zinni rose now, collected her basket and her thermos and, with a heart full of gratitude, she made her way home again.

Chapter 15

Gideon had been transformed. Jane May parked her car in the public lot and made her way among a moving throng to Main Street. It was closed to traffic and the trees lining both sides glittered with tiny white lights. On its way down, the sun illuminated the mountains that ringed the little town, casting their peaks here and there in a pink glow. The faces of the people gathering were golden in the disintegrating light. A bluegrass band tuned up on a stage at one end of the street and children weaved in and out among the legs of grownups, shouting to each other. Colorful banners hung from the lampposts, inviting, "Come Home to Gideon, a Small Town With a Big Heart." Aromas of funnel cakes and popcorn and grilling hamburgers twirled around each other and coalesced into a savory haze. Jane's mouth watered. She approached a booth, bright and beckoning with paintings of lemons and hotdogs adorning its facade. A young man in a white apron and tee shirt from a local church was flipping burgers. He turned from the grill and asked what he could get for her.

"Oh, I think I'll start with a hamburger and a cup of that lemonade."

"Coming right up." He smiled and turned back to the grill and Jane May watched the swelling crowd as she waited for her burger. She was overcome by that particular sense of well-being that a small town summer festival can impart. For the moment, all was right with the world. She was a part of something. Something wholesome and light. Something grounded in community and neighborly conviviality. Something that felt like home. The band struck up the first chords of a song and she began to tap her foot and the smiling man in the white apron said, "Got your burger and your lemonade right here."

Jane May wandered through the crowd until she found a bench and sat down to eat her supper. The burger was juicy and delicious, the lemonade, cloyingly sweet, made her wince and then laugh as she took the first sip.

This was the overly sweet lemonade of county fairs and homemade stands, and hot, lazy summer afternoons rocking on the porch. The lemonade that made your mouth pucker and your teeth begin to rot. *But my goodness,* she thought, *it's delicious!*

"Hey lady! Miss Jane!" Charlie was jumping up and down and waving at her from the other side of the street. When she saw him, he came running over. "What'cha eatin'?"

"I'm having a hamburger. How are you, Charlie?"

"Fine. Did you have a funnel cake, yet? They're my favorite."

"No I haven't and I don't know if I can stand any more sugar after this lemonade, but I like funnel cakes, too. Where's your mother?"

"She's working in Miss Alice's booth, selling pies. You should go by and say hey." Their conversation was punctuated by the clang of a bell and raucous cheering, as someone swung a sledgehammer hard and hit the mark, winning a stuffed bear or a funny hat. The cacophony of sounds and smells and the openness of this darling boy's face and the breezy evening all conspired to make Jane think that stopping by Alice's booth and saying hi to Nanette and maybe picking up a piece of pie to take home might be a good idea.

Charlie ran ahead and Jane ambled down the street, the plastic cup of lemonade sweating in her hand. The band was in full swing now and a few people down near the stage were dancing in the street. The big red ball of the sun was perched on a mountain peak, casting everything in its fiery glow. For a split-second eternity, the whole world hung suspended in a hush. And then the orb slipped from its perch and slid behind the mountain and the curtain of night was lowered slowly onto the stage, the scene resumed, the people danced, the children screamed and laughed, and Jane May Gideon let go of the breath that she'd held for that moment and continued down the street behind a small boy who was running now toward his mother.

"Mama!" he called, as he ran. "Look who I found! That lady, Miss Jane!" His hands softened his collision with the booth, as he slid to a stop.

"Goodness, Charlie, slow down!" Alice laughed. "You'll knock my booth over, boy!" She reached over and tousled his dusty hair. Nanette was behind her, slicing pies and placing the luscious triangles on paper plates. There was a mountainous stack of sky blue plates beside her and, waiting to be divided, an impressive array of pies fanned out on the long table. Alice and Nanette wore blue aprons with the Alice's Pie in the Sky logo. From the outside the booth looked like a miniature version of the bakery with its sky blue awning studded with fluffy white clouds. Inside, cut-outs of bluebirds, fat pies, and more clouds, hung from the supports, twirling in the breeze from a big box fan.

It was a charming scene made delectable by the assortment of pies. There were fruit pies, meringue pies, tiny individual tarts, and large fluffy cream pies. Pies with latticed crusts, golden and glistening and sparkled with sugar, and mounded pies, bursting with filling, their top crusts embellished with intricate bows and birds and hearts. One pie was prominently displayed in the front of the booth, on a metal pedestal. This one was stuffed with peaches and covered with a fine, delicate crust. It featured an heirloom ceramic pie vent, in the shape of a bluebird, singing its heart out from the center of the pastry. The same pie vent that had allowed steam to escape from the pies that had cooled on the windowsills of Alice's childhood home, explained a hand-lettered sign propped beside the pedestal. And the childhood home of her mother before her. The whole business—Alice's Pie in the Sky—had been built around this little porcelain figure which had taken on the status of a sacred object, even being housed in a small glass case in the shop when it wasn't doing its job venting pies.

Charlie's collision with the booth had rattled the pedestal that the featured pie squatted upon so Nanette was peeved and on edge before the exchange with Jane even began.

Nanette stood, slowly wiping the large slicing knife with a damp cloth. She admonished her son silently, using only her eyes. He ducked his head and shuffled his feet, trying to shake off the discomfort of her gaze. Jane May's sense of well-being diminished incrementally as the seconds ticked by. The knife-wiping added an unnerving element to the awkwardness.

"Charlie, who's your friend?" Alice broke the spell and Nanette put down the knife and stepped forward to the front of the booth.

"This is Miss Jane. She lives at the inn, down by the stream." The boy perked up again as he introduced Jane.

"Well hello, Miss Jane. I'm Alice. Pleasure to meet you. What's your favorite kind of pie?" Alice stuck out her warm, slightly sticky hand and Jane's feeling of well-being increased again by a fraction.

"Oh gosh, I don't know. Pecan? No lemon. Definitely, lemon meringue."

"Well, have we got a treat for you then," said Alice as she turned to the pie table and scanned for lemon meringue. But as she was scanning, Jane spotted a pale, honey-colored slice and she couldn't help herself.

"Is that chess? Oh, my grandmother made the best chess pie and I haven't had it in years!"

Alice laughed and snatched up the chess. "Good choice! Chess is good. No frills. Just the basics: sugar, eggs and butter."

"What more do you need?" said Jane.

"Exactly! You'll like this one." Jane reached into her pocket and Alice waved her off. "New friends always get a free slice."

Jane May's sense of well-being skyrocketed as she bit into the pie, its sweet creaminess filling her mouth and a big smile lighting up her face. She covered her mouth and exclaimed around the pie, "Oh yes!" Swallowing, she declared that it was exactly like her grandmother's pie. And then she remembered that she hadn't spoken to Nanette yet. So before she took another bite, she said hello and Nanette responded in kind. The inevitable awkward silence was delayed as Jane finished her pie and Nanette waited on two chatty customers while Alice set Charlie up behind the counter with a slice of strawberry. He said that he didn't have a favorite and didn't see how anyone could. He didn't like rhubarb, the one time he'd had it, but other than that, they were all his favorites and he intended to try every single kind of pie that Alice could come up with.

Jane blotted up the stray bits of crust with her fingers. Charlie finished his, too, in three gulping bites. He jumped down from the stool he'd been perched on. "Mama, can I go ride the pony?"

"May I, Charlie," she corrected.

He laughed, and mimicking her, said, "No silly, you have to help Miss Alice!"

She fished in her pocket and handed him a couple of bills. "Come on back here and check in with me afterward, you hear?"

"Yes Mama, I hear and I obey," he intoned the words like a sleep-walking zombie. Then he was gone in a cloud of boyish magic, and the inevitable awkward moment had arrived. Alice had taken over the pie cutting, leaving Nanette nothing to do but wait on customers, and at the moment, there weren't any. Jane desperately wanted to walk away, but had drawn a blank on how to accomplish that in a civilized manner, so both women stood in the uncomfortable silence, until Jane regrettably spoke.

"So, that boy of yours is a handful, I imagine."

Nanette glared and between clenched teeth, she asked, "What do you mean?"

Jane recognized immediately that even though she'd meant nothing, finding the boy completely charming herself, she should have chosen a more neutral topic. All she could do now was to fawn and back peddle. She did both of those with abandon, but only seemed to make the situation worse.

"I am so sorry, Ms. Gideon, that my boy continues to bother you. I will make sure that he doesn't do it again."

Oh dear, thought Jane, *this isn't going well at all.*

"Nanette, please," she said, "I didn't mean anything at all. Only that he's quite spirited. I'm very fond of Charlie. Please don't be angry with him."

"Spirited? Do you mean hyperactive?"

"No, certainly not." But Nanette couldn't hear Jane now. She had taken a position and she was locked in. And her position seemed to be that Jane was a meddling busybody.

"I'll tell you what." Nanette's feet were planted. With her fists on her hips, she leaned forward slightly, toward Jane. Alice came up behind her and laid a hand on her shoulder and simply said her name. Nanette waved her angrily off. "You leave the raising of my son to me. I'll keep your house clean and leave fresh towels for you because that's my job. Beyond that we don't need to have any dealings with each other." Nanette turned to Alice and said in a falsely calm voice, "I need to go find Charlie. Can you handle this for a minute?"

After Nanette had gone, Alice left the booth and went around to the front where Jane was standing, shaking, and she put her arm around her and said, "Oh Honey, her bark is way worse than her bite. She doesn't mean anything."

Jane did her best to fight back tears. "I always do this," she sniffed. "Every time I see her, I seem to say the wrong thing and she gets so angry."

"Listen, it isn't you, Hon. That girl's got real old anger she's holding on to. She's jealous too, of you, you know."

"What? Why?"

"I shouldn't speak for Nanette, but it's a real old hurt with Mai Zinni. Lots of other hurts too, but that one's sticking in her craw now, with you coming to town and all. But if you just give her some time, she might come around eventually."

"I just don't understand," Jane sputtered in frustration, "I barely know that old woman. I've only even met her a couple of times. Why do people keep talking about her?"

Alice led Jane back into the booth. They sat on the two stools by the pie cutting table and Alice began to talk.

"Nanette went to Mai Zinni years ago, after her no-good husband had left her broke, and with a baby boy to raise. She was a good girl, and she had her roots here, but Mai Zinni knew that she wasn't the one."

"The one for what?" Jane asked, peevishly.

"I'm gettin' to it, Honey. Nanette was desperate and she had some knowledge of the plants already. She couldn't believe that Mai wouldn't take her on as an apprentice. Mai Zinni cared for Nanette and she loved little Charlie, right from the start. She paid her a little to gather herbs and mushrooms in the forest and to deliver her baked goods to me, but what Nanette asked of her she could not give. And she couldn't explain why not. Thankfully John took her in. It's been good for both of them. All of them. Little Charlie loves John and John loves him. Mai's happy that John isn't all alone over there. And she always says she will know the right one when she meets her."

"Okay." Jane could see why Nanette was disgruntled with the old woman, but why her? "I still don't understand. The one for what? And what does this have to do with me?"

"I've said too much already, but you try not to worry about Nanette so much. It's nothing to do with you, really." Alice handed Jane a slice of pie in a parchment bag. "Here's your lemon, Sugar. You don't have to choose a favorite." She gave Jane a quick hug as a customer approached the booth.

Jane accepted both the pie and the hug and made her way toward her car, shaking her head as she went, her sense of well-being quite diminished now, but pie in hand, she knew it would return eventually.

PART 2

THE MOTHER

Gael lay tangled in the embrace of the man, content in the aftermath of love. Her body was grateful for the contact and the release. It had been a long time since she'd laid eyes, much less flesh, on another. She didn't expect him to stay around for long. He'd stumbled on the tiny shelter that she had created in the roots of a huge hemlock tree and called home for several years. She had found him, a bloody heap, half out of his mind in the clearing next to her little shelter. He'd been bone tired and wounded. Starving too. She dragged him in, cleaned him up, poured trickles of spring water into his mouth and kept watch, lest his attackers found him here and tried to finish their dreadful work. They hadn't. Either they'd hurt him as much as they wanted to, or he was presumed dead. Both options seemed plausible. He had been brutally roughed up. He lay unconscious for twenty-four hours before waking groggily and asking where he was. He barely made sense for the first few hours, but once Gael had gotten some food into him, a stew made from foraged mushrooms and greens, and a hunk of rough bread, lucidity began to dawn in his strange sad eyes. He was able to sit up and he let her hold his head while he drank from the earthenware vessel she held to his lips. She was mesmerized by those eyes. One a deep soulful brown and the other limpid like a blue pond. Some might have called those eyes the mark of the devil. There was so much fear afoot in the world. But Gael looked into them and felt that she was looking into windows beyond which lay beauty and mystery. She had tended him well and in the last hours of one crystal clear night, exhausted, and both grateful, they gentled each other, without words, or need of words, toward an easy ecstasy.

Afterward, the man groaned in pain as he disentangled himself from her limbs and eased up to a sitting position.

"Does it hurt much?"

"A bit, but I can take it," he boasted.

They both laughed and she kissed him tenderly as if he were someone she loved. And in a way she did love him. Even though she didn't know him at all and maybe because of that, she loved him without fetters, without notions, without expectations. Purely. Innocently. Still, she didn't expect him to stay and so was surprised when he said that he wanted to.

"I've nowhere to go," he'd said. "I'd like to stay on for awhile, if you'll have me. I'll heal up soon and then I'll be handy. I can hunt and keep you in wood for fires, and haul water." His voice trailed off when she smiled and laid her hand on his arm.

"Stay," was all she said.

When he had been there with her for six cycles of the moon and they had developed a comfortable, friendly routine that included loving under the stars, and inside the hollows of the ancient tree, and on leaf beds in the forest and by the stream that ran near, and once in the fork of two massive limbs high up in the tree, he looked at her with his sorrowful eyes and said, "I have to go."

She turned away in order that he not see her vulnerability. Before he came, she'd had no idea how much her solitude had cost her. When she set out all those years ago with her beloved childhood pet, Gruffyn, she'd only meant to have a little adventure. She had always thought that she would return, triumphantly, to her village. She had imagined her mother's joy upon seeing her. She would stay and help her mother, as she always had, until she married one of the boys she had known since she was a child. It would be a fine life. She just needed to see some of the world first. But it was not to be. There was always that danger. Stay safe at home or follow your heart, your dreams, and risk the road to return being barred. The fates had not seen fit to allow her to go home then and when they did, so much time had passed and so much distance. She had become a grown woman and a different person than the one who'd left. She wondered if anyone would even know her, or she them. And would they be angry at the pain she must have caused her mother? Still, she meant to return, truly she did, but it hadn't happened and then one day, while traveling for supplies, she'd gotten word that her mother had died. Crushed by regret and a feeling of utter abandonment, Gael had retreated into the forest with her grief and other than brief trips into a neighboring village for whatever supplies she could not forage, she rarely had any human contact at all. The villagers regarded her with curiosity when she came into town and behind her back they called her Owl Feather, because she had befriended a little screech owl and it sometimes rode on her shoulder. She knew what they called her and it suited her just fine. She would chuckle and say to herself, "Come along Owl Feather, let's go brew something up."

So when the man made to go, the hollow space that opened inside her was familiar. Still she couldn't stop the longing his leaving stirred up in her chest.

He stayed for three more days and then one chilly morning, when the leaves were just beginning to change on the trees, he kissed her long and deep and then disappeared into the woods without a backward glance.

She had not told him about the child that swam now under her heart. What would have been the point?

Chapter 16

"Memories," Mai Zinni was saying, "make people all sad. *I remember this and I remember that and I want it to be like it was.* Here's the thing, can't nothing ever be like it was. That's gone, it's over. Don't even exist anymore. Your memories, though—your memories are safe. They are real, at least to you. You own them. They're yours. Can't nothing change that. There's no need for all the longing and the yearning to go back somewhere. That somewhere ain't real anyway. It's gone. But what you got—memories—that is real. That's as real as you and me standing here. That's someplace you can go whenever you want. You can wander for days if you like, but you'd do better to spend a goodly amount of time in the here and now. It's the only real thing there is." Mai Zinni paused for a long moment during which she seemed to doze off. Jane waited patiently. Finally Mai spoke, "And you can change the past too."

"What do you mean?"

"Well, if it's gone . . . if it ain't even real, then you can remember it however you want. See?"

"Hmmm . . . ." Jane May pondered this before speaking. "Isn't that just revisionist history? Or worse, lying?"

"Or healing the past. Time ain't what you think, Child. Everything is happening all the time. Everything." Mai Zinni paused for effect, "All at once. See?"

Jane May certainly did not see, but she declined to say so, hoping that maybe in time the meaning would become apparent. Sometimes this happened when Mai Zinni talked. One day, out of the blue, what she'd said would just suddenly make sense. Meanwhile the two women sat, side by side, with this bit of seemingly incomprehensible wisdom between them, squatting on its haunches, looking from one to the other, waiting for acknowledgment. Jane May chose to move on.

"But what about bad memories?"

"Ah," said the old woman as a sly half-smile blossomed on her face, "turn those ones into birds."

This is how it went most times with Mai Zinni. She talked and Jane May listened, soaking up her cryptic words like they were water and she'd been wandering in the desert for a thousand years. Many times the words seemed pleasantly idle, but then later, maybe that same day, or lying in bed at night in the thin place between waking and sleep, or even days later, they would push themselves into the front of Jane's mind and lodge there. She would turn the old woman's words over and study them from every angle and then tuck them away again like jewels into some pocket of herself, where they would remain until she needed them or, unbidden, they would return to her, demanding her attention. Other times Mai's teachings seemed so convoluted, so obtuse. And sometimes they sounded just plain crazy. But Jane May kept coming back for more. She couldn't have explained this to herself, except to say that the old woman's voice was like a balm, rubbed into her battered life, and the more of it she got, the more she wanted.

No one who knew Mai was surprised by any of this. Since Jane May pulled into town on the wings of spring, everybody figured she was the one Mai Zinni had been waiting for all these years. Though it wasn't talked about much, the people of Gideon knew that the old *Deborah* woman who lived deep in the forest and had the gift of healing and sight was waiting for someone to impart her secrets to. The things she knew had been handed down for generations from mother to daughter and although Mai Zinni had had a daughter of her own, Little Star was long gone, wanting nothing to do with the old ways.

Jane May Gideon was surprised, though. She thought that what she was doing, when she'd packed up her things and left her home, was going off to be by herself for awhile. To rest. To give herself time to figure things out. She wasn't looking for anything except a little peace. Or at least that's what she'd told herself. She certainly wasn't looking for herbal lore, or any of that, or a teacher of those things. And if she had been looking she would never have imagined a crazy old witch woman living alone in the mountains to be the teacher she sought. But, although she herself was only just becoming aware of it, it was clear to most everyone else that Jane May Gideon was becoming an apprentice to the old woman.

Jane May had come the long way this morning to visit Mai Zinni. Wandering down the woodland path that she'd first stumbled onto almost two months ago, she still didn't understand the logistics of this passage. There was something about the way the path spiraled around and passed the waterfall and crossed the stream and wound up in Mai Zinni's front yard that didn't quite make sense, but Jane had long since stopped trying to understand and just accepted it. Although she could take the other way in, which was much shorter and more direct, she preferred to duck into the rhododendron thicket, which was in full glorious bloom now. She loved to meander down the path, strewn with petals in every shade of pink, and through the woods in the company of birds and small furry things and always something else, some unseen presence that was comforting, familiar. She couldn't put her finger on it, but it was as if someone long-ago loved and lost had returned.

As comforting as this presence was, on this day thoughts of Jane May's daughter, Isabelle, weighed heavy and her heart ached. Isabelle, angry and unable to forgive. Though Lord knows, Jane May didn't forgive herself or feel worthy of anyone else's forgiveness. She would have done anything to earn Isabelle's, if only she had any idea where her daughter was.

The fights had been heated, the words bitter, the feelings twisted and desperate for months, and then one day Isabelle didn't answer the phone when Jane called or the door when she went by. After several days of this awful silence, Jane had used the key that Issy had given her for emergencies and gone in to find the apartment mostly cleaned out. The landlord said that she'd left suddenly, with no notice, and so had forfeited her deposit—sorry. No she hadn't left a forwarding address or even a note. There had been a young man with a truck and they had packed everything they could fit into it and that was all the landlord knew. But he was going to call Goodwill to come get what was left unless she wanted to go through it.

She had sifted through everything that Issy left behind, looking for anything. Some clue as to where she'd gone. She found nothing, and a truck came and hauled off all the second hand furniture. After they'd left, Jane sat on the floor in the middle of the empty apartment. Her grief could no longer be contained, and she wept. The pool of sunshine she'd been sitting in moved off and left her in shadows as the afternoon wore on.

Finally she dried her eyes and went home.

Ben. The subject of much of the fighting. Jane didn't trust him. He wasn't honest, she could read it in his eyes. Or maybe she just didn't trust any man anymore and had projected that onto him? At the time she couldn't understand why Isabelle couldn't see him clearly, and she was so afraid for her, if not for her physical safety, then surely afraid for her heart and her spirit. She desperately wanted to protect her only child from all the hurts that the world waits to dish out and stupidly, stupidly, she believed that she could do this. And all her wanting to protect her daughter had done was drive her away, and now she didn't even know where Issy was.

She'd gone to Ben's apartment and as she expected, he was gone too. Since then there hadn't been one word from either of them. Lenny wouldn't talk about it. "Let her be, Jane," he'd said, repeatedly, infuriatingly. "She'll call when she's ready to." The police wouldn't help because Isabelle was over twenty-one and had obviously gone willingly with Ben. Jane had thought about hiring a private detective, just like in the movies, but she knew that Issy didn't want to be found and when she spooled the scenario out, she could never see a happy ending. And so she prayed. She prayed to a vague deity, whom she'd long since lost touch with, a deity who seemed remote and uninterested. She got more comfort from a mother image and so that's how she prayed, but even that felt hollow. "Blessed Mother, please take care of my Isabelle." Night and day she asked for protection for her daughter and for forgiveness and for Issy to be happy wherever she was. And she grieved.

Jane sat down on the big flat rock that she'd warmed herself on that first day and she wept again. She wept for her child and for herself, for her marriage, her old life, and all her hopes and dreams, which were dust now. She wept for the road home, which was closed to her, and for the future which looked like a vast beige desert, all dry sand and no sign of water. And when she had wept all her tears out, she lay down and fell into a deep sleep.

Here was the fire and the big cats and the woman dancing with fireflies shooting out all around her but now there was someone else. She could sense a presence, but she couldn't see anyone. It was as if she were standing away from the scene, watching the woman stomp and sway, bending and lifting up. Suddenly she knew that someone was right beside her. She turned and there was a child, a girl. Jane locked into the girl's eyes, one blue as the sky, the other, a deep, intense brown. She couldn't look away, she was sinking into those eyes, and then she was drifting down, down, down in water, but she wasn't afraid. The water was warm and clear and the child was with her, holding her hand and smiling at her as they went deeper and deeper. Now there was long wet grass swaying and brushing against Jane's legs and the girl was pulling her along and then there was a wreck, like a shipwreck, only it was a house, with shutters hanging awry and window boxes full of soggy flowers and strange sea creatures. They swam through the front door, which was hanging on its hinges, and into the living room. Everything was there, but ruined. Barnacles had attached themselves to the old linen couch with the faded flowers, the pictures were hanging askew, their glass clouded, a vase of flowers had fallen over on the coffee table and the flowers were dead and slimy. This was Jane May's house. The house where she had been happily married and then miserably too. The house where she had brought her daughter home from the hospital, perfect and tiny, and laid her in the white crib with the little quilt that she had sewn so lovingly from her own old dresses and Lenny's faded work shirts. Most of her life had been lived in this house. A sob bubbled up and when she tried to suppress it, she inhaled the salty seawater and couldn't breathe. She was choking and panic rose and threatened to swallow her whole. And then the little girl was beside her again, smiling and pulling her up and up and together they broke the surface.

She was in the woods on the big flat rock and the sun was golden and little dust motes and winged things danced on their beams and the dream drifted away like smoke. With a sigh, Jane May stretched and rose. She continued down the path toward Mai Zinni's house in the woods.

"You seem preoccupied today, child." Mai Zinni was boiling water on the old wood stove in her little kitchen. She and Jane had gone out to pick herbs from the woods around the house when Jane got there. Jane May loved these days. She loved following Mai Zinni with the basket. "Ooh, look at all them pretty violets. Pick all of them you can and get a mess of leaves too. Old Violet, she's the queen of the forest." They had a huge pile of heart-shaped leaves chopped and waiting in a big stoneware bowl to be made into tinctures and infusions, and next to them the sweet little purple flowers, divided into two piles. One batch, they would eat in their salad of mixed greens, gathered under Mai Zinni's keen eye. The other would be made into *violet sweets*; dipped carefully one-by-one into a beaten egg white and then into fine white sugar, they would be laid out on waxed paper to dry and then eaten like candy or used to decorate little cakes. Mai Zinni sold these treats and others to Alice's bakery from time to time. She didn't take orders. She let Nanette know when she had a batch and the young woman would pick up the goodies and deliver them to town. Alice knew that Mai Zinni's treats came when they came and the townsfolk knew this too and considered themselves very lucky to happen into *Alice's Pie in the Sky* on a day when Nanette had made a delivery. Word spread quickly on those days and the tender delicacies didn't last long.

Before long the violet flowers would be gone, so the women had made the best of it, by meeting up and picking them wild two or three times a week.

"I'm sorry, Mai. I guess I've got a lot on my mind. I'm really missing my daughter today."

"Tell me." There is comfort in those words when they are spoken with gentleness and sincerity and Jane May did tell. She told it all, from meeting Lenny at a music festival when she was only seventeen, to being taken completely by surprise when she held her sweet daughter in her arms for the first time. Surprised at how her heart expanded to enfold this little one, but her love for her handsome young husband did not diminish at all. In fact, it only grew. A miracle. She told of all the joy and all the regrets. The way they had gradually moved further and further away from each other. Her failings with Issy, with Lenny. "I let them both down. All of us, myself included. I let us all down. I had become detached, drawn into myself in a way that didn't allow them in." She told it all the way up to finding Lenny in bed with a woman she'd thought was a friend. In their own bed. The bed that Issy had been conceived in. She told Mai how shocked, how shattered she had been by those betrayals. Too shattered even to try to protect Isabelle from any of it. And later, the defiant, powerful flush of feeling when she'd met Jack—*I am alive! I am!* Then later, finding Issy gone and finally, fed up with being in the town where she'd spent her whole life and unable to get ground under her feet, she'd left too and wound up here. The whole story poured out like water. The older woman soaked up the words and took them, willingly, from Jane's heavy heart into her own. And having been shared, the power of those words was significantly diminished.

Jane May felt that she had been both emptied and replenished. What a relief to tell her story and have it be received and held so gently by this strange older woman whom she was beginning to love. It was as if an ancient and heavy weight had been lifted from her shoulders. She hadn't realized how tired she'd become of carrying the story alone. The burden of it had exhausted her.

"Let's eat." She was famished now and light-hearted.

And so they did. They broke the hearty bread that Mai Zinni had baked that morning, slathered it with butter and honey, and shared the green salad garnished with tiny purple flowers, while the leaves infused in mason jars in the window and the delicate violet sweets dried on the counter.

Grace comes unexpectedly, and lucky is she who recognizes it in the moment rather than backward after it has slipped away again. And Jane May did recognize this state of grace and she was thankful. A small, secret smile bubbled up from deep within and she felt peaceful and contented for the first time in a long while.

Chapter 17

Isabelle was confused. Her father had blown their family to pieces by having an affair and she was angry with him. Enraged really. But she could find no outlet in him for that anger. He refused to engage with her about it.

"It's none of your business Issy," he said with maddening calm. "Human relationships are complex. This is between your mother and me."

She sputtered and stuttered and became angry with herself when she could not articulate what she was feeling. *Could this be true*, she wondered. *Is it possible that I am not involved in the breakup of the institution that brought me into being?* Wasn't her parents' marriage the very foundation of her life?

The two had met for lunch at her urging. "I need to understand this," was what she'd opened with and had been immediately shut down by him. The news of his infidelity had just broken and was raw and volatile for all of them. She found it intensely embarrassing, among other things. He was old in her eyes and she felt that he should behave accordingly. That was, in a manner befitting an older man—parental, more or less chaste. He certainly didn't need to be exhibiting any kind of sexual passion or desire. She didn't mind the thought that her parents had sex with each other, but she didn't want to overhear it or think about it or see overt signs of it in their day to day life. And for him to go outside the marriage . . . . Well, besides the obvious, that he was disrespecting her mother, it was just gross.

Issy had a very fixed idea about who her parents were. Or at least she had had such an idea. Now it had been blown wide open and she was disoriented.

"How would you feel if this happened to me, Daddy?"

"Shit, Issy. What are you doing?"

"I'm trying to understand!" She was whining now. Imploring. And the farther she went down that path, the more closed he became.

His arms were crossed over his chest, his mouth was set, a vein throbbed at his temple. "I can't help you with that. Maybe you just need to grow up."

That did it. She jumped up and stumbled awkwardly from the booth near the back that she'd claimed upon arriving minutes before him. "Just forget it!" She was fighting tears. And then getting a grip on herself, she said, trying to match him in coldness, "I guess you're right, Dad. This has nothing to do with me. I'll be fine. It's time for me to grow up."

She had meant to sound measured and already grown up, but she was only a freshman in college and at that moment she'd felt like a very young child, who was begging for love and not getting it. She stomped away before she gave into an almost overwhelming urge to fall on the floor and kick her feet—or to kick him.

"Goddammit, Issy."

But she didn't look back, just flew out of the restaurant, leaving her chicken salad uneaten on the table and her father shaking his head.

She continued to speak with him when he called, but they kept their conversations brief and confined them to matters easily spoken of: how she was doing in school—sometimes well, other times, not so well—items he'd seen in the local paper about people she knew, the weather. Occasionally she hung up on him when he chastised her for letting her grades slip, but usually they got through the strained communications. After talking to him, she was always sad and mentally muddled and she often acted out, without really thinking about why. She would drink too much or start a fight with her roommate, or go home with some boy that she didn't know well, and then be consumed with remorse later.

During that time she began to call her mother after these conversations. It never went well. They would talk for a few minutes about school or her friends or the weather and she would always find something to take issue with Jane about.

"Honey, I'm worried about you. Your grades are suffering. You seem depressed. Are you okay? Don't you think it would help to talk with someone?"

That was all it took for Issy to launch into a sarcastic tirade. "Sure Mom, I'm fine. I'm great really. Why wouldn't I be? No need to worry about me. Just make sure that you're okay. How's the therapy going? I just want you to be happy, that's all that matters." If Isabelle felt sad after her conversations with her father, she hated herself after these talks. *Why,* she wondered, *am*

I so mad at her? He's the one who's been a jerk. She would vow to be gentler with her mother, but then she would forget all of it whenever she heard Jane's voice. It touched something inside her that hurt and that set her off. Something cloyingly familiar.

Issy was spiraling down and out of control and she felt completely alone. Her room-mate's parents had divorced when she was ten and Issy sometimes wanted desperately to ask her about it. How she'd felt, how she still felt. The girl's parents had both come to move her into the dorm at the beginning of the year and, just like Issy's own pathetic parents, they were stiff and formal and from the looks of things, couldn't stand each other. The two girls might have bonded over this shared experience, but they didn't. Issy still held out hope, a vague, unarticulated wish, that her parents would somehow figure out how to return to the way things had always been and by befriending her roommate, she would be giving in to the inevitable. And she wasn't ready to do that.

Eventually Issy dropped out of school and returned to her hometown. She persuaded her father to help her pay for an apartment until she could find a job and she took up with Ben Davis, a boy she'd known in high school. The two had dated briefly in senior year, but then Issy had gone off to college and Ben had gone to work in his father's construction company, while he saved money for school. Ben had continued to call her, but she'd brushed him off until now.

The catalyst for change came from inside Issy herself. She had always had a strong sense of her Self. She might go down a wrong road, but she never stayed on it for very long. But Ben was the guiding force that kept her on track. She had recognized something in him the first time they'd met. A steadiness. A purity of heart, and she clung to those qualities in him now, as if her life depended on it.

Jane, she knew, could not stand him, and that only reinforced her feelings for him. Her mother was bitter and she hated all men now and there was an ugliness in it that gave Issy a feeling of power. They fought all the time, and became more and more estranged. She maintained a tenuous relationship with her father because he was holding her up financially and she couldn't afford to cut ties with him. But as soon as she could, she intended to. She didn't need anyone but Ben. And yet, even with Ben, she held a part of herself back. He wanted to move in together. It would have solved her financial problem and allowed her to cut her father off sooner, but she said no.

"I love you, Issy." He said the words one night after they'd had amazing sex at her place. A graceless silence ensued and lingered. Finally Ben rose and dressed slowly, in the light from a streetlamp. He looked at Issy for a long moment and then left, closing the door quietly behind him.

She cried herself to sleep and broke up with him the next day. In a couple of weeks he called and they made up. The cycle repeated itself in various iterations for a couple of years.

One day Ben came to her apartment and gave her an ultimatum.

"Isabelle, we can't go on like this." He declared. "I love you. I only want to be with you. I'm not your father and you are not your mother. We don't have to make the mistakes that they've made. But the bottom line is this. There are no guarantees in love or in life for that matter. You are going to have to decide to trust me. To trust us." He was breathing hard, both his hands hung by his sides in a sign of surrender. "If you can't do that, I can't be with you anymore."

Issy was struck by how the sunlight had pushed its way in through the slats of the venetian blinds in her apartment and lay in stripes across his body and on the floor at his feet. He was so beautiful, with his soulful eyes and mop of dark hair. For a moment she became fascinated by the pattern the sunlight was painting, but then he broke the silence with a proposal, so unexpected, so bold, that it brought her back, suddenly, to the matter at hand.

"Issy. I want us to go away. I don't think we're going to make it here. We need to make a clean break. We've got to start over. We need to go now. Will you come with me?" His question hung in the gravid air between them for a long moment. Neither knew what would happen.

"Yes," she whispered, and then louder, "Yes! Yes!" She flew across the space between them and was enfolded in his arms. She hadn't known until that very moment that she loved him. And discovering that, her confusion lifted and certainty settled over her like a shawl, light and comforting. "Yes. Let's go now."

By the end of that day, they'd packed all of their belongings into Ben's truck and were heading west toward the setting sun. They didn't have a destination in mind, but they were young and free and in love, so they sang with the windows down and they laughed. And when they'd driven for many hours and put hundreds of miles between themselves and the old life, they bedded down in the back of Ben's truck and it wasn't until the crescent moon rose in the sky and Ben breathed steady and deep beside her, that Isabelle felt a pang of regret for the pain she knew her mother would experience when she discovered them gone.

Chapter 18

Charlie crept along the forest path. It was a favorite game of his—trying to be as silent as a fox in the woods. He was barefoot and thoroughly enjoying the cool moss on his soles. The game was so much easier in spring and summer when the ground was soft and quiet. In the fall, the dry leaves made it very difficult to move about undetected. This morning though, he was able, with little effort, to sneak up on a nest of rabbits. He was so happy in the woods. His mama felt okay about letting him go unattended while she got her work done at the inn. Periodically she'd go to the edge of the woods and call to him and he would answer and, reassured, she'd turn her attention away again and he would return to his adventures. For as long as Charlie could remember, he'd been able to talk to animals and they talked right back to him. His mama said that when he was just a little baby, she would lay him on a blanket outside and birds and squirrels would come right up to him and bring him little gifts like acorns and worms and sometimes feathers. He would wriggle and coo and squeal with delight, she said. He had friends at school, but they rarely invited him over and when his mama agreed to have them, usually they couldn't come. He didn't mind. He had plenty of friends in the forest. Uncle John had told him when he was younger that his Indian name was Little Brother, because the animals all saw him this way. He thought of himself as Little Brother. Whenever he met a new friend in the forest, he would put his hands together in front of his heart and say solemnly to them, "Hello. I am Little Brother. Don't be scared, I'm your friend." He couldn't remember if he'd gotten this from someone else or made it up himself, but it had become a ritual and he followed it faithfully.

Little Brother paused on the trail to listen to a rustling in the brush behind him. Slowly, slowly he turned, taking care not to make a sound. He hoped it was the cat he'd found the other day and tried to show to John, but it wasn't. From the underbrush emerged a rotund creature with tawny fur.

The animal sat on its haunches and looked at Charlie. It was a great mound of a creature, nearly half Charlie's height. A whistle pig. Uncle John had told him they could make a sound like a bird call and the mountain folk would sometimes eat them. Charlie didn't like the thought of that and he said to this one, "Hello Friend. I am Little Brother. Don't worry, I won't eat you." The groundhog twitched its nose and continued to look at the boy for a minute before waddling off. Charlie followed. Down the path went the two, boy and groundhog. Charlie tried to imitate the waddling walk of the fellow as it continued on its passeggiata through the forest. Eventually, the animal darted into a hole and after a few minutes of waiting, Charlie grew bored and headed back toward the inn. It was beginning to feel like lunch time, and he didn't want to be late and make his mama mad.

As he walked along the soft path, the wheels of Charlie's young mind were whirring and spinning. He loved the early summer, the way a green curtain descended on the mountains after the long, brittle-silver months of winter. He loved not having to wear a coat or boots. Even though his mama was always reminding him to put on shoes, he'd gotten away before she had noticed his bare feet this morning. He much preferred being barefoot in the forest. "None of the other animal's mamas make them wear shoes," he'd grumbled when she tried to waylay him one day. "My feet can't feel the dirt or the grass when I wear 'em." Still, she insisted and he would dutifully lace up his tennis shoes and then take them off as soon as he was out of sight, leaving them in the hollow of some tree. But today she hadn't even noticed when he kissed her and bounded off toward the woods, bare feet hardly even touching the path.

Uncle John understood Charlie a lot better than his mama did, but even so, he wouldn't argue with her. "Do what your mama says, Boy," the old man would declaim in a mockstern voice. But sometimes when Nanette wasn't looking, Uncle John would give him a wink.

This was the closest Charlie got to having a father. He knew he'd had one once, but he could barely remember him and so he didn't miss him much, except that most of the other boys at school had them and that made him feel kind of fenced off, like the old lion he'd seen once at the zoo, all alone in his enclosure.

He liked to play ball and his mama encouraged it, but at the games, he felt like the only kid with no dad there. John didn't like to come and sit in the stands, because he didn't like people much, except for Charlie and Nanette and old Mai Zinni. Well, Charlie couldn't tell if he liked Mai Zinni or not most of the time. And Mr. Mac. He liked him all right, but that was about it. Anyway, Charlie had stopped playing ball because it hurt his feelings to see all the dads messing up their boys' hair and saying "Good game, Son," and "How about pizza?" after the games. Some of them got all riled up and yelled at the umpires, "What are you, blind? That wasn't even in the strike zone!" Their sons were embarrassed and hung their heads, but even that seemed like something that was missing from his life.

John was his friend though. He taught him lots of things, like how to look for tracks to know what animals had been around and what birds made what songs. How to tell one tree from another and what their names were. And how to make a fire and how to put it out, although Charlie wasn't supposed to ever do that unless a grown-up was with him. Last fall, Uncle John had helped him build a wikkiup in the woods. The teepee shaped shelter leaned against a big tree and Charlie had spent many happy hours, sitting inside and making up stories about the animals. Once when he'd come to it after a snowfall, he'd found tracks coming out of the shelter that looked like a big cat had made them. Excited about the find, he'd run back to the inn to get Uncle John, but when they returned, the snow had begun to melt and the tracks were gone. A few times, John had taken him hiking in the mountains and once they'd even camped overnight. Charlie knew he could talk to Uncle John about things he couldn't talk to his mother about—man things. And he felt that John believed him sometimes when his mama didn't. Like the other day when he'd found the spotted cat in the woods, but lost it before he could show anybody. John didn't act like he was crazy or just being a kid or something. He really listened and Charlie guessed that's what fathers did.

Nanette was just coming out of the laundry house when Charlie skulked up the path to the parking lot. He didn't know what time it was, but he thought he'd been out too long and was prepared for a tongue whipping, so he stood, head hanging, bare foot kicking at the gravel, but instead she said, "There's my little man. Are you having fun, Pal? Enjoying your Saturday? About ready for some lunch?"

"Yes, I'm about starved!" She didn't notice his bare feet. He followed her into the kitchen of the main building and hid his dirty feet under him in a chair and waited while she made a peanut butter and jelly sandwich and sliced a banana.

"Mama?"

"Um?" Anyone could see that her mind was somewhere else today and that meant a good time to ask for something that might otherwise be hard to get.

"Could you make the safe zone a little bigger? I'm bigger and I should be able to have more of the woods for myself."

"I'll think about it, Buddy," she said as she set a plate down in front of him.

He'd let one grimy foot dangle and was swinging it hard and knocking the leg of the chair. Sometimes *I'll think about it* would turn into yes and sometimes not. He pressed on. "I know how to be smart and safe in the woods and I never get into trouble."

"I said I'd think about it, okay?" Anything that started with *I said* mean it was time to hush up, but that was so hard.

'Mama, you look pretty today." He knew he'd gone too far when she raised an eyebrow at him.

"Hey! Where are your shoes? Didn't I tell you not to go into the woods barefooted? Didn't I?" Uh oh.

"I'm sorry, Mama. I just forgot 'em." Would that make her soft again? No.

"Charlie. You are trying my patience and I don't have much left today. Don't ask me for anything else until I can see that you do as you're told. Now finish your sandwich and get on home and do your homework."

Chapter 19

Charlie put John in mind of himself at that age. The boy was happier than John remembered being and for that he was grateful. Like Charlie, John had been born with no father. Charlie had one, but he weren't no account. John's was dead. Pretty much the same thing, as far as John could tell. If a father weren't no use to you, didn't much matter if he was dead or alive.

John had driven up onto the Parkway this morning, as he often did, to get away from all the distractions in the world. He much preferred to be distracted by clouds and birds and plants. He'd parked the truck and walked a short distance up a little used path to an overlook with a wooden bench. The bench had seen better days, but it still supported him and provided a majestic view of the Blue Ridge Mountains, layer upon layer of ancient, scalloped, hills, reaching as far into the distance as he could see. He unfolded a camp chair and set down a cooler with a beer and a sandwich inside, settled himself on the bench and pulled the brim of his hat down over his eyes. There wasn't a better way to spend a day than this. John's mind continued to meander back through time.

Like Charlie and Nanette, it had been just John and his mama. Unlike Nanette, though, his wasn't much of a mama. A sad little woman, she cried a lot and mostly let little John run wild and do whatever he wanted. Charlie was luckier in that department. Nanette was determined to be both mother and father to the boy. If anything, she went too far in that direction, always needing to know where the boy was and what he was thinking. Sometimes John thought the boy could use a little more freedom. Somewhere between what he'd had and this. But Nanette was a good mom and Charlie was lucky to have her.

John's father had died before he was even born, so that was that. You can't miss somebody you never even knew. But it leaves a boy with a father-shaped hole inside himself that can't ever be filled.

When he got big enough for school, the other kids always asked him,

THE BRIDGE TO HOME

"Who's your daddy?" Ain't got one, was all he knew. His mama just said he was dead, wouldn't even tell his name, if she knew it. So the kids called him Jesus. "Poor Jesus, with no earthly daddy. Who's your Joseph, then?" John thought they might have benefitted from a little more time outdoors, minding their own business, and a little less time in Sunday School, learning to mind everybody else's.

His Joseph, in fact, was a crusty but kind old retired lobsterman named Barley. Barley let John and his mama live in the tiny apartment over his garage. He watched John whenever his mama was at work and he wasn't in school. He took the boy out on his boat, The Jubilee, a creaky old wooden fishing boat with a wheelhouse and a little room below deck, where John loved to play or read. Sometimes, lulled by the rocking, on a hot afternoon, he would surrender to the delicious monster, Sleep, and have wonderful dreams about sailors and pirates and giant sea creatures. John loved that boat. It had once been painted blue but had faded out to the color of water, making it seem to disappear sometimes in the drink, which is what Barley liked to call the ocean.

Once, when John and Barley were out on the open sea on a cloudless day with the engine stalled, being rocked like babies by Mother Ocean, John had drowsily asked, "What does Jubilee mean?"

Barley closed his eyes and thought a long minute. "It's a grand celebration, full of dancin' and singin' and joy, I guess." After that John would often lie in bed at night, listening to his mama's quiet sniffling and trying to imagine such a thing.

Still, he hadn't been a morose boy. Maybe it was the imagining that kept him from that sad affliction. Always in his mind was the image of the grand celebration of joy. And, of course, he had never actually experienced loss. He was simply born into a world where everyone else had had more than their fair share of it.

Barley was already an old man when John was born, so though he truly seemed to love the boy and his sad mother, he couldn't offer them much. His lobstering days were well behind him by then and although he lived comfortably but simply on savings and social security, he had little to share.

John's mother worked as a waitress at a cafe on the wharf. She wore a pink and white uniform that hugged what few curves she had and she came home bone tired and smelling of greasy fish. She could barely say a word to him before she'd had a long bath. The boy knew his mother was home when he heard the door slam around four every afternoon. She would groan as she hung her purse on a hook on the wall and again as she struggled with the door of the ancient Kelvinator. When she'd pried it open, in would go the bags of leftover food the cafe owner let her bring home at the end of her shift everyday. Whatever there was would be their supper that night. Might be a couple of soggy lobster rolls or some greasy fried cod. Once in a while, hamburgers. His mother wrapped these in foil later, after her bath, and put them in the oven to warm up. She never removed the condiments and so John was a grown man before he knew the pleasure of a juicy hot hamburger with a crisp cold leaf of lettuce, the bite of a fresh onion and the wonderment of a thick slab of vine-ripened tomato. The wilted, soggy mess that he was usually given for dinner was certainly no cause for a jubilee. He winced at the memory now and wondered if no one had ever taught her to cook properly or if she was just too tired and beaten down to care. He hoped for the first explanation, but strongly suspected the second, meaning that his life had been pretty much doomed from the start. Being born to a mama that couldn't even muster a care for her own child wore on his natural optimism and did not bode well for a joyful life. The world had done little to prove that wrong. Although there had been moments . . . brief periods when he thought, maybe, just maybe he could see a reason for singin' and dancin'.

    John had learned long ago, at his mama's knee, not to trust those happy moments. They never seemed to last long before something would shatter them.

    He had only been eleven the day his mama didn't come home at all for the last time. There had been times before when she was late, but she'd always called Barley and asked if he'd watch her boy, that she'd be a little while. John didn't know what she did at these times, but he didn't mind when Barley would come creaking up the stairs to the apartment and the two of them would stay up past John's bedtime watching TV or playing cards. In the morning Barley would be gone and his mama would be back, like always, scurrying around in her pink uniform. Shaking him out of sleep to say goodbye, your cereal's on the table, get to school on time, y'hear!

    But one day she didn't come home and old Barley came a-creakin' up the stairs and his face was the saddest thing John had ever seen. Barley sat him down and told him that his mama had been found floating in the marina that morning. Nobody knew if she'd fallen in or what. John couldn't remember anymore how he'd felt or what he had done for the rest of that day, but he always had it in his mind, that she'd gone for a walk after work, by the water, and that something had caught her eye in the depths. A beautiful shiny fish or a mermaid or something and she'd fallen leaning over to get a better look. Somehow this made him feel better about it. Less sad. Maybe she'd died full of wonder or curiosity and not just plain dead tired after a long shift at the diner. After that, he moved into the house with Barley and the two of them hammered out a kind of life. A routine of comings and goings, meals and TV, punctuated by lazy afternoons on the boat—the best part. It was comfortable, comforting, but rarely joyful.

As John neared high school graduation, he began to notice more and more that Barley was getting forgetful. He locked himself out frequently, which was odd, because no one in their small fishing village ever even locked their doors. John would come home to find Barley sitting on the steps, usually disoriented and dehydrated. He would have to climb in through a window and let them in. The old man began to leave the stove on and to forget to pay the few bills that they had. John began to feel lonely and anxious. And sometimes he got irritated with old Barley, which made him feel ashamed. He was pretty sure it wasn't the old man's fault, but he felt so sad and he didn't know why and that made him angry, so he would lash out at the only friend he'd ever had. "Barley, what the hell!" he snapped one night when the lights flickered and went off. "Did you pay the electric bill like you said you would?"

Instantly he felt like a heel when he saw the confusion on the old man's face. "It's all right, man," he said, as he fumbled for the lantern that they kept on a high kitchen shelf. The power often went out when there were storms, but this evening was as placid as a deep mountain lake. "It's okay, I'll fix it tomorrow. Let's go sit on the porch. The moon's full. Come on, I'll get you a beer." And the two men, one young and waxing full of promise, the other waning, shuffled out into the salty summer night air.

John became afraid to leave Barley alone and that interfered severely with school and his part-time job. Never even mind any kind of social life. John had remained on the fringes in this little town all his life, never feeling like he fit here. He had, however, developed a lanky, shambling handsomeness that drew attention from the local girls. This baffled him, but also pleased him a little. Sadly the old man was becoming such a burden that he didn't have much time to devote to the girls who hung around, ducking their pretty heads and hoping for some attention from the boy with the strange and beautiful eyes.

One day a nice lady, identifying herself as a social worker, came to the door and asked a lot of questions about the living arrangements that John and Barley had worked out. The end result was that Barley went to live in an old folk's home on the other side of town. John was so close to eighteen that they left him alone and let him live in Barley's house until it sold and the new owners were kind enough to let him rent the apartment where he had lived with his mama when he was a boy.

John had faithfully visited Barley every single day for a couple of years after his graduation. He went full time with his job at the marina, gassing up boats and washing them, and doing any odd jobs that the marina owners wanted, and he stayed in the only place that he had ever known. He even briefly dated a local girl named Adele and the two of them fumbled around in the tiny bed in John's apartment over the garage, and discovered a few age-old secrets.

Increasingly though, Barley didn't know John when he went to visit, and one day John arrived at the home and Barley's room had been cleaned out and he was gone. The manager handed over a cardboard box and patted John on the back.

He wrote a letter to Adele that he hoped would allow her to move on without too much thought of him, threw his meager belongings into the pick-up, and headed south.

John was startled out of his ramblings, by the buzzing of the cellphone in his pocket.

"Damnation!" he cried after a split second of thinking that he was experiencing a heart attack, and muttered, "what is it, now?" *Why in tarnation do I have to have this thing anyway*, he thought as he fumbled with the buttons on the phone. Zee had insisted that he have it and keep it with him. "What if I need you? What if Nannette needs you and you're away from the inn?" she'd said. The world would go on, that's what.

"Who is it?" he snapped into the device.

"Sorry. It's me, John. Mai Zinni. I was just calling to see how you're doing."

"I'd be fine, if you and ever' body else would stop pestering me."

A silence. A smile. How was it that he could feel her smile through the phone line? He'd just as soon not have that magic power. Why couldn't the woman ever leave him alone?

"Okay. Well, I was thinking about you, that's all. Have a good day."

"I'm tryin'." Shaking his grey head, John punched the phone off and returned it to his pocket. *Might as well go on home now. Day's rurnt from all this dang meddlin',* he thought as he folded his chair and picked up the cooler. Down the path he ambled, under a canopy of tender green, breathing in the smell of summer.

Chapter 20

Jane pulled the old blanket close around her shoulders. She would never get over the coolness of a mountain evening in summer. By now, where she'd come from, it was swelteringly hot around the clock. The punishing heat wrung every last drop of enthusiasm from all but the most determined, or those with access to a swimming pool or the beach. By late May, a heavy wet blanket of ennui would have covered the land, enfeebling some of the dazed people and enraging others. Crime shot up during the summer months in the Deep South, whether a function of the hot, humid weather, or stultified young people finding themselves temporarily without structure in their days, no one knew for sure. The heat addled brains, stifled ambition, clouded judgement, the will even to walk to the box and check the mail, all bent back into a couch prone slump. Violence flared, but could not sustain itself for long. Anger pulsed like a temple vein and then shaking its head like some prehistoric beast, circled round and laid itself in a humid puddle of warm shade with an impotent harumph.

But here in the mountains, a miracle. A show. The warm days were followed every evening by cooling breezes. Daily the lights went down and as if on cue, the crickets and fireflies ushered in a mild and magical twilight. Wisps of peach and rose feathered the sky to the west and the ancestral mist rolled silently up the sides of the ancient mountains. Later, like a curtain, the mist was pulled back and pinpoints of light dotted the inky sky. It was easy to understand why most Southerners who could afford it had retired to the mountains in the heat of summer, before air conditioning, and many still did. The populations of small towns exploded for a few months and roads became congested with timid drivers, afraid of the curvy mountain roads.

In the three short months since she'd arrived in Gideon, it had become routine for Jane May to go to Mai Zinni's cottage in the woods almost every day. Without ever verbalizing what they were doing, a comfortable sort of loose schedule had developed between the women. They would walk and gather herbs in the forest or work in the kitchen with roots and leaves and fungi gathered earlier, grating, grinding, boiling and making tinctures, salves or infusions. Slowly, Jane May was learning from the old woman. She asked questions and took notes and made drawings in a small notebook that she kept with her always and Mai Zinni was patient and never got frustrated with her slow and stumbling attempts to memorize the names of all the *kindred*, as the old woman called the flora of the forest, and to match them with their properties for healing.

Bloodroot—astringent, antibacterial, anti-inflammatory, it can treat fungal growth and ringworm; Heal-all—for wounds and snakebite, also digestive ailments; Violet—for treating sores and moving lymph; Willow bark—for fevers and rheumatism; Betony—a good mouthwash for the gums and also lowers blood pressure; Yarrow or Snakegrass—for treating swelling and gout and stimulating the appetite, but be careful, it can cause an allergic reaction.

Jane found that she loved getting to know these plants and their properties and their names. She and Mai Zinni would often take them one plant at a time. They'd spend a whole day on, say, Stinging Nettles. They would walk into the forest, cotton sacks on their backs, and wander until they spotted the deep blue-green, serrated leaves growing in pairs on tall stalks, usually in the wet, low places, where the soil was rich, or along fence rows or the edges of cultivated fields. The older woman would take out a small knife and gently cut through a piece of stalk, exposing a hollow interior, threaded through with pink.

"Careful with 'em or they'll bite you," she showed Jane the tiny delicate white hairs that would shoot drops of acid if they weren't handled correctly. Jane wore old leather gloves whenever she worked with the nettles, but Mai Zinni never did. "We're friends," she'd say. "They know me, they trust me. Besides, I like the little tingle they give me when I handle 'em. You'll learn." Sometimes they would sit down among the plants and rest for awhile, letting all their senses open to the energies of the green beings.

Dropping into silence, the symphony of sound that is always present in the forest would be almost overwhelming to Jane. She could hear the wingbeats of tiny insects, and something like breathing, some primal in and out, an ebbing and flowing that underlay all the other sounds. She tried to articulate this to Mai Zinni once and the older woman said simply, "Pachamama—Mother Earth," and Jane May had understood for the first time that the tiny blue dot that she called home in the vast universe was a living, breathing organism. She was filled with such love at that moment, and such sorrow, for the harm human beings had carelessly done to their home.

"Just feel the kindred," Mai Zinni said, "let 'em speak to you." At first Jane sat quietly, thinking to herself that the old woman was a nut, but a harmless one, and what else did she have to do but sit here in the forest and rest among plants anyway. Gradually, though, the more time they spent doing this, the more Jane May began to feel them. She could sense an aliveness, an energy, and it seemed to lean in toward her whenever she focused on it. It was as if the plants, the *kindred*, acknowledged her somehow. Welcomed her. She still felt slow and clumsy, but Mai Zinni recognized an aptitude in her, a gift. She said she had a way with the kindred. A way that made the older woman nod and smile, and filled Jane with pride.

"She got the gift, all right," Jane had overheard Mai and Mac one day. She'd arrived early and was pleased to see Mac in the kitchen. She stood at the open front door about to knock, but couldn't resist the temptation to listen in to their conversation.

"Really?" He said, eager to hear more. "I thought she might. That first day when she came into the shop, I told you I thought there was something about her. Something hungry, yet confident, something calm and uncluttered underneath her current uneasiness. So you think she's got it?"

"Yep. She's definitely got the gift. I've seen it." Mai Zinni declined to say more, even at his urging. She liked to keep close council, Jane certainly knew that. She cleared her throat and knocked on the door, alerting them to her presence. *They were talking about me. I've got 'the gift'*, she thought, suppressing a smile.

The two women had spent much of the afternoon in the forest, among the plants and the animals. Afterward, they put together a light supper at the old kitchen table as the late afternoon light slanted in through the little window above the sink. As always Mai Zinni blessed the meal before they ate, "Beloved, fill us with your grace and bless us with the gifts of these our kindred. May this food feed our bodies and nurture the seeds that you have planted in us. So must it be."

They ate in silence, savoring every bite and Jane May felt so contented that she forgot, for awhile, everything else that she knew of the world. How she wished to stay in this safe, warm place.

After supper, they strolled out into the early evening, the between time, when dusk has just begun to fall and daylight hasn't yet gathered her things and gone home. That liminal time, which was home to the creatures of the fringes, the edges of things. As the fireflies began their luminous frolic, all manner of animals came to the edge of the forest and stood silently, unwilling or unable to come fully into the embrace offered by their human friends. Fox and rabbit, raccoon and groundhog, bobcat, wild turkey and owl gathered in the shadows. They kept their friendly distance, holding their separateness like dark cloaks around themselves. They were a comfort to the women, their mere presence an offering, an invitation to join the community of God's creatures, to be a part of the river of Life, gracefully flowing, free from the human struggles of acquisition and competition. Jane never felt, more than in these between times, the connection between herself and all living things. The allrightness of everything. The natural flow of life. The spinning of the planets, and upon one of them all of the creatures of Earth and perhaps other beings upon other orbs, all one, all the same in some elemental way.

They sat sat in old worn chairs in front of Mai Zinni's fire pit and there they talked deep into the night. It was Mai Zinni who did most of the talking. Jane soaked it all up like a child eager to learn everything about this strange new world she'd found herself in.

At times like this, Mai Zinni might talk about any subject that struck her fancy, or she would tell old Cherokee folktales, yarns spun out like ribbon about Little People, or Grandmother Spider, or the scary old Raven-Mocker, whose banshee cry of a dark night could terrorize the most stoical of hearts.

Once she began, "There is another world underneath, just exactly like this one in every way. The streams that come down from the mountains are the trails to this underworld, and the springs at their heads are the doorways. But to go there, you'd have to fast for a long time and have one of the underground people for a guide. And they don't much like us. I don't know nobody that's ever been there, but it's there for sure, I do know that."

Jane had asked, "How? How do you know this, Mai?"

"Just do," was Mai Zinni's terse reply.

"Well, if the underworld is just the same as this one, how would you even know if you were there?"

"Exactly. Might be there right now." Mai Zinni chuckled to herself and pretty soon, Jane joined in.

"The inside of your head must be a wondrous place, Mai!"

"Ha! Sure is. Yours, too."

On this night the moon was new and hiding, its darkness allowing the stars to burst forth from the black velvet canopy like tiny glittering diamonds. The women sat around the fire pit and leaned back in their chairs, gazing at the constellations just as people have done for millennia and Mai Zinni began to speak of a starry formation that wasn't visible at this time of the year in this part of the world.

"The Bridge to Home, the ancients called it. Orion's Belt. First People came from there, down onto a mountain very close to where we are now. A mountain that is very powerful. There's a ledge near the peak that's thirty feet of pure quartz crystal."

"Sounds beautiful," murmured Jane, beginning already to be mesmerized by the dancing flames in the pit and Mai's melodious voice. "I'd like to go there sometime."

"You will. Soon."

Jane May opened one eye and looked at her mentor who was innocently stirring the fire with a forged iron poker that looked like a snake. "Just how far is it to this mountain?"

"Well, take you about an hour to get to the trail head, then it's a good solid five mile in."

"Mai Zinni, do you think you can do a hike like that?"

"Do *you* think *you* can do a hike like that, more like it." Mai settled herself back into her chair.

"What do you mean? By myself?"

"Yep," was all Mai Zinni said and the realization of what she was commanding slowly sunk in to Jane May's brain. Mai would brook no argument, nor answer any questions, though Jane May had plenty of questions. The old woman's taciturnity was legend and Jane was receiving the brunt of it on this cool summer evening.

Two days later, up at dawn, Jane May had loaded her pack, with all the necessities for an overnight hike through the Shining Rock Wilderness and up to the top of the mountain, into her car. Shining Rock was an electromagnetic vortex, located at a convergence of ley or energy lines, according to the book on the subject, which Jane May had found at *The Light Within* in the intervening days before the hike.

"I must be crazy!" Jane muttered, "A nearly fifty year old woman taking a ten mile hike into a wilderness area by herself." She had only the most basic camping experience and that was quite out of date. She'd been a young woman, newly married and in the throes of hormonal love, when she and Lenny had driven across America, camping in campgrounds and also remote areas off any beaten path. She had to admit to herself that Lenny had taken care of everything. He'd rounded up the proper equipment, packed the car, set up the tent whenever they'd stopped for the night, lit the lanterns and the stove—what did she know of camping? Nothing. She was incredulous when Mai Zinni told her what she wanted her to do. Incredulous. And terrified.

"You have got to be kidding! I will die. You will never hear from me again. I will be eaten by panthers."

"There ain't no panthers in these hills. Haven't been for years and years." The old woman pronounced it *painters*, which made Jane smile in spite of her terror, picturing, in her mind's eye, a large friendly cat, wearing a beret and standing before an easel, flinging paint onto a canvas.

"Are you sure about that Mai?"

Mai Zinni smiled her coy little smile and explained the purpose of the trip. "You going to make offering to the mountain. To the First Place. And by sleeping there you will really know her. She will give up secrets to you. If you just walk up and look around, maybe pick up a piece of quartz for your shelf, and come back down, you don't know nothing. You just been a tourist. No, Child, you gonna lie down with her. You gonna get intimate. You gonna find out why you are here, why you been called to this place. You have been called, you know?"

"Mai, apparently you don't know me at all. I'm completely out of shape,

I'm a scaredy cat and I have no sense of direction, whatsoever. I'll never find my way."

"Apparently it's you don't know your own self, Missy."

And that was that. Jane May had learned enough by this point to know that any protesting was futile. Mai Zinni didn't back down, she just shut down, and all of Jane's arguments blew away in the wind. Of course she would do this insanity. She would probably do just about anything this crazy old woman wanted her to do. Here in this old one, Jane May had found something that she had been looking for all her life. Mai Zinni offered comfort, strength, courage, companionship, and guidance. She was teacher and friend, mentor, mother, and soul sister all rolled into one. Jane May had allowed herself to be swept along in this crazy plan to climb a mountain and sleep in the wilderness and now the moment of reckoning had arrived.

Mai Zinni's place was between the inn and the trailhead where she would embark, so Jane had stopped her car at the pull-out and Mai Zinni was waiting for her, sitting on a rock, holding a paper bag in her lap.

After going over the directions to the trailhead and a few other salient points, Mai Zinni handed the paper bag to Jane and said, "I made you a sandwich. You got everything you need now. Go on and git so you can be to the top in plenty time to set up camp." With that, she blew a little kiss and turned on her heel and headed back down the path to her house. Turning once, she pointed her gnarly old finger at Jane and said, "Pay attention, y'hear?"

Jane May stood by the car for a moment, then shook her head, got in and cranked the engine.

"Might as well get on with it," she said out loud. "Just go ahead and meet my fate head on." Gravel shot out from under the tires as she pulled onto the main road and headed for the Blue Ridge Parkway with a lump in her throat and a song in her heart.

Chapter 21

They say, that which doesn't kill us, makes us stronger. *Maybe so,* thought Jane May. She was definitely not dead, and she felt quite strong and full of herself late the afternoon of the day after she'd set off alone into the Shining Rock Wilderness, home of the First People, their Garden of Eden.

It had been with fear and trepidation, and also a sense of excitement that a plump, middle-aged woman had strapped on a heavy backpack just yesterday morning. She'd gotten her bearings on an old compass that Mai Zinni had given her, along with a quick lesson on how to read it, and made a beeline down the Art Loeb trail for Shining Rock.

A couple of hours into the hike, Jane sat down and fished out the sandwich and apple slices Mai Zinni had made her for lunch. Settling herself on a large, sun-warmed rock on a high bald, she ate and when she'd finished, she lay back on the rock. Shading her eyes, she saw a vortex of birds, spiraling like a tornado. Hundreds of birds. A kettle of hawks, migrating southward. But this was summer, too soon for them to head south. And yet here they were and the sight took her breath away. The birds seemed to come from every direction and they flew into the swirl and were absorbed by it, becoming part of the dark twister, which hovered and whirred, spinning crazily overhead. More and more birds continued to come, blending themselves together until spinning and spinning and spinning, the bottom of the black tornado began to widen and open up and inside was a light so bright that Jane had to squint and shield her eyes from it. Jane May wanted to be part of that light. She wanted to fly up and be sucked into the vortex. The light gradually condensed and localized into first a column and then a thin beam. This beam shot out from the bottom of the vortex and pierced the heart of the woman lying upon a sun-warmed rock, high atop a mountain peak in the Shining Rock Wilderness area. Jane May arched her back to meet the light as it entered her body.

Afterward, she lay, eyes closed, in the warmth of the sun, and wondered if she had imagined the whole thing. When finally she rose to continue her hike to the summit, she spied, in the distance, a black and spinning vortex, moving away from her, in the direction that she was going. It hovered over the peak of the mountain, barely visible in the afternoon haze, before disappearing.

The woman who emerged from the wilderness the next day was changed in ways both great and small. If you had met her on the trail, you would have seen a strong woman, striding with purpose. You might have noticed the way she carried herself with confidence. And she did carry herself. For the timid, soft, barely competent Jane May Gideon was still here, indeed she rode quietly in the back pack, tucked between a space blanket and a rain poncho (just in case). This timid one wasn't even much of a burden for strong confident Jane today. She shouldered her pack with ease and found her way back to her car as if she had an inner compass that had been pointing true north all this time.

Chapter 22

"Uncle John! Uncle John!" The old man woke with a start to the shouting.

"What the . . . ? Why're you hollerin' boy?" John had slept on the screened porch, as he often did these days, finding it cooler than the house in the relative heat of early summer.

"You ain't gonna believe it!"

"Could you tone it down a notch?" Scratching his whiskers, John rose slowly and ambled in to heat water for coffee. He put the kettle on the burner as the screen door slammed and Charlie appeared beside him, jumping up and down.

"Uncle John, I saw Punkin again! I found him in the woods and he took me to his den!" Charlie stopped and his forehead wrinkled, as he realized what he was revealing. "I was out of the Safe Range, Uncle John." The boy hung his head and dark hair obscured his eyes. Then looking up, he said, "I know it was wrong, but please don't tell Mama. Punkin and me, we looked right at each other. Right in the eye! He wouldn't never hurt me, Uncle John, I just know it. Mama wouldn't understand, but you do, don't you?" The pleading brown eyes looking up at John nearly melted his old heart, but he recovered.

"Now, you know your mama makes rules for a reason. What is that reason?"

Charlie shifted his weight from one foot to the other and made a whiny sound.

"What is the reason, Boy?"

"To keep me safe," he said with resignation, "because she loves me. I know all that Uncle John, but Punkin, he's my friend, and you know it. You can talk to Mama. You can make her understand. She just needs to make the Safe Range a little bit bigger. I'm bigger, so it should be bigger, too."

John laughed. The boy made sense. "Why don't you show me this den and then we'll see." Charlie nearly knocked the old man down when he threw himself at his knees. "I knew you'd understand, Uncle John! I just knew it!"

"All right, all right, now get! Give this poor old man some peace, for a change." Turning back to the stove, he said, "Come on back tomorrow after your mama's gone into town for the shopping and we'll take us a walk."

"Thanks, Uncle John!" The screen door slammed behind him.

Why in the Sam Hill does that boy have to run everywhere he goes? John wondered to himself. He wondered other things too, darker things, things that had no answers. He was old and tired and wished he could just lie down and sleep for a thousand years.

The old man lowered himself into a kitchen chair and tried to shake off the fear and dread that was creeping in between the chinks in the walls of his mind. "Damnation!" he muttered as he angrily reached for a book lying in a stack on the old wooden table. Tattered and worn, the stained white cover read simply Tao Te Ching in red letters. He remembered finding it in a quirky little used book store out west all those years ago. Or maybe it had found him. He'd been wandering the stacks, idly perusing the titles, when he'd stumbled over something on the floor. Bending down to see, it had been this very book. John looked up. "All right," he'd said out loud, "All right. I hear you."

When he had placed the book on the counter to pay for it, the clerk, a very attractive young woman with long blonde braids, had smiled and said, "Be content with what you have; rejoice in the way things are. When you realize there is nothing lacking, the whole world belongs to you. Verse sixteen."

Had things been different, John might have smiled back and they might have struck up a conversation and his whole life might have gone off in a different direction. But as it was, he tucked the book under his arm, murmured his thanks and shambled out of the store, his resolve intact, to return to Appalachia and do right by his daughter, although he had no idea what that could possibly mean.

John opened the book now, randomly as he had done so many times before, looking for some kind of explanation . . . something that would make sense finally, and read:

If you don't realize the source,
you stumble in confusion and sorrow.
When you realize where you come from,
you naturally become tolerant,
disinterested, amused,
kindhearted as a grandmother,
dignified as a king.
Immersed in the wonder of the Tao,
you can deal with whatever life brings you,
and when death comes, you are ready.

John drained his cup and sighed as he rose to set it in the sink. "I guess I'm ready," he said aloud, to no one in particular.

Chapter 23

"Mai, it was fabulous! The most beautiful place I've ever seen, honestly. How come I never heard of such a thing? A crystal mountain!" Jane May had unpacked, showered, and rushed to her mentor's house. Unable to contain herself, she could hardly wait to share her joy with the older woman.

"Um, that's real good, Child," was all Mai had to say. Her old grey head remained bent over the herb bundles she was tying with twine in preparation for hanging them to dry.

At first Jane didn't notice her friend's distraction. She just barreled ahead with her exuberant account. "The moon was full! Did you know that? I didn't even need a flashlight it was so bright after the sun went down. And Mai, Oh my God, it was beautiful! I felt like I was the only woman alive." Slowly she realized that Mai Zinni wasn't responding or really even listening and she became annoyed.

"For heaven's sake, Mai! It was your addle-brained idea for me to go and now you don't even seem to care at all . . ."

"It ain't that, Dear One."

"Well what is it then? Tell me."

Mai Zinni declined to answer. Instead, she walked out of the front door and through the hedge and into the forest beyond.

"Crazy old witch," Jane muttered and followed the flash of Mai's blue skirt into the forest just as she had followed it to the cottage on that first day.

The old woman seemed to be running and Jane followed her deeper and deeper into the thick green woods as she hurried through the underbrush. Out of breath and sweating, Jane was relieved when she came into the clearing and saw Mai Zinni there, standing in the middle of it, arms raised high, eyes closed, nostrils flared, sniffing the air.

"What in the world, Mai?" she panted, "Are you crazy?"

Mai Zinni cocked her head slightly, as if listening to someone whispering in her ear. "Shhh." And then, after a pause, "something's comin'. Something bad."

Goosebumps rose on Jane May's flesh and the hair on the back of her neck prickled.

"What?"

"Don't know. Can't get clear on it. Just a bad feeling—a knowin'." The old woman sat down then on the ground and began to rock back and forth, humming quietly.

Jane May was at a loss and so she sat down too, next to her friend, and waited with her while all of her joy seeped out and was absorbed into the soft ground. Finally she spoke. "Come on Mai, let's go home before it gets dark. I'll make you some supper." The younger woman helped the elder to her feet and supported her for the winding walk back to the little cottage.

"I'm so sorry, Dear." Mai Zinni was sitting at the table, cradling a cup of chamomile tea in her hands. Jane May was at the sink, washing vegetables for a stew.

"It's all right, Mai. Do you feel better? Would you like to talk about what you saw?"

The old woman shuddered. "No, I want to hear about your camping trip. Tell me."

So Jane told her. She told her everything, but now she was calm and composed. There was a chill in the air on this evening, so they stayed in the house and the last golden light of the day streamed through the windows, illuminating their faces as they ate their little supper, and words flowed easily between them.

After Jane had cleared the table and washed up, streaks of pink and gold shot across the sky in every direction and melted into indigo blue, and they were quiet for awhile. Finally, the night fell and they settled themselves in front of a fire that Jane had laid in the stone fireplace. The two women were cozy in faded, overstuffed chairs. They sat long into the night talking in the glow of firelight. Jane May told about her fear and how it had gradually fallen away as she walked. How she felt taller and stronger with every step and how when she rounded a bend and found herself face to face with a bear, she wasn't terrified. Startled yes, and cautious certainly, but not afraid, and that seemed remarkable. For a few long moments, she and the bear stood and sized each other up. Finally the bear had shuffled off into the brush, and Jane May had continued on her way as well.

"Um hmm, she gave you her medicine, old mama bear did." This time Mai Zinni listened with enthusiasm, the afternoon's minatory vision in the forest apparently forgotten.

"Oh Mai, as I climbed higher, I came to a spruce forest. The floor was made of needles and moss and the smell was divine! Sugary, like Christmas. I felt like I was walking through all the Christmas mornings in all the world and I could feel the joy and the disappointment of those mornings all at the same time. And it was like Christmas morning represented something larger, do you know what I mean?" The older woman nodded. "It was like that sugary smell touched off a flood of some kind of feeling in me. I saw how sorrow and joy and regret and contentment are almost the same thing, or at least they co-exist all the time. I don't know, it's like it's clear in my heart, but I haven't the words." Jane looked at her friend now, and on Mai Zinni's face in the light of the fire, she saw something so pure and so sweet and it washed over her like honey. Understanding. This old woman listened and heard and understood what she was saying. For the first time Jane May felt that she'd really been heard.

Jane went on to describe pitching the small tent and eating the meager supper that she had prepared.

"No cooking up there in the wilderness," Mai had said, "No fire, neither. You just gone eat a sandwich and some fruit and then tie your garbage up high in a tree afterward. Don't keep nothing in the tent or near you that might seem like food to a wild thing."

After the encounter with the bear on the trail, Jane did not question this advice and pulled her trash and food bag high up into a tree with the nylon rope Mai Zinni had given her.

Jane told how after her early supper, she'd discovered the quartz ledge that Mai had told her about, and how it had taken her breath away, and she had sat there as the sun went down and the sky bloomed with the dying of the day and a huge raven had circled and circled and several times gotten close enough that Jane might have touched its black wing tip, had she not been afraid of toppling off the ledge and plunging to her death. And then the magnificent orange moon rose slowly as if being hoisted by some unseen, lovesick giant. Jane had risen too, then, and she had stood quietly, raising her arms to the moon, and then she had begun to sing. "Yes, Mai. I was singing a song I didn't know. The stars came out, one by one. Even though the moon was so bright, I could see the stars. A really bright one rose over the peak of a mountain in the distance. And this song, these strange sounds, just flowed out of me and it felt so natural and so familiar somehow. It was almost like a language."

"Um hum. That's real good. What else?"

Jane looked across at the beautiful old woman illumined by firelight. Her eyes shone in the glow, her skin was burnished gold. For a moment, she wasn't Mai Zinni, but someone else, someone familiar.

My dream! She's the woman from my dream. Jane was thrust back into the dreams she'd always awakened from in a fog of forgetfulness. She could hear the drumbeat and feel the big cats' eyes boring into her. She could see the beautiful woman dancing. The bzzz-pop of the sparks shooting out of the fire.

But the nature of dreams is ineffability. And this tiny recollected glimpse receded just as fast as the dreams themselves had and left Jane shaking her head as her vision reframed her friend into an old woman again.

"I said, what else. Where are you, Child?"

"I'm sorry, Mai, I guess the fire is making me drowsy. I should probably go home now. It's late. We'll talk more tomorrow, okay?"

"Sure Baby." Mai Zinni rose and embraced Jane, then returned to her chair, as Jane went out the back door, heading for the short trail that would take her to her car.

Sometimes it's yours and nobody else's. Jane was learning to discern. To hold things. To keep her own council. And that was good. What Mai Zinni had hoped for had happened. The younger woman had touched her own courage on the mountain. She was beginning to reclaim her wild heart. Old Shining Rock could do that.

When Jane arrived the next day, Mai Zinni was in a talkative mood.

"Sit down, Love Bug, I want to tell you a story 'bout the first time I myself spent the night on Shining Rock alone. So many years ago! And I was just a child, really. Barely thirteen, when my grandma sent me overnight to the mountain. A vision quest, she'd said. I felt so brave when I set out with my homemade backpack filled only with food and a bedroll and a little compass. The same one I gave you. I was so proud that my grandmother thought I could do this. I would not let her down. No, I would not. I made my way up the long trail to the top of the mountain and made a camp and ate my little supper. I sat on the crystal ledge and watched the day wane and an enormous raven circled, getting almost close enough for me to touch, just like it did for you."

Jane May gasped as she heard this.

"But as the stars popped out of the darkling sky one by one, my little child's heart began to falter. It was cold. And I was so alone. I'd slept on Granny's screened in sleeping porch many times, and felt brave. But this was different. I was all the way outside and so far from home!

"Somehow I fell asleep under that big dark sky in my little bedroll, only to be awakened hours later by a shouting sound. 'AWR, AWR, AWR.' I sat bolt upright, my eyes must've looked like saucers. I searched the dark for the source of the awful sound. 'AWR, AWR, AWR.' It seemed closer. My heart was beatin' so hard and I'd gone to shiverin' and I couldn't stop. Then I noticed movement on the edge of the clearing where I'd bedded down. I peered into the dark. Poor little scared girl child. As I looked, a long-legged vixen came out of the night and made her way slowly toward me.

"Oh the sweet thing! Relief mixed with excitement coursed through my veins and I held out my arms and the fox walked right in as if we were long-lost friends. She stayed until morning, spiraled into my body and when the sky greyed up, she rose and with one glance backward, trotted off into the mist. I ate my breakfast, broke camp and came home, a different girl. Ever since that night fox has been a powerful ally for me. She comes whenever I need to be reminded of my own courage.

"But listen, my mama was so mad! For weeks after that she had forbidden me to see my Granny at all. 'I can't trust her no more! What kind of grandma sends a little girl off into the wilderness by herself? You ain't ready for that. No, hush now, I won't have any more of it!' She railed and ranted for days about it.

"I cried myself to sleep every night until finally Mama relented. She needed a baby-sitter. She had to work after all. Late one night, I woke up to hear Mama and Granny Street speaking in mad whispers in the next room.

'You have to promise me!'

'I can't make a promise like that, Child.'

'Then I'll take her far away and you'll never see her again.'

'Sophia Louisa, you always was a hard-headed child yourself. You know this little one has the gift. You know it.'

'I don't know any such thing! She is a normal child, mother. This nonsense stops right here and right now.'

'Nonsense. Normal.' Granny Street spat the words out. 'Girl, you are talking about our family's legacy. A gift that's been handed down for generations as far back as anyone can remember. This is our heritage. This is who we are.'

'Heritage.' Mama could spit words, too. 'What good has this so-called heritage, this gift, ever done any one of us? Tell me that? It ain't done nothing but bring heartache Mama, and you know it.'

"Propped up in bed on my elbow, with my ear against the wall, I could hear my grandmother sigh and lower herself heavy-like into a chair. *Oh no*, I thought, *don't give up, Granny*. But then Mama sighed too and sat down with matching heaviness. *A truce!* They always managed a truce, these two, and I always knew I could count on Mama and Granny to compromise in my favor, in the end!

'All right, Mama,' said my mama to my granny.

'All right, then. You've made a good decision, my dear one,' said Granny Street.

"Mama snorted and that was that. From then on, Granny Street openly taught me the ways of the family. And I soaked up the teachings like a sponge. I was a good student, too. My mama never once said it, but I think she was proud of me."

"Oh Mai, I know she was! She had to be." Jane sat quietly and let Mai Zinni's story soak in. Finally she said, "Mai. Is that what you're doing with me now? Teaching me the ways of the family?"

"Well now, that is a good question, my dear." The two women were sitting on Mai's porch in the creaky old rocking chairs and for a long time, the back and forth of the rockers and the purring of Period, curled in Jane's lap, marked time like the ticking of a clock. "A very good question, indeed." The corners of Mai's mouth turned up at the ends, ever so slightly, as she continued to rock.

Jane leaned back in her chair and sighed. "Mai, can I ask you something else?"

"I reckon I can't stop you, can I?"

"Are you Deborean?" The word hung heavy in the air between them and Mai Zinni made no move to answer, so Jane went on in a tumble of words, "I've heard of the Deborean Clan. There's not much on the internet about it." Mai snorted at this, but Jane continued, unable to stop herself. "I mean it kind of makes sense doesn't it?" Jane had wandered into uncomfortable territory and she sensed that she should stop talking, but she couldn't. Not yet. "I'm just so curious. Have you been taught magic? Spells? Are you going to teach me these things? Are you some kind of witch, Mai?"

A long silence followed in which Jane May had time to review all that she had said. She wished sincerely that she could take back at least some of her words. Maybe she should have stopped at the original question. Maybe she should have skipped it altogether.

Finally, Mai Zinni spoke. But first she let out a long sigh. "Child. You got a powerful urge to label things. To get 'em into neat little boxes. Let's say you get me stuffed into one of your boxes. Then what? Are you done? Think you know me? Think you know all about me?"

"No Mai, that's not what I meant at all," Jane's voice faltered as she realized that probably was exactly what she meant. *Let's get this woman figured out once and for all and be done with it.*

"Be careful, Sugar Pie, of thinking you got anything, anything at all in this old world figured out. Stay curious. Keep wondering. Live in the questions. That's how you'll come to understand things."

Chapter 24

"John?" Mai Zinni could just make out a shadowy figure beyond the hedge that encircled her house like protective arms. She'd stepped out onto the front porch, unafraid. "John, is that you?" The shadow shuffled and shifted its weight from one foot to the other. "John, come on in here, it's damp out." John Hawkes slid through the gate and up the walk and paused at the bottom of her steps. "You got something on your mind?" She waited, accustomed to his silences. "Come on in the house now." She turned and went in and put the kettle on to boil and he lingered in the dark.

Mai Zinni and John had known each other for so long that a kind of language had developed between them. Neither could have told the rules of this language or its origin, but both were fluent and even though he had not yet spoken a word, volumes had been communicated and understood.

"Come on. Sit," she said with her back to him. She'd sensed him come in and quietly close the door. She knew that he was standing in the doorway to the little kitchen, his head hanging down, and she felt his turmoil. And his sorrow. The turmoil she didn't share with him anymore, having resolutely put that down for her own survival years ago. But his sorrow? Oh yes, that was hers too. They bore it together and were inextricably bound by it.

"John, what's got you riled up tonight?" She set a mug of herbal tea in front of him, steam curling up like a spell.

"I guess it's the moon. I can't sleep when it's full like this."

"I know." She reached out and lightly touched his hand, and he pulled it away, as she knew he would. Mai Zinni had learned long ago to approach this man as she would a wounded animal in the forest. She was calm and gentle, and when finally he looked at her, she took advantage of the brief moment to communicate to him with her eyes her assurance that he had nothing to fear from her. Still he was skittish, always, and angry. If she wasn't careful, he could shape-shift into something mindless and fierce and then they were all in danger. Not physical danger, John was not capable of hurting her, but they were at risk of dropping the loose threads that held their story together and if that happened, who knew what would become of them. Mai Zinni shuddered at the thought.

"Have you slept at all?"

"A little."

"Did you dream?"

"Damn woman! Your questions wear a man down!"

So that was it. He'd been disturbed in the other world. Mai Zinni took a sip of her tea and began to softly hum. John shook his head in agitation, but she continued. She got up and lit a candle and placed it on the table, casting both of them in a soft glow. Then she went and quietly closed the shutters over the kitchen sink, smiling sadly at the big round moon as she did. All the while, she kept humming the soothing tune. When she heard John take a deep breath and slowly exhale, she let the song come to a rest.

"Tell me," she said. And so he did.

"It was just like always. I am at the bottom of a dark well, feeling lost and then a door opens onto a meadow, or a field. It's full of sunlight, it's golden." He went silent again.

"Tell me," she repeated.

"The woman. She's picking blue flowers."

"What does she look like?"

"You know what she looks like!" He spat the words out and Mai Zinni quickly moved to calm him. "Okay John, it's okay. You're okay. She's picking flowers and what happened?"

John pushed his tea out of the way and laid his head down on the table. "I'm tired, Zee. I'm so goddamned tired."

"I know my dear, it's all right. Just rest now. I'll make up the couch for you."

She did and she led him there and drew the old quilt up over his bony shoulders and kissed him ever so lightly on the forehead and in the morning he was gone, as she knew he would be.

Mai Zinni sat out on her porch with her tea and the morning mist all around and let her mind wander backward.

She'd been up on the bald, picking wildflowers. It was the time of the cornflowers, blue bottles, her grandmother had called them. She'd taught

Mai how to use them for an eye tonic and also to make a pretty blue dye. It was a beautiful, sun-washed day and her long black hair swung free around her shoulders, the wind lifting and twisting it.

For the first time in months, she felt the sun warm her and her heart softened a little bit. She had been clinched up tight ever since her mother's death. She was afraid. Only twenty-one, she'd lost everyone she'd ever loved. Her father had died when she was a toddler, and her beloved grandmother had kept Mai Zinni while her mother went to work to support them. It was Granny Street who had taught her the names of all these wildflowers and herbs and the uses for many of them, both medicinal and ritual . . . she had taught her to think of the plants as kindred spirits. Her grandmother had told her stories from the old days about her ancestors and her heritage, stories about her own mother Bel, Mai Zinni's great-grandmother, who was a Cherokee woman of the Aniwodi, the Red Paint Clan. Bel had married a Welch immigrant. And Bel's mother before her, Lois Inez, had traversed the Trail of Tears in 1838 on a cradle board strapped to her mother's back, all the way to Oklahoma, and had been brought back four years later on horseback, by her father, after the death of his young wife. He had left the little girl with relatives who'd stayed behind, hidden in the green folds of the mountains, and ridden off without a word, never to be seen again. Mai Zinni loved to hear these stories, even the tragic ones. They gave her a strong sense of rootedness to this place. When Granny Street talked of these people, young Mai felt surrounded by helpers, old ones who loved her and cared about her. She never tired of hearing the tales and many she had heard over and over again, from the time she was a very young child, sitting in her beloved grandmother's lap or working beside her, picking herbs and flowers in the forests and on the balds. Mai Zinni's mother, Sophie, worked long, hard hours cleaning the houses of townspeople in order to support herself and her little girl. The price she paid was intimacy with her daughter. Mai Zinni was immeasurably closer to her grandmother than her own mother.

Granny Street had died in her sleep only three years before and then six months ago, her mama, and now Mai Zinni was completely alone in the world. Oh, she was loved and she knew it. The whole town loved her and thought of her as their own. They were still leaving offerings of casseroles, cakes, homemade bread and the like on her doorstep, all these months after her mother had died. She knew they loved her and she was grateful for it, but still, it wasn't the same. Her mother had been an only child and so had her father. As far as she knew, she had no aunts or uncles or cousins.

But on that day, all of the sadness had lifted somehow and she felt glad to be alive again. She felt hopeful. She was gathering wildflowers on the bald and humming to herself when she looked up and saw him. She was not afraid, not even from the first moment, when she had no idea if he meant her harm or not. She knew that he did not. She knew it in the way that she knew her own name. He was a stranger, and yet she knew that he was there at that moment, in that place, just for her, and even though she'd had no inkling that she'd been waiting for him, she didn't question that either. It felt right. It felt like perfect timing.

From that first day, Mai Zinni and John were seldom apart.

The people who knew her were delighted and embraced the young man completely. He had proposed marriage shortly after that first meeting and Mai Zinni had accepted. The town readied for a joyous event after so much sorrow. She would be given in marriage by Mac Harkness, her childhood friend. Mai knew that Mac loved her, even though he'd never spoken of it. Her feelings for him were strong and affectionate, but not reflective of his. She was grateful and loved him more because he wanted only for her happiness and so made John his friend.

Chapter 25

The brass bell jingled as John Hawks entered the dim space. Shafts of dusty sunlight poked at the floor, but there was no other light.

"Hullo there," he called out, waiting for his eyes to adjust to the semi-darkness. "Anybody round?" No response, just a slight rustling of papers near the cash register in the wake of the front door opening. "Mac? You back there?" John moved slowly toward the heavy brocade curtain, careful not to upset anything as he went. He pulled back the curtain and peeked through, not wanting to frighten his friend if he was engaged, as he often was, in some process of divination. Mac tended to give his full attention to any task set before him, whether it was reading the cards for himself or someone else or just dusting the shelves. John had observed him once, reverently lifting every item and caressing it with a dust cloth, as if it were a priceless jewel. He had watched his old friend for a full ten minutes, before he felt that he had crossed over from bemused observer to intrusive spy, and he'd cleared his throat loudly to get Mac's attention. Mac had laughed to find his friend had come in without his knowledge, and he had put down the cloth, offering up a warm smile, and transferred his full attention to John. And that is what happened this morning too, as Mac came, humming, down from the upstairs apartment. He was lost in thought and made it all the way to the bottom of the stairs before catching sight of his friend. Upon seeing John, Mac's face lit up with merriment, and he rushed to embrace him.

John was not in a mood for frivolity this morning, and did not want to be distracted. He waved the other man off and started talking.

"I'm here for a reason, Mac. It's not all fun and games with ever' body, you know."

Seeing John's distress, Mac quickly adopted a sober demeanor and, pulling back the curtain, ushered his friend into the dusky private space, making soothing sounds all the way.

"Sit John, I'll make tea. While the kettles boils, I'm going to turn the lights on in the shop. Running a little late, this morning. Wait here, okay."

John sat at the round oak table that had seen its share of seances and tarot readings and happy meals with friends and family, and that was just in this life time. The hundred year old table undoubtedly held secrets that no one living now would ever uncover.

More recent secrets had been revealed around its worn perimeter too but Mac was a master secret-keeper. His usually open and happy demeanor belied this genetic trait. Mac came from a long line of people adept at keeping close council.

This gift in his friend was highly prized by the reclusive John.

As John waited for the tea to brew and Mac to join him, his mind wandered and he thought of Mac and this place. Good Golly, he'd spent a lot of time here over the years. He'd watched his friend with the people who came into the shop, and admired him. Mostly tourists, they were, but the occasional serious student of esoterica would make their way to him. Mac had a strict policy about his sporadic customers. Whether they be frivolous tourists or locals, looking for some witchy gag gift, or serious students of the occult, they were given as much time and thoughtful attention as they needed. Mac had an uncanny gift for reading people. He could tell if they wanted to talk or be left alone to browse. Sometimes he would slip behind the curtain and leave a person alone to peruse the wares. He'd told John that he had found that, because of the nature of his shop, people were often reticent about coming in, and when they did muster up the gumption to enter, they could be timid about handling the items. Sometimes, if they had the sense that they were alone, a boldness that they might not even know they possessed would come forward. Sometimes people were afraid and sometimes that came out as aggression toward him, but that was rare.

Mac's attitude toward the arcana that cluttered his shelves and hung from his rafters was that if one was seeking: seeking answers, help, illumination, guidance . . . God, then one would find that, down whatever paths one chose to look. And that's what most people were seeking. What in fact is built into everyone's DNA to seek. Mac had a strong mental image of God as a wind, a breath, who before sending little babies into the world, twisted into their double helixes the longing to find Him. Or Her.

John was certainly familiar with the longing for God, but he wasn't sure about any of the rest of it. He felt a stab of regret for the darkness he was bringing into this lovely space today and that reminded him of a story that Mac had told him years ago. They had never mentioned it again, in all the intervening time, but the memory of it still raised John's hackles.

A woman had come into the shop early one morning. In fact, Mac had seen her from the upstairs window, pacing the sidewalk in front of the door, waiting for the shop to open. It was quite early, but *The Light Within* was new then and Mac was always happy to have a customer. It was, as he'd known it would be, a struggle to keep a shop like his open in a small mountain town like Gideon.

Mac said that there were locals who, even if they didn't practice the old ways, at least knew of them. Perhaps their parents or grandparents had adhered to ancient practices like dowsing, or root work, herbal cures or protections, but it was a new world, a modern world, and most people wanted to keep up-to-date with that. People remembered things though, and sometimes when the going got tough, they longed for the old ways and they would come to Mac, seeking help or advice. But most of his trade was done with tourists, people from elsewhere who were passing through and liked to spend a day poking around in quaint, historic downtowns, which Gideon delivered. They would wander in, the bell on the door announcing their arrival, and frequently they'd buy a candle, or a wind chime, or a sun catcher, little gifts for their friends back home, or maybe a souvenir of the trip for themselves. Sometimes they would see his sign that advertised Tarot readings and shyly inquire and he would lead them through the brocade curtain, set a cup of tea in front of them, and tell them things about themselves that they knew deep inside but hadn't been able to see clearly before. He certainly wasn't rich, he always said, but he was content with this life.

He didn't recognize the woman pacing in front of his shop that morning. *She must be a tourist*, he'd thought to himself, as he hurried down the stairs and unlocked the heavy door, holding it open for her to enter.

From the moment she brushed past him, he had been uneasy.

"Good morning," he'd chirped. "Welcome."

But the woman had said nothing, just filled up the space with malevolence.

"What can I show you this morning?"

"Well," she crooned, turning to him once she was inside and the door was closed, "Isn't this charming." She held him in her gaze, her irises like cold blue flames and he felt himself wither. *Do I know her*, Mac wondered. Something about her presence made him uneasy in an ancient and strangely familiar way.

"Have we met before?" Mac's voice had a strangled quality.

Shards of laughter hit the floor and scattered like broken glass. She moved closer to him.

Mac backed up until he was pressed against a wall and for a fraction of a second, she loomed over him. He was caught, mid-gasp, as she retracted into the small neat package that he'd seen from his upstairs window. Body like a cat, muscular, no extraneous fat whatsoever, she was dressed in a red pantsuit, devoid of decoration, except for a small gold pendant hanging at her neck. A symbol that he'd never seen, but seeing it now, he shuddered. Her perfect blond bob smelled faintly of something burnt.

She was wandering the shop, letting her fingers lightly brush first a statue, then a deck of cards. He knew that he would need to smudge the place as soon as she left. And he hoped that that would be soon. He emerged from the corner she'd backed him into.

"Can I show you something in particular?" Feeling his strength return, he advanced a couple of steps in her direction.

"No." Her voice had a dreamlike quality. "I just want to see what you're about here."

"Well, please feel free to browse and let me know if I can answer any questions for you." With that he moved to put the heavy wooden check-out counter between them. He wasn't about to take his eye off the woman.

As he watched her over the top of his glasses, she moved around the shop, touching one thing and then another, pausing now and then to study something, picking up a book and thumbing idly through, sniffing a candle . . . Mac could hardly wait to get this creature, for that is how he thought of her, out of his shop.

"It's a lovely day, isn't it? Have you been up on the Parkway?" Hoping she would get the idea to go there now, he prattled on about the rhododendrons and mountain laurel, but she was having none of it, appearing instead to be settling in for a prolonged stay.

He offered her tea. She refused. He wished intently for another customer to come in and break the spell she'd put over the place. None did.

Watching her from his perch behind the fortification of the counter, the air around her seemed to shimmer and he watched with repugnance as she took on the form of a snake. Her slim body in the red pantsuit arranged itself into an S shape and her tongue flicked obscenely. Mac blinked and the snake was gone, leaving only the woman behind, but he would never forget it. He waited, stunned and immobilized, until she finally glided toward the door, leaving a faint scent of sulphur in her wake.

"Thanks for coming in," he muttered.

"You take care now," she said. "I'll be around. We'll meet again." The door swung open and the incongruous comforting sounds of birds singing and people greeting each other wafted in along with a wide, happy swath of sunlight. And then there was nothing but the relief of the bell, fading into infinity. Mac never saw her again.

There were, Mac always said, forces of evil in the world. Whether they had arrived here soulless, or had their souls broken and stolen by violence or grief, he didn't know, but he had surely encountered one of them on that lovely morning, and he had never doubted their existence since.

John had arrived in Gideon a few days after the experience, and Mac's attention had turned to happier things. Years later, he told John the story and they had spoken of it only the one time. Remembering it now, John felt sorry. Sorry for all the pain he knew that he had caused Mac and also Mai and Little Star over the years. Maybe he could ease that pain for all of them. Well, for Mac and Mai anyway. Their daughter was lost, a fact which had long ago settled itself into John's bones. He took sole responsibility for that. Regret can swallow a man, like a black hole, folding him into its relentless darkness. John felt that his own soul had been lost.

Mac's voice brought John out of his head and he shuddered briefly.

"Here's your tea, Buddy. What's on your mind, today?" Mac set two steaming mugs on the table between them and lowered himself into a chair.

"I need your help, Mac."

Mac turned toward John and allowed his face to come into line with his heart. How he loved his old friend. He had known John since he first came to Gideon, all those decades ago. He had seen his friend through ups and downs, joys and sorrows. He had walked his beloved Mai Zinni down the aisle and given her to this man in marriage, even though he cherished her beyond all others himself. He had known John before he dove deeply into himself, never to fully surface again.

"I'm here John."

And with those three words, a torrent of pent-up anguish was released. Only Mai Zinni and Mac knew John's whole story. Oh, plenty of folks knew parts and made up the rest. There had been speculation over the years by the townspeople, but only those two knew the whole true story and that fact made them both, at once, John's worst nightmare and the only medicine that allowed him any rest at all. At this moment, he was soul-sick and badly in need of medicine. He had sought it out at Mai Zinni's cottage last night, but it hadn't worked. In fact, as often happened, it made him worse. He didn't see how he could take the torment of the truth any longer.

"I've decided to end my dried up miserable life. It's time. Don't know why I hung around this long."

"John, no!" Mac gasped.

"No, I ain't got time to listen to any platitudes meant to soothe my ravaged heart. I just need your promise that Zee will be taken care of. She should receive all the proceeds from the sale of the inn, which I hope Jane May will buy. We've talked about it, Jane and I, and while she ain't said she will, it seems right and likely to me that she should buy it and stay here in Gideon. After all, she's got no reason to go back to where she came from. Too much has changed for her already and from her divorce she's got enough money to be comfortable here and to afford the inn. People like her. She would keep Nanette on, I would insist on that, and that would help her to take care of Charlie. She would be good at running the inn, better than I've ever been, with my moodiness and codgerly ways." So in John's mind, it was all settled. He needed to know that Mac would check in on Zee regularly. And that he would handle the particulars. John didn't hold truck with lawyers, as Mac knew, so he had written down what he wanted and he was asking his friend to make sure that it happened that way.

"I don't have much. Nothin' really, 'cept that old ramshackle inn. But I want her to have all the money from it. Make sure it don't go to no long-lost relatives or no damn lawyers or nothing like that. Can you do that for me, Mac?"

Mac sat, stunned.

"Yes, of course, but . . . ."

"No buts, ya hear? This ain't up for discussion."

"John," Mac pleaded now, "Don't do this! Your life is worth so much more than you know."

"To who? My sorry-ass beat-up life ain't worth nothin' to nobody and you know it!"

"It's worth something to me. You're my friend."

"I said," John's fist came down hard on the table and his face twitched, "this ain't up for discussion. If you're my friend like you say, I need you to agree to some things. Will ya?"

Mac hung his head for a long moment. He blinked away tears and nodded, without meeting his friend's eyes.

"No, look at me."

Mac lifted his head and looked at the man sitting before him. John was broken. A shadow of the handsome young man who had rolled into town, all those years ago, full of bravado and ready for anything.

This man staggered under the weight of sorrow that rested so heavily on his shoulders. He had been valiant, stoic in his effort to carry what he had not asked for. He had doggedly dragged that burden across more than four decades and he was stumbling now, tired and in desperate need of rest. But was this the only way to find it? Mac knew it wasn't, but he also knew that his friend hadn't come to this lightly or quickly, and was not likely to be dissuaded, and his heart was heavy with this understanding.

"I'll do it, John," he said quietly. "Whatever you need from me, it's yours. Just please promise me that you'll give it a little more time. A little more thought. So many love you, John."

"Yeah, I'll think on it some more. I will." John rose from the table and laid his hand on Mac's sagging shoulder. They remained this way for a moment or two, Mac filled with sorrow, John with resolve. A wisp of a breeze caressed Mac's face as the lifting of the brocade curtain marked John's passage.

Chapter 26

As she walked the drumbeat got louder and louder and the glow from the firelight grew brighter. Cresting the top of the hill, she could see the woman dancing, her form silhouetted against the firelight. She had her back to the fire, facing seven panthers standing at the edge of the forest in a semi-circle. They watched her and her stomping and swaying grew more frenetic. Sparks arced from the fire exploding in mid-air—bzzz-pop. As they popped, they wheeled up, up, up in the sky toward the enormous orange ball of the moon. Just as the woman's dancing seemed to reach a climax, the drumming stopped. The woman turned and looked directly into Jane May's eyes. She was the most flawlessly beautiful woman Jane had ever seen. Her skin, smooth and caramel colored, was decorated with blue markings. There were lines, spirals and dots on her face. Swirls twined around her arms and caressed the top of her firm and ample breasts. Her eyes, deep and dark, penetrated Jane's own. She felt a yearning radiating from her solar plexus. She stood transfixed and the woman changed. Her image became amorphous, liquid almost, and then regathered and solidified into a much older person. With her face, leathery and deeply-etched, and her smaller stature, came recognition—Mai Zinni! This was Mai Zinni, had always been Mai Zinni. But it was also Jane May herself. She awakened in the dream and found herself there. She knew, with a dreamer's knowing, what it meant to be a woman and to be vibrantly alive, and at the same time, to be marching resolutely toward death. She understood how all the stages of her life, from the maiden child that she had been, to the mother who had carried life in her womb, and carried that life still, in her heart, and to the old crone, who she would be, bent under years of experience, were all parts of her right now, and always had been. Her struggles with these disparate parts had been painful. She could still remember that first red flower in her underwear at school, her knowing that everything would change now, but how? The angst and humiliation that were the true hallmark of youth. And then the pain of birthing and the conundrum of how to stay sane in the world when her heart now resided in her daughter's body as much as her own. The struggle to tame the terror of what might happen to Issy, when being smothered by motherlove was just as big a danger. The discomfort of looking in the mirror at forty and seeing the beginnings of the transformation. The lines, the sagging, the thinning, the plumping. Watching with smug envy her daughter and her daughter's friends, blithely flitting down the years with their unmarked skin and their barely used bodies, and knowing that they didn't appreciate their current perfection any more than she had at their age. The late night fears about dying alone, unloved and unwanted. Fears of being sick or in pain.

As Jane May stood, immobilized but cognizant in the dream, the old woman approached her and didn't stop. Jane May shuddered, as she was entered and lifted by the spirit of the dream Other. She felt herself to be momentarily suspended above the earth, containing the whole of her life, past, present and future, curled like a spiral in the center of her body. She was buoyant and light for a moment, the spaciousness inside herself as vast as the starlit sky above. And then she felt it pass through her and leave her, just as it had entered, and she was set back, gently, on the ground, the word *Rise* forming in the air all around her.

Jane May Gideon woke in almost utter oblivion, nothing but the word *Rise* in her mind. Nothing else but a sense of being lifted.

Sunlight drifted down through the green canopy, filtered like honey through the window, puddling on the bed where Jane lay, slowly, slowly, ascending from the dream world.

"Rise," she murmured. "Rise? Rise." Struggling to remember, she closed her eyes, not wanting the distraction of waking, of sunlight on the bed, of birdsong, of her phone ringing—

"Damn!" She fumbled for the phone as the dream darted, irretrievable, into the recesses of her consciousness.

"Hello, who is it?"

"Who do you think it is? You seen John this morning? I can't get him to answer his phone. Damn fool." Before Jane could answer, Mai added, "I'm coming over. Meet me up at the inn."

"Wait." But the line had gone dead.

"Mai Zinni!" Jane called as she came up the path from her cottage, "I'm here. Where are you?"

The old woman stepped out onto John's back porch, brows drawn together, shoulders slumped forward, "He's not here," as if the question had been about John, and not about her. "He's lost."

Jane May put her arm around Mai's shoulders and led her into John's house. "Why are you so worried, May? I'm sure he's just gone out for something. He'll be back soon."

Jane May put water on to boil in John's tiny kitchen, while Mai Zinni continued to open drawers and root around the sparsely furnished rooms, searching for some clue, some note or item, that would let her know that he was okay, that he would be back soon.

When the tea was ready, Jane May collected the old woman and led her to the back steps.

"Let's sit down for a minute and see if we can sort this out."

"He's lost. For the love of God, can't you see it?" Mai Zinni began to cry and a strange thing happened. Her old weather-worn face, crinkled and grooved, began to smooth out. It was as if her tears were filling in the rivulets created by the relentless flow of years and time was turning in on itself. Jane May stared into this face that she had come to love and realized that she had seen this transfiguration before. It was a dream . . . there was drumming, and fire . . . Jane snapped back to the present, as Mai Zinni stood up beside her and began pacing the pine straw carpeted lawn. The old woman, who had been momentarily young, was old again . . . had returned to her soft, familiar self, and Jane shook her head once to reorient her mind.

"Lord, Child, quit staring at me! Have you lost your senses?"

"Mai, I can't understand why you're so worried. Looks to me like he's just gone to town for something."

"You don't know nothing!" The old woman spat the words out. She was becoming more and more agitated. She began to mutter to herself as she paced, but Jane couldn't make out any of the words, although there seemed to be a rhythm to them.

The pacing stopped suddenly, as did the muttering. "Did he say anything to you yesterday about his plans for today?" Mai seemed to be trying hard to get in gear, to make a plan, but every idea she had for moving in that direction fizzled out as soon as it saw the light of day.

"No Mai, I barely saw him yesterday. I was in and out all day. Wait, I did see him early and he said, now that you mention it, that he was going to see Mac."

"Of course. Of course. I should've thought of it earlier. Call Mac, will you? He'll know what's going on. Mac'll know."

Relieved to be able to retreat from Mai's anxiety for a minute, Jane May returned to the cottage to make the call. She had to locate her cell phone, which had not seen much use since she arrived in Gideon, other than the call she'd received from Mai this morning. She found it tangled in the bedclothes where she'd dropped it. It had lost its charge. She found the charger, which was curled up like a snake in the fruit bowl in the kitchen, plugged it in, and stood by the wall, scrolling for the number of *The Light Within*.

That's odd, she thought to herself as it rang and rang. *Mac should be opening the shop by now.* Jane made her way back up the hill to be with her friend, and to try to bring some calm to the situation.

When she got there, she found Nanette with her arms around Mai Zinni, who was sitting on the porch, tears streaming down her face. Jane May felt her body tense at the sight of the younger woman, and she could see Nanette do the same as she eyed Jane over the old woman's grey head. *We don't have time for this now.* She willed herself to put her feelings about Nanette aside. "Mai, what is it? Did you find something?"

"No. Can't find nothing. I'm just so scared."

"I'm sure he's all right. He's probably just gone into town to get something. Or maybe he went up onto the Parkway." Nanette purred into Mai Zinni's ear. Everyone knew John's fondness for the Blue Ridge Parkway. "That's what he's done, Mai, don't you think? It's a nice day and he's gone up to spend the morning on the parkway. He'll be back soon. Don't worry."

"Yes," Jane May agreed. "He'll be back soon, Mai."

Nothing Jane or Nanette could say, however, soothed Mai Zinni's sense of dread.

"I saw this coming, I knew it." The pacing had resumed and if anything, the old woman was getting more and more worked up. "Oh John, we didn't know, we're not to blame. Don't you leave me here like this. Don't." And then, turning to the two younger women, "sure, you're probably right." But Jane could tell that she didn't believe it.

Later, Jane would wish for that moment. The moment right before they knew. The moment just before everything changed. The last moment when Mai still held a tiny shred of hope in her heart that John would put down his burden and forgive himself, and her, at last. But at this moment, Jane had no idea what was going on.

Jane and Nanette rose as one at the sound of crunching gravel and saw Mac Harkness pull his behemoth of a copper colored Cadillac ponderously into a parking space.

Mai Zinni's knees buckled. Jane May and Nanette eased her down into the soft grass.

Chapter 27

The flames leapt higher and higher in the rusty cauldron. The old woman occasionally poked at them with the iron stick in the shape of a serpent, wrought with spirals and crescents and vines. She was hunched over, her eyes hooded. Everything about her, a warning that said KEEP AWAY. By her side was a large basket filled with shiny green leaves.

Jane May whispered to Mac as the two stood watching, "That's Galax. It's used for wound healing and an infusion of the roots can treat kidney problems. Is Mai hurt? Is she ill?" Mac sighed to see his old friend in so much pain. He couldn't explain any of it to Jane. Mai would have to do that and she clearly wasn't interested in talking.

It soon became clear that Mai Zinni was sewing. She reached into the basket and pulled out a leaf and held it in place as her knotted fingers deftly stitched it to another leaf. In fact, she had a long row of leaves trailing across her lap and onto the ground on the other side of the basket.

"What in the world is she doing?" Jane May whispered.

"Sewing a pall. That's how the Old Ones did it, with the green leaves of the Galax."

Mac and Jane May stood just outside the hedge. Jane May chewed at her thumbnail as she watched Mai Zinni working away at her sad task. Mac laid his hand on her shoulder, in a gesture meant to comfort. It didn't, Mac could tell. Nothing he could say would comfort her. Jane was as bereaved by Mai Zinni's grief as she was by the loss of John. Mac understood this. She had arrived in Gideon completely lost and here she had been found, mirrored by these people in a way that she had probably never seen herself. John and Mai and Mac, too, had seen a strength and a spark in Jane that she herself had long since lost contact with. Now John was gone and Mai Zinni, who had become as a mother to Jane, seemed lost just as surely. His heart went out to Jane as she stood helplessly outside the hedge, watching something that she could not possibly understand.

Mac had brought Jane with him to check on Mai the day after John's body had been found, and pausing in her sewing, Mai told him to take Jane May away and keep her away. Jane turned angrily, like a child, and made to head back to where the car was parked on the road. Mac's hand went out to stay her leaving, just as Mai Zinni spoke.

"Wait. I got something to say."

Jane May paused, brushing aside tears, but not turning. Mac stood, helplessly suspended between the two women.

"I can't help you, Child. Not now. I know this is hard for you to understand, but I ain't got nothing to give you now. I didn't plan any of this, and if I could undo it, I would. You got to leave me now. You too, Mac. I got to have some room. I got to be by myself. I got nothing to give now. You got to get. I cannot help you."

Mai Zinni's voice, which had begun softly, almost kindly, had become impassioned, fevered.

"Please." She looked up and made eye contact as Jane May turned to face her. The younger woman took a tentative step forward then stopped.

After a moment, Mac took Jane's elbow and guided her around the house and down the path that led to the road where they'd left the car. They took the short path. The one with no magic, no glimmering. Only gloom and shadows.

It had been two weeks since John's body had been found up in the high meadow where he'd met Mai Zinni all those years ago. He'd left a letter with Mac and Mac had passed it on to her.

"I plan to take advantage of the migration of the monarchs to make my escape." Mai Zinni had known exactly where to look for him. He had hidden his truck and walked a long ways down the trail that led to the meadow. Their meadow. A red-tailed hawk had been circling and circling, as if keeping watch over his body. John had specified that he wanted to be cremated. Mai had sewn the Galax pall, and it had draped his simple coffin for the Sitting-Up, the night before the cremation took place. She and Jane and Mac stayed with John's body all night, and a few others from town came and went, quietly. Nanette brought food and liquor. Her eyes had dark circles beneath them, hinting at the grief she felt over the loss of the man who had taken her in when she so desperately needed it. Three men sat around a large drum in the foyer of the funeral home, beating a mournful tattoo to usher John's spirit on to the other side. They played all night, at Mai Zinni's request, only taking short breaks. This was unusual for the funeral home, but not unheard of. Mai was adamant, and Mac had made the arrangements. Mai Zinni would have liked to have kept John's body at her house, washing and anointing and laying it out herself in the old way, but Mac persuaded her to let the funeral director take the body into town. They didn't have a service after the cremation. John wouldn't have wanted that, and Mai couldn't bear the mourners. After the wake, Mac had driven her home.

He followed her in.

"Leave me," she said, but he could not.

He slept on her couch under a quilt and listened to her quiet weeping through the night. As day broke, he slipped into her bed, and she did not resist as his arms snaked around her. Mai's shattered heart was almost more than he could bear. Finally, in his embrace, she slept fitfully for a few hours, waking as a hawk circled, screaming, over her clearing in the forest.

"Mac...."

"I know, Dearest, I know." And he rose and prepared to leave. Turning at the door, he stood and let his gaze rest on her familiar face. A face that he had loved for as long as he could remember. He loved her so much that he had never told her. And he never would.

In the time since, Jane May had maintained the distance that Mai Zinni had asked for, but she delivered hearty soups and did her shopping, leaving the bags on the porch. Jane had respected that Mai didn't want to talk, that she was deep into mourning for this man, but she didn't fully understand the depth of the grief. To comprehend that, she would have had to understand who they were to each other and she did not. She had observed their mostly contentious relationship and been bemused by it, often wondering if they'd been lovers at some point, or hadn't but wanted to be. She had asked Mac more than once, but he was loyal and vague and she'd gotten nothing out of him. Mai Zinni had never wanted to talk about it, and if the conversation strayed toward her relationship to John, she would cut it off by changing the subject. When that happened, there was nothing to do but let it go. So Jane remained oblivious to the reason for the breadth of the old woman's loss, and it was frustrating and hard to bear, and Mac understood her frustration, but could not help her with it. Jane May came to see Mac often in the days after she was banished by Mai Zinni. They sat at the old round table together and it was a comfort to both of them.

"I feel unmoored, unable to decide the smallest things. What to have for breakfast? Whether to do my laundry today or wait until tomorrow. Nothing really seems to matter. Nothing feels right in the world."

"I know, Dear, I feel the same way, but it will pass, eventually. We just have to wait for Mai to do her grieving."

"I know it's selfish of me Mac, but I miss her so much. There's so much I want to tell her."

"Tell me," he said.

"Isabelle made contact with Lenny." It felt so good to share this news. She's had it bottled up inside herself for days now. "He passed on a cell phone number to me. I tried and tried to call it, I'm desperate to hear Issy's voice, to heal the rift between us, if it can be healed." She had left several messages, and once Isabelle had tried to return her call, but she'd been out walking in the woods and missed it. Issy had left a message though, in which she sounded somewhat conciliatory, which gave Jane hope that maybe her daughter also pined for her, and they would be able to find their way back to each other at some point. Whenever she thought of her beautiful, lost girl, a sensation like sinking came over her. As if she were in water and weighted down with stones, unable to make her way to the surface.

"That's great, Janie! I know you've waited a long time for this." Mac placed a hand over Jane's hand on the table and the warmth of the contact caused her to moan and tears to leak from her eyes and fall onto the table. "You'll reach her and be able to make things right again."

"I'm sorry, Mac. I'm so sorry. I'm selfish, I know, but I miss him, too, and I can't understand any of it!"

Mac stood and encircled her with his arms. "Hush now, it's all right. We all miss him. Everything will be okay, I promise." And he desperately hoped that it would.

Chapter 28

Nanette stepped out of the laundry house and called for Charlie. She was worried about the boy. Since John's death, he was spending more and more time alone in the woods. What did he do all day? She knew the boy was hurting. He had to be. He had loved John like a father. In fact, John was the closest thing that Charlie had ever had to a father. His real father, the idiot, hadn't the fortitude to come around since Charlie was an infant. John had scared Ricky half to death and after a couple of visits, he'd apparently decided that it wasn't worth the fear that John bred in him to know his own flesh and blood, and he'd just wandered off. Nanette figured she and Charlie were better off without him. He never had two nickels to rub together, so child support had always been out of the question, and she didn't want Charlie growing up with a violent role model.

They'd been happy, almost like a family, the three of them, until John had gone and . . . well, she couldn't think about that. She had to think of her boy and how she was going to take care of him.

After John's cremation, Mac had called her into his shop and told her that John had laid the groundwork to take care of her and Charlie.

"Ha!" she'd snorted. "He took care of me real good. Charlie too." Poor old Mac. She sometimes thought he was too kind and gentle for his own good. The way he looked at her almost made her want to relent, but she was too angry. She thought she'd never get over how angry she felt at John for what he'd done. How do you explain that to a boy? Charlie had just closed up when she had told him the news. She'd found him behind their house one morning on his knees, keening, and it had torn her heart out. She'd taken him in her arms and he'd thrashed about for awhile, finally settling down, his sobs subsiding into hiccoughs. After that day, though, he hadn't wanted to talk about it. She had tried once or twice, and he had simply said, "It's okay, Mama. We'll be all right. Don't worry."

He must be lost in some kind of kid denial. He could probably use counseling, but how in the hell could she afford that. John had taken care of them by leaving a small trust fund and requiring that whoever bought the inn would have to keep Nanette employed. Good grief! Clearly he'd been out of his mind. No one was going to care about her or Charlie now. He wanted Jane to buy the inn and she certainly didn't care about Nanette, and Nanette couldn't stand her either. Why, the woman had gone to John and accused Nanette of some kind of child abuse, for Christ's sake! Really, she could spit nails right about now. She was so mad at the whole world. And Mai Zinni, the old witch, had just retreated into her shell and was no good to anyone—out there alone in the forest rocking and moaning to herself, stirring a fire in that cauldron of hers.

She'd have to apply for jobs in town, but what about Charlie? School didn't start up for another month and even then she didn't want him to be a latchkey kid. He was alone enough as it was without having to come home from school to an empty house. Maybe they should leave and go . . . where? Oh Lord. How could John have done this? And where was her boy?

"Charlie, Charlie!" She called until she was hoarse and near hysteria and then there he was. It was a foggy morning and he appeared like an apparition out of the mist right in front of her.

"I'm here, Mama. What's a matter?"

"Where've you been, you little scoundrel? I was worried about you!" Nanette sank to her knees and squeezed the boy until he cried out that she was hurting him and he couldn't breathe.

"I'm sorry. You've just been spending so much time alone in the woods. I've been worried about you. I know you miss Uncle John. Don't you want to talk about it?"

"I'm okay, Mama. Sure I miss him, but he's always with me."

"What do you mean?" Nanette wiped her nose on her sleeve. This boy of hers was an odd one. An old soul, Mai always said.

"Well, he told me once that I was never alone and that whenever I needed him, all I had to do was close my eyes and think of him and he'd be there and he is. Not the way he was before. A different way. Do you understand, Mama?" Those earnest little eyes bore into hers until she felt herself softening. Maybe everything would be okay. Charlie was strong and smart and maybe he could get along with just her.

"Yes, I think maybe I do understand, and you know what?"

"What?"

"I love you and you are my good little man. But you have to tell me what you're doing all day in the woods. Are you staying in the Safe Range?" John had spoken with her a few weeks before he died about the Safe Range. He'd said Charlie was older and he thought it should be expanded and she had agreed, but now she could plainly see that Charlie had played John in that devilish way he had, and she wondered if she had been right to agree to the expansion.

"Yes, Mama. I don't go no farther than the boundary."

"Any farther."

"Or that."

"Aren't you lonely?"

"No. I got friends in the woods."

"What do you mean, friends?"

"You know, animals."

"Oh, yes," she said, "squirrels and bunnies and things?" It was so charming the way animals had always taken to Charlie, even when he was a baby. Once a wren had flown into his nursery window through a hole in the screen and sat on the edge of his crib, singing a song to him. She had come in to get him up from his nap and found him sitting up, holding his chubby little baby finger out for the bird. She'd been charmed but had, of course, shooed the bird out and repaired the screen that afternoon.

"Uh huh, squirrels and bunnies and things," Charlie said.

"All right then, you be safe and if you want to talk to me about anything, you know you can, right?"

"Yes, Mama. And you can talk to me, too."

"Okay, Charlie." She laughed "I will remember that."

Chapter 29

Reticent and still stinging from their earlier encounters but determined to smooth things over, Jane May knocked on Nanette's door early one morning while Charlie was having his breakfast. She could see Charlie through the screen door, lying on his stomach, a bowl of cereal in front of him, his attention focused elsewhere as he slowly brought the spoon to his mouth and slurped. She heard the low murmur of a television set, the beast that currently held Charlie's attention. As she watched, Nanette came into her line of vision, sailing through the room, words drifting behind her, "Watch what you're doing, Baby, don't get milk on the rug."

Jane May was touched by Nanette's tone. Affectionate and gentle. Not at all the harsh way that Jane had seen her with Charlie when they first met. She knew that she needed to learn to be less judgmental of people, to give them a chance. Maybe she was that harsh with herself. Or maybe she'd learned it when she was still small and malleable, and it was so deeply imbedded that it was difficult to root it out. As Jane pondered these things, Nanette caught sight of her standing at the screen door, peering like a child into their life.

"Can I help you?" Nanette was defensive. She always seemed ready for a fight.

"I'm sorry. I, I . . . I came over to bring you . . . this." She lifted the foil covered paper plate that she'd been holding in her hands. "I thought you and Charlie might enjoy some homemade corn bread. I brought soup, too." She bent over and lifted the jar of soup that she'd set down on the stoop. "I'm sorry," she repeated, and then felt silly.

"Oh," Nanette seemed chastened, but was obviously still on alert. "Oh. Well then, come on in." She opened the door and Jane entered.

As the screen door slammed behind her, Charlie looked away from the TV, and his eyes lit up when he saw her. Jumping up, he turned his cereal bowl over, and chaos ensued. Jane set the cornbread and soup down on the kitchen counter and spun around, looking for something, anything, to clean up the mess. Meanwhile, Nanette was already there, sopping up milk and bits of cereal with paper towels, and scolding her son at the same time. "I said, pay attention, Charlie! Good grief, you are a bull in a china shop!"

"I'm sorry, Mama." The boy hung his head. Here were the Nanette and Charlie that Jane knew, and again, she felt that she was the cause of this sorry dynamic.

"I should go," she muttered, as she backed out of the living room and turned toward the kitchen door to leave.

"Wait."

Jane May turned at Nanette's voice.

The younger woman was standing now, a bowl full of wet paper towels in her hand. "I'm sorry. It's nice of you to bring us soup and cornbread. Actually cornbread is Charlie's favorite, isn't it, Charlie? Tell her."

"Yes'm." He continued to hang his head, while he surveyed the scene from under his shaggy mop of black hair. Wondering if it was safe yet, he ventured, "I love cornbread so much, I could eat it all the time and nothing else. Um, hummmm." He licked his lips and Jane laughed, hoping it wasn't the wrong thing to do.

"All right, son." Nanette laughed too. "Thank you. That's enough. We get it," and turning back to Jane, with a megawatt smile on her face this time, she said, "he really, really likes it."

Jane relaxed and smiled. "I'm glad. I made too much. It's hard sometimes to cook for one. Especially soup. I just keep adding things and the pot gets bigger and bigger. It's good to have someone to share it with. I mean I'd take it to Mai, but . . . ." A shadow passed over Nanette's face.

"Yes, why don't you take it to Mai." The moment was gone. Jane May had ruined it. Nanette had closed herself off again. But Charlie was watching, and he was not about to let the soup and cornbread out of the house.

"Aw, Miss Mai's got plenty to eat," he whined. "Can't we keep it, Mama, please?"

"Oh yes," said Jane, brightening. "Please keep it. I had you and Charlie in mind while I was making it. I really did, and I'd be honored if you'd keep it."

"Fine," said Nanette. But her hackles were up and along with them, the wall that separated these two women had been raised again as well. "If you're sure Mai Zinni will be okay without it."

"Oh goodness." Jane smiled weakly. "I'm sure she's fine." Actually, she knew Mai wasn't fine, but this clearly wasn't the time to discuss that. Charlie smiled anxiously at his mother, and then at Jane, and eventually Nanette acquiesced and smiled as well. A small, tight smile this time.

"All right then, well, I'll be on my way now. So sorry about the cereal. Enjoy your day." Jane was out the door and on the way down the path back to her cottage before she could do any more damage. *That was a disaster,* she thought, *and it's my fault. Why did I have to even mention Mai Zinni? What an idiot. John was surely mistaken in thinking that Nanette and I will ever be friends. Every time we see each other it seems to get worse.*

PART 3

THE CRONE

THE BRIDGE TO HOME

It had been ages since the villagers had seen the old woman they called Owl Feather. She used to come to town regularly, to get supplies and she must be starving or dead by now, they thought, but they hesitated to go into the forest and see about her. She'd never done but good by them, healing their hurts with her herbs and potions, helping them to find their strayed animals, delivering their babies. And yet, they were afraid of her. Afraid of her power. The things she knew. She seemed to be intimate with some force that they were not familiar with, and it frightened them. Some of them suspected her of using her gift for nefarious purposes from time to time. No one could really point to anything specific, but there'd been talk through the years. A woman alone, sovereign unto herself, in need of no one, is a threat and a danger in the minds of some. Of course she did bear a child many years ago, and oh, but there was plenty of talk about that. The fey little one, a girl-child, was fathered by a black wolf, or a lion, or a demon. The truth of it, a waylaid traveler, just seemed too ordinary. And the child. The child with those strange eyes that seemed to pierce through to the soul of anyone she looked upon. She came into the village, trailing in the wake of her mother. She was fair enough, nothing remarkable though, until she turned those eyes on you. Brighde! Her gaze could send chills up the spines of the most down-to-earth citizens. She was unfriendly as well, which didn't help. From living alone with only her mother and the wild things of the forest for company, she was wary of people, and hid behind her mother's skirts, peering out with her wild eyes. Women would gather their children up and bustle them away when she was near. She could have benefited from a little human friend, but alas, that luxury was not in the cards for this one. She lived her entire life with only the wild animals and plants for companionship. Her mother taught her the ways of the forest and she learned to hunt and trap small animals for food, always giving thanks for their lives before she cleaned them and again before she ate them. "It is an affront to the Holy One." Her mother told her, "To take a life without honoring it and offering amends." The one who was called Little Owl could make a fire of wet sticks and moldy leaves. The fire wizard, Owl Feather called her. As the little one grew into a woman, mother and daughter grew into friends. They'd talk around the fire at night, comparing notes on things they'd found or seen that day. Or on the ailments of the villagers who sidled into their clearing periodically, glancing over their shoulders to make sure no one had seen them coming. The people in the village had, almost all at one time or another taken advantage of the knowledge of the two women, but not one of them would have stood up for Owl Feather and her daughter. Cowards are plenty, but courage is hard to find in a frightened world.

There came a day when Little Owl, returning from a dawn hunting foray, gathering a meal to break the fast, couldn't rouse her mother from sleep. She applied everything that she knew about healing to the sleeping woman, but in three days time, Owl Feather ceased breathing and Little Owl had to face the fact that she was completely alone in the world. She cried over the body of her beloved mother, until the sun had almost burnt out for the day. Finally, she sorrowfully pulled a blanket over the only face that she had ever loved, picked up her gathering basket and stumbled into the woods where her trembling fingers plucked enough round leathery leaves to fill the basket. She returned after dark, feeling her way through intuition back to the little house in the roots and her dead mother. She blew the fire that still smoldered in the fire ring back into being, sat down on a log and began to join the leaves together with a bone needle and sinew. She worked through the night, bent over her task, while the Milky Way flung itself, a grand parabola across the sky and Orion's Belt stood, a bridge to a home that she could not remember. Little Owl rocked back and forth and hummed a low song. She bit back the tears that wanted to come. There was no more time for that. She would have to step fully into her power now or die.

The sun came shooting shafts of sunlight through the trees into the clearing the next morning, but Little Owl didn't stir at first. She lay under a heavy skin, by the dying fire. Beside her was a beautiful green blanket made entirely of glossy green leaves, which were tinged with the slightest hint of red, signaling that soon the light would die, the leaves would fall, the bears would go into their suspended, sleepy state, and she would be alone for the first time in her life in a cold and icy world.

Finally, she opened her eyes, unfolded her sore frame from the ground, and entered the root house and wrapped her beloved mother's body in the shroud that she had made. Then she went into the forest and gathered several large fallen limbs and with great effort, fueled by her sorrow and her fear, she rolled them back into the clearing and laid a bonfire. Going back into the root house, she gently lifted her mother's green shrouded body, which she was surprised to find had become quite light. When had that happened? Had she been leaving for some time? The tears fought hard to come then, but Little Owl fought harder and won. Squaring her shoulders, she laid the shell of Owl Feather on top of the bonfire, and as the light from that day died, and the moon rose and the stars pricked the night sky, she lit the fire in several places. The woman who was once a girl now stood by, with head bowed and shoulders slumped and the fire, which would consume the body that had brought her into this world and kept her safe her whole life, caught up and roared.

Slowly her head came up and her shoulders lifted and she began to dance. Dipping and swaying, leaping and twirling, she moved around the funeral pyre in an ancient, untaught tarantella. A fitting ode to a lost life and also this new one that would have to be lived into. She didn't notice at first, but as she danced, animals had come out of the forest and stood at the edges, watching her, perhaps offering solace for her loss, respect for the one who'd passed over. Mountain lion, coyote, bear, deer, and fox all stood silent. Crow, owl, and hawk paused to mark the transition of a kindred spirit. Witnesses to the passing of a friend.

From that day forward, Little Owl was no more. The villagers assumed she had gone to make her way in the world, and the older woman must be saddened by that loss, because she averted her eyes on the rare occasions that she came into town, sheltered under a heavy shawl draping her head, casting her face into shadows.

Chapter 30

Jane May had spent the morning aimlessly driving around Gideon and out into the countryside. Once or twice she pulled her car over and picked wildflowers that she'd seen growing on the side of the road as she passed by, but mostly she'd lost heart and even the kindred weren't speaking to her like they had before. She'd grown weary of trying to keep herself distracted and returned home, thinking she would put a chair outside and spend the day reading. She parked and collected her purse and water bottle and as she turned to go inside, she felt eyes upon her and, looking up, saw what might be a large animal standing in the shadows just across the creek. The dust had barely settled from her car wheels, the shadows were deep and the distance was wide, so she couldn't be sure what it was. But there stood something, shade dappled and large and somehow not menacing, but turned toward her. Her breath caught, her heart stuck in her throat, and something inside spoke to her and said simply, stay. And she did. She stayed and faced the creature. It was probably a dog, she thought, and so she waited. The two stood like that for what seemed an eternity. In those moments, something was communicated to Jane May Gideon. A message about her own power, quiet and strong, rooted deep inside her. Power that quickened like muscle and blood, not needing to strut or to testify. Full unto itself. Something that had been threatened in her life, but not killed. Pushed down, but not buried. How startling to realize its presence. A remembrance from some place long forgotten.

A memory came now of herself as a young girl on her grandfather's farm, standing with her friend Scout, looking into the peach orchards. It was dusk and a dark, familiar thing had curled itself around her heart and begun to squeeze. A thing that she had known for as long as she could remember. It always came at the end of the day, in the shadows. It was insistent and heavy. Ponderous, as if a slow but enormous beast were settling itself on her small, fragile chest. She didn't know how to speak of it, and so told no one except Scout. "Scout," she whispered now, "It's here. It's squeezing me." She whimpered and the dog moved closer to her, resting his shaggy head on her thigh, and she was comforted.

The peach orchards made, by day, lovely rows of dappled sunlight and fuzzy ripening fruit, haloed by buzzing bees, branches forking into wonderful nooks that a young girl could climb into and while away a whole day, hidden from adult eyes. But they were, by night, strange and foreboding. Furtive shadows darting in and out among the trees. The eyes straining to make out something threatening, something scary. A scream shattered the quiet and Jane May wanted to run, but couldn't. She was frozen in fear. Scout was on full alert, ears back and hackles raised. And then it came again, the screaming, stabbing the air around them. Scout's lips curled back and a low snarl of warning issued forth from his throat. Frightened, Jane had begun to cry, but when she wound her hand into the soft fur of the big dog's nape, courage straightened her small frame, raising her to her full height. "Scout," she whispered again, just as a fierce rustling erupted in the dark undergrowth in front of them. "Scout," this time with more urgency. "Listen to me, Scout. We've got to be brave. We'll stand right here. We won't run, no matter what." The dog shifted his weight from one side of his body to the other and back again, planting himself firmly between the girl and the unknown, and she added, "Don't leave me, Scout." A calm descended then on Jane May. *It's all right*, she told herself. *Whatever happens, it's all right. I am fine.*

They stood there, girl and dog, for a long time, listening. The rustling moved away from them in rattles and bursts, until eventually, silence fell over the orchard and the two turned together and headed home.

The next morning, Jane's grandfather supposed that it'd been a panther they'd heard. He'd heard it too, from the shop where he had been working. There were reports of sightings in the area from time to time. He took Jane into the den and pulled out a heavy encyclopedia. He laid it on the coffee table and flipped through the pages until he found a picture of the animal. Instead of fear, Jane felt a mixture of pride and awe and something proprietary, like kinship. This was her panther. Even though she hadn't actually seen the beautiful animal, she knew that she had been brave and faced her fear. She carried that feeling with her for a long time, but somewhere along the way, she'd forgotten. She had misplaced her courage.

But here she was again, standing fully in her own power and telling herself, *It's all right. Whatever happens is all right. I am fine.*

Finally the animal, whatever it was, turned and loped off into the trees. Jane May stood, watching the place in the woods where it had disappeared and feeling comforted by the encounter, and also blessed. By the time she reached the front door though, she'd convinced herself that the shadows, the light, and her eyes had all conspired to play a trick on her, and it had only been a dog or maybe a fox. *Silly Jane*, she said to herself, *shaking her head, there are no panthers in these mountains.*

She went inside to the bathroom to draw herself a hot bath. She filled the old claw foot tub almost to the rim with water so hot it formed a humid cloud that enveloped the room. To the tub she added a handful of Epsom salts, a few drops of lavender oil and a sprinkling of dried herbs that she'd gathered in the forest with Mai. She brought all the candles she could find in the other rooms and placed them around the tub and lit them. The green light filtered through the leaded window and cast flickering leaf shadows on the walls and floor. Jane May stood in the middle of the room and closed her eyes. A wellspring of sorrow opened up. Her daughter, her marriage, her life, the world, John. But right now, and most of all, it was the loss of her friend and mentor, Mai Zinni, that hit her the hardest. She allowed her clothing to drop to the floor and her body to sink into the hot water. She merged with it. She became the water, fluid and warm. Flowing forever toward the sea. Her tears lent their salt to the river and made it ready for merging with the ocean. She felt the tides waxing and waning, storms brewing and subsiding, rivers always flowing, flowing to the sea and sometimes raging out of their banks, soaking the earth and bringing destruction in their path. She was the rain coming down and the dew on the grass and hot steam rising. She rushed and tumbled and gurgled and gushed. She rose and fell. She gathered herself into spiral twisters and hurricanes and blew with a raging force that could not be contained. She evaporated. And then she began again.

And then, Mai Zinni was there. "Well done, daughter, well done. I never really left you, but sent others to stand by and watch over you." She was speaking in that deep, fluid voice that she used when doing spells and calling on her spirit guides. That voice that could bring Jane May round or put her under. The voice was pulling her gently up now, like a hand reaching deep under water, bringing her slowly back to the surface. "Well done. You are ready. Rise now."

Jane May opened her eyes and waited for her mind to adjust itself to her surroundings. She was quite alone in the bathroom and not surprised by it. She stood and let the water bead and slip from her skin, the shadows play across her body. Was her body becoming beautiful? Or was she just learning to accept it for what it was? She admired her strong legs and feet, her toenails, painted red, the one concession to vanity that she allowed herself. She held her arms out and inspected her hands, veiny and sinuous, solid peasant hands, hands that had known work: they'd held a man, a baby, they'd planted seeds, weeded gardens, prepared and served food, helped a little girl to ride a bike and learn to swim, sewed clothing, held another man for awhile.... Turning her palms up, she surveyed the square terrain of intersecting lines, the faint shadow of a wedding ring callous on the base of her left ring finger. She placed her right hand on her belly, silvered and lined from birthing her daughter all those years ago, and soft from having lived for a half a century. It was a map. A map of the world. She was, in that green moment, the whole universe. Jane May Gideon threw her greying head back and laughed. The laugh spread to her toes and rose up through her heart and her throat and her eyes and bubbled out like honey through the top of her head and covered her in gold.

Ah, the miraculous healing powers of a long, hot bath. Later, dressed and refreshed, Jane knew that she could wait as long as it took for Mai Zinni to come back. Heaven knows, Mai Zinni had done plenty for her over these last many weeks. Had changed her life in fact, or guided her in changing her own life. Mai always said that Jane had everything she needed inside her, but it had taken so long for her to rediscover that for herself. *Maybe it is true, after all, that I already have every single thing I need.*

Maybe I will buy the inn, thought Jane May later, as she sat outside in the dappled sunshine of late afternoon. That was what John wanted. John knew that Jane May had some money from her divorce settlement and that she could take care of the place. She smiled thinking of the confidence the old man had felt in her ability to run his inn. Before he died, he had brought it up a time or two. "Think about it," he'd said. "It's a great idea. You'd be good at it." She had laughed at the time, but had secretly begun to fantasize about fixing it up and maybe adding a little cafe to offer breakfast to weary travelers and locals. *It could be fun*, she thought. *maybe I would be good at it.*

After John died, Mac told her about his visit to *The Light Within* and his request to Mac. John wanted Jane to buy the inn and the proceeds from the sale to go into two trusts, which Mac would oversee. One trust was to insure that Mai Zinni had money to live on, albeit modestly, for the rest of her life. The other would help Nanette and Charlie. Jane May wondered for the thousandth time what connection bound John and Mai Zinni one to the other. From her point of view their relationship seemed warily tolerant, and yet a fathomless grief had held Mai Zinni in its grip since the morning John went missing.

Maybe she would never understand it. Right now a trip to see Mac seemed in order. It was time to take a step toward the inn. Toward a new life. Maybe Gideon was beginning to feel like home.

Chapter 31

Mac held the door open for Jane May as she left *The Light Within*. She stopped and embraced him before she left. "Thank you, Mac," she said, "I feel like this is the right thing, don't you?"

"I do, indeed, Dear." He smiled and patted her arm. "I know this is what he wanted and I know you'll breathe new life into that old place."

With the wheels in motion for her to buy John's inn, they both felt relief. Mac had been delighted to begin paperwork for the sale. He had, in fact, turned over his chair jumping up to hug her when she'd told him what she wanted to do. It felt, in some small way, redemptive. This was what John had wanted. Mac still felt, and would no doubt always feel, the sting of his friend's death, so helpless had he been to change the course of events.

Mac had loved John with a fierceness that sometimes confused him. He had never had a real family, but John and Mai Zinni had felt like one to him, and now John was dead and Mai Zinni might as well be, she'd shut herself off so thoroughly from him. Mac was lonely and when Jane May had appeared in the shop this afternoon, his heart had leapt. She seemed like part of their strange little family now. A family created out of love, not blood. He'd grown quite fond of her, they all had, these past few months. And she had changed since she'd come to them. The sadness that floated around her was still there, but lighter, and Jane May seemed stronger, more confident. She laughed easily and graced them with her lovely smile more frequently. She seemed happier in her skin, and Mac knew that much of the credit for that lay with Mai Zinni. Jane had spent hours and hours with Mai, gathering herbs, walking in the woods, sitting around the fire listening to stories. Mai had taught her to be still enough that Chickadee would come and eat out of her hand. He had seen this once and no one could have failed to be delighted at the wonder on Jane May's face as the tiny bird with the little black cap lit on her palm and peered for a moment into her eyes before snapping up a sunflower seed and flitting away. He had held his breath, just as Jane May had, and then smiled to himself as she squealed with delight. Whatever business he had that day at Mai Zinni's cottage was left undone, as he turned and walked back to his car, not wanting to disturb the easy camaraderie between the two women.

But that had been before. Before John had given into his demons and plunged sweet Mai Zinni into a pit of dark regret and gut-twisting anguish. Oh yes, Mac could imagine what she was feeling. And it broke his heart. It was very hard to believe that they would, any of them, ever regain their joy.

But they had before, hadn't they? Found their joy again? When the darkness seemed impenetrable and final, all those years ago. When John had vanished and they thought they'd never see him again. But they had. He'd come back. He couldn't stay away, goddammit, he'd said, and that's when he'd bought the inn and settled down. And then when Little Star had left without a word, taking the unborn child, all those years ago, Mac had felt the despair again right along with Mai and John. He had thought that they would never recover, but they had. They had. Maybe not fully. Maybe not completely, but they had gone on. They had laughed sometimes and the hurt had become merely a dull ache, forgotten, occasionally, for days. And then Jane May drove into their lives, and Mai Zinni and John had both seemed invigorated with new energy, new purpose.

And now? Maybe with Jane buying the inn, just maybe Mai would come out of this dark cave and everything would be all right again. Maybe.

Chapter 32

Jane May found her old friend right where she knew she would. Among the green spirits of the forest. Her kindred. Mai Zinni was most at home when she was with the plants and flowers and mosses. She and Jane May had spent countless pleasurable hours walking among the plants as the older woman gave names and medicinal uses for them. Jane May especially remembered one such day.

"Rattlesnake Plantain," the old woman whispered, as she knelt beside a green-leafed whorl that hugged the ground. Each shiny green leaf was bisected by a bright white line and laced with lighter green veining. From its center sprang a tall, hairy flower stalk with tiny white flowers clustered around it.

"Leaves make a poultice for snakebite and rashes," she went on, "good blood tonic and used to treat scrofula."

"What's scrofula?" Jane May asked, but Mai Zinni hushed her and hurried on ahead, looking this way and that.

Suddenly, the old woman veered off the path and dropped out of sight. Alarmed, Jane May ran to catch up with her and found her in a ditch hunkered down in a stand of pretty plants with butterfly shaped leaves and simple, multi-petaled white flowers.

"Oh!" Jane May's breath caught at the lovely sight.

"Birthroot." Zinni pinched off a leaf and handed it to Jane May, orange juice oozed from the broken stem. "Eat it."

She slowly bit into the leaf and was surprised by the taste. "Sunflower seeds! It tastes like sunflower seeds."

"I guess so then."

"Why's it called Birthroot?"

"Called Bloodroot too. And Indian Red Paint, Red Puccoon, Sweet Slumber and some-times Sang-Dragon. Helps with laboring and brings on the moontime. The roots are also good for aching joints and to cure the runs. Wound healing, too."

Jane May's head was overflowing with information and she didn't think she'd retain any of it, but she always did seem to remember, at least some of it. It would all be repeated over and over on subsequent walks, and eventually she realized that this ancient knowledge was seeping into her brain, into her very cells. She had begun to feel kinship with these plants.

"Chickweed!" Jane May exclaimed, falling to her knees. "I recognize it. Look Mai." Jane May looked back at her mentor who was stopped in the path, a faraway look on her face.

"What's wrong? It's chickweed, isn't it?"

"Yes, Sweet One, it's chickweed. Good work." Mai Zinni came closer and squatted down beside Jane. "Stellaria, she's called. Little Star. Like my girl." The faraway look intensified in the old woman's eyes.

"Tell me," said Jane. But she didn't. A story had been bursting to be told that day, but Mai Zinni had suppressed it, and no amount of gentle cajoling would bring it forth until it was ready to be told.

The old woman looked up now and saw Jane May standing in the path. Jane had taken a risk, coming here without an invitation, but something told her it would be okay, and sure enough, there was a softness about Mai Zinni that Jane hadn't seen since John's death. An opening. She took advantage of it and sat beside her friend on a fallen Hemlock.

Jane could see that the time had come to tell and the old woman's story began to unwind and spin out like spider's webs.

"It was 1959 and my mama had just died. I didn't know how to live in this world all alone. Oh the town folk cared for me and they brought me food and tried to give comfort, but I was deep in a well of despond. My daddy died when I was just a wee thing and my mama and my granny raised me. They were all I ever knew of love or family, and they were both gone." Mai paused for a long moment and Jane May waited.

She sighed and went on, "Then, one day, there he was. This beautiful young man. It was John, you see. My sweet Johnny." Jane May wondered now, how she could have been so dense. Of course it was John. That explained everything didn't it? Well almost everything. It explained why

Mai Zinni was so bereft at John's death, but why hadn't it worked out for them?

"I first saw him up in the high meadow. I was picking those pretty blue flowers that grow up there. My mama loved them and they made me feel like she was still near. I liked to put them in jars around the house. It was a small comfort." She paused and sighed again. "Anyway, he just appeared before me. Like a ghost, only not a ghost. Flesh and blood." The old woman blushed at the remembering. "Sweet flesh, I'll say. Anyway, we were together all the time. Pretty soon we married, and a couple of years later, came our girl. Little Star. We called her our Nina Magena. She was the love of both our lives. And so beautiful. Lord. She hung the moon and the stars. She was a sweet child and smart. She loved the kindred and knew all their names. She could tell the names of the stars too. Her daddy loved to take a quilt out after supper, on a warm evening, and we'd all lay there and look at the heavens. He knew them all and soon she did too. Even in winter when it was warm enough, that was the best, when the Great Winter Circle was high in the sky. We'd go out and quick find Orion's Belt, *the bridge to home*, the Old Ones called it. From there, we could get our bearings.

'Castor and Pollox!' our little one would shout. 'The twins!'

'Where's the old dog star?' John would ask, pretending like he couldn't remember.

'Daddy! You know. Be serious!' repeating their inside joke. 'Sirius is right there.' She'd giggle, stabbing the sky with her little stubby finger. God we were happy then."

Jane May waited. Mai Zinni's head was in her hands. Maybe she was crying or maybe she'd fallen asleep.

Finally, Jane asked gently, "What happened?"

"Well, I reckon you know the story. She grew up, she grew wild, she grew angry. She got pregnant. With my grandchild. *My grandchild*. And then one night, when I thought she was safe in her bed, she left. Without a trace. She left and took all my joy and my hopes and dreams with her."

"Oh Mai. I am so sorry. What did y'all do? Did you try to find her?"

"Y'all! You and your infernal talk! There weren't no y'all. Her daddy'd up and left his own self years before that. He came back, but we wasn't together anymore. I guess that was why she was so mad. She couldn't understand how he could leave us. Probably she blamed me. And truthfully, I was mad myself, and I guess she got tired of the pall that hung over our life all the time. I know she struggled to get out from under it, and she didn't understand it. There wasn't any way for her to understand it. We barely could ourselves."

After a few minutes of silence, Mai Zinni rose stiffly and stomped off. When Jane May caught up to her and tried to reopen the conversation, the old woman simply raised her hand and kept on walking.

But Mai Zinni was ready to tell the whole story today. After a while, she sat down again and allowed Jane to catch up and sit beside her.

John had been magic to Mai Zinni, she said, in the time before the horrible knowing, when they'd been innocent and clean. His name had been nectar in her mouth. Johnny. And now. Well, now there was only the rusty taste of regret. A sorrowful tenderness was all that remained.

How could anyone have known that the olive-skinned young wanderer who showed up that spring of 1959 had any connection to Gideon? He blew into town as if on some kind of celestial cue and breathed new life into poor young Mai Zinni, who spent all her time that spring alone on the mountain, gathering herbs and sitting by herself. No one knew what to do with her, how to comfort her. Her bereavement was so deep and seemed so final. Then John Hawkes flew in and her heart grew wings and the whole town was happy that their little Mai Zinnia was blooming again.

He was a handsome young man and kind, with the most unusual eyes anyone had ever seen: one a deep, pensive brown, the other a clear, soulpiercing blue. He said he was from Maine. He was nineteen years old. He was heading to Texas to see his mother's relatives who he'd never met. He thought he might have had enough of Maine. His father had died before he was born. His mother had died when he was a young boy and the old man who'd taken him in had gone into an old folk's home and, recently died too. There didn't seem to be anything keeping the young man there, so he'd let the road take him where it would, and it had brought him to Gideon.

On his way into town that first day, he'd pulled the old truck over to the side of the road and, wanting to stretch his long legs, had walked up a well-worn path and found himself in a meadow. He closed his eyes and stretched his arms up over his head, breathing deeply of the clean air and sweet grasses. When he looked again, there she was, bending over and picking blue wildflowers, her black hair curtaining her face, the sun warming her back and shoulders and creating a glow around her. He stood entranced until she straightened and turned and saw him. From that moment on, for the next eight years, they were rarely apart.

And then, one day, he'd remembered that he had been on his way to Texas to see his mother's people. Now he had a beautiful wife and the prettiest little daughter anyone had ever seen. And he wanted to show them off to someone who was tied to him in some way. So the three of them had packed up and headed to Texas in search of John's people. Oh, if only they could've spun the whole world backward and not done that. Maybe they would never have known. After all, what good did the knowing do? Their lives had been ruined, nothing but torment had come from that damnable visit to Texas.

Leaving their lush green mountains, in the lazy days of late summer, they had driven west and then southwest. Stopping along the way to stretch their tired limbs and refresh themselves with food, and water from spigots behind the overgrown facades of gas stations, and the occasional cold soda. Little Star was four years old, and so could not be expected to sit in a hot old truck with very little in the way of shock absorption for too many hours without a break. They stopped in cheap motels and laid their heads down on rickety beds with questionable mattresses and once, on the last night of their ill-fated trip, they slept in the truck, mindful of their dwindling finances, but completely unaware that they were hurtling toward devastation. It was probably Little Star's favorite night.

Mai Zinni had brought along blankets and pillows and she used them to create a nest on the narrow bench seat between them for the child when she became tired. Also, sometimes, Little Star would curl up at Mai Zinni's feet with her doll and, wrapping her arms around her mother's ankles, she could nap for a little while, during the heat of the day.

But on this one magical night, worn out from traveling, but bolstered by their love for each other and their daughter, John and Mai Zinni had made up a cozy berth in the bed of the old truck and, after eating cold sandwiches, the three of them had snuggled in under the stars. John began to spin a tale, as he often did when his daughter was settling into sleep: a tale of far-away worlds inhabited by princesses and dragons. Mai Zinni found herself beguiled by his voice, and the sentient breeze gently lifted her hair, and with her daughter nestled in the crook of her arm, and her bare foot wound around her Johnny's ankle, she let herself slip away downstream of consciousness and into a dream.

She was floating in space, engulfed in a silence unlike anything she had ever experienced. Around her was complete blackness. She had no awareness of her body or her identity, but she had awareness. Complete, omniscient, total awareness. In the dream, her solitude was vast and boundless. The silence was total. She felt wrapped up somehow in this vastness, floating, floating.... "Mama!"

Catapulted back into the bed of the pickup Mai Zinni's eyes flew open and she was staring into the heavens and stars were streaking down the firmament and falling with abandon, or letting themselves simply drop with silent whooshes from their hooks in the black sky. Little Star was on her knees, head thrown back, pudgy little hands to her face. "Daddy! Mama! The stars are falling! The stars are falling! It's so pretty, is it okay?"

"Yes, my darlin'." John laughed, taking her in his arms, "It's more than okay. It's a show put on just for you, tonight, by God, Herself." Mai Zinni fell deeper in love with him whenever he referred to God this way! He was a man so ahead of his time, or very, very behind his time, depending on your perspective. Mai Zinni winked at Jane, and continued her story.

He possessed a completely natural love and understanding of the feminine in the world and in himself. He was fully a man, all right. Mai Zinni could certainly attest to that. But so comfortable was he in his masculinity that he had no taboo against his own softness, his gentleness, and Mai felt that this made him the best father that her Nina Magena could possibly have, not to mention the lover of every woman's dreams, and a harbinger of a new age for the world. This man seemed to auger a time of equality and harmony, when men and women were not at odds with each other but embraced and honored each other's similarities and differences. A time beyond patriarchy and matriarchy both, and into deep natural balance instead. A time when men and women worked together, side by side, complementing each other's powerful gifts for the good of the whole world.

The back of the old pickup truck was so filled with love and joy and expectation that night, it was as if sparks flew up from it to meet the ones coming down from the hand of God. It seemed that night as if nothing could ever touch the bubble of light that this little family floated in. But bubbles are fragile, delicate, and in the end, unsustainable.

Chapter 33

The dusty bleakness of the road that led to John's mother's family might have alerted a less optimistic group to what was coming, but they were blind in their joy.

"Well, it sure is dusty here. I guess they haven't had rain in a while. I'm sure it will be nice and cool in the house. Maybe they'll have lemonade, Neeny. You love lemonade!" Mai Zinni spun a web of pleasantries around her family as they approached the house. There was not a tree in sight and they felt as if they'd been approaching the house for hours. As it came closer in the bug splattered windshield, they could make out, through the swirling curtain of dust, a large, unadorned white frame house with a sagging porch and leaning chimney. Its windows gaped in defeat. As they got closer still, the front door swung open, and a large man in dirty overalls and a black hat lumbered onto the porch and shielded his eyes as he watched their approach. Mai Zinni noticed that three turkey vultures came silently flapping, spiraled overhead, and settled in a gnarled and stunted tree. Sentinels. Witnesses. A small shudder wrung Mai's slender body as she pulled her daughter close and plastered a smile onto her own face.

The Preacher was a fearsome man. He towered above them all. Little Star was frightened and recalcitrant from the start. John had called them from the road, so they were expecting the little party.

The Preacher's wife joined him on the porch and, before even inviting John and his family in, she tried to force the child into a display of affection, "Give your old granny some sugar, now," she demanded.

Little Star retreated behind Mai Zinni's skirt and refused even to look at these people. Mai Zinni was uncomfortable, but wanted to get off to a good start with John's family so she was trying to pry her daughter from her hiding place and reassure her that no harm would come to her when John stepped in and swooped the little girl up and onto his shoulders, deflecting the affected intimacies. He stuck out his big hand toward his grandfather, who took it, disarmed by John's confidence. Then, with his daughter still perched on his shoulders, he lowered himself to embrace his grandmother. "This is my wife, Mai Zinni, and my daughter, Little Star." John had momentarily stunned the dust-grey pair and they invited everyone inside, although nothing was offered once in the house, and awkwardness prevailed, until John again charmed them all by complimenting his grandparents on their homestead. "It's a nice place you have here. Did my mother grow up in this house?"

"Why yes," murmured the older woman, hanging her head. Everyone in the room felt the heaviness emanating from the preacher, who had somehow gotten a Bible in his hands in the moments since they'd all come inside. He seemed to wield the book like some sort of shield. Little Star's tiny hand slid into her father's and grasped it tightly.

"We've come a long way and would be mighty obliged if we could trouble you for some water," John smiled down at his daughter.

His mother's mother sprang into action as her husband lowered himself ponderously into a large and lumpy chair. Uninvited, John led Little Star to a humble plaid sofa facing the old man, and Mai Zinni shuffled into the kitchen to see if she could help with the refreshments.

When they were all reinstalled in the living room with ice water in cloudy glasses and some stale store-bought cookies for the little one, The Preacher cleared his throat and all eyes turned in his direction.

"Our daughter shamed this family when she turned her back on us with no regard or respect for all that we had sacrificed for her. When she came crawling back with her little half-breed bastard boy, wanting our charity, it was just too much. She like to have killed her mother and me." The old man's wife hung her head again. The Preacher stood now, looming balefully over the little group. "I can't say we are too happy to see her spawn in this house today." He was now holding the Bible above his head in one hand, as if he might hurl it at them. "It says in the good book that fornicators will not inherit the kingdom of God." He was getting worked up now and Little Star shrank into her father's side and whimpered. Mai Zinni instinctively moved toward her husband and child. "It says in the good book that adulterers," here he paused for effect and looked from John to Mai Zinni, "adulterers shall not inherit the earth. *I, the LORD thy God, am a jealous God, visiting the iniquity of the fathers upon the children unto the third and fourth generation of them that hate me.*" The Preacher then pulled from the pages of the book two photographs, which he hurled, one at a time, at John. With the first photograph, a winsome young woman with her head thrown back in laughter, John's mother, he shouted, "Fornicator! We should have known when we first laid eyes on her. A demon child, tainted with sin. Couldn't never do nothing with her. Wouldn't mind. Started whoring around practically soon's she could walk."

With the second photo, a somber but handsome dark-complected man, wearing a uniform and standing by a delivery truck, he shouted, "Adulterer! Not even man enough to own up to what he did, he shipped her off to Maine and forgot about her."

John's grandmother sobbed quietly into a handkerchief. A sorrowful thing that looked like it had sopped up oceans of tears.

Turning his cruel gaze on her, her husband growled in a low, controlled rage, "quit yer crying woman. Get yer sorry hide outta this room and let me tend to this bidness." John's grandmother slunk silently from the room.

And now Little Star was crying and Mai Zinni had taken her into her lap and was rising to go when she saw the picture of the man, in John's hands.

John had never seen a picture of his father, had spent his whole life imagining what he looked like. Was he handsome? Was he tall? Did he bear a resemblance to his son? And now here was a picture at last. The man who looked back at him from the picture was dark and closed, shy. He seemed to be draped in a mantle of sadness. He didn't see much of himself there, except for his dark skin. He knew he looked more like his mother. But still, he was glad to finally see a photograph of his father. He looked with wonder and wistfulness at the likeness of the man whose absence had been the grand theme of his life.

And now here was his beautiful wife, her eyes locked on the photograph in his hands, confusion morphing into horror spread across her face. She took the picture from him, gingerly, gently, as if it were a pernicious treasure of some sort. She brought it to her face and examined it closely, brows knitting together, head shaking side to side. The picture floated from Mai's fingers and slid under the bulging, dust laden sofa, as she ran from the house and fell to her knees in the front yard.

John jumped up, lifted his daughter into his arms and ran to his wife. "Zee, what's wrong? What is it?" She was throwing up, in the dusty yard, her body heaving. Little Star had begun to cry.

"Oh God." Mai wiped her mouth on her sleeve and looked up into his eyes, "Oh God!"

"What? You've got to tell me, Zee. What is it?"

"That man in the photograph."

"What about him? I don't understand." Panic rose in John's voice. He had put Little Star down and she stood beside her mother, now, whimpering.

"Johnny. Johnny, don't make me say it." Mai Zinni sobbed now, kneeling in the dirt.

Little Star tried to help her up, tugging on her arm and pleading, "Get up Mommy. Please get up. I want to go home."

"The man in the photograph, John. Your father. That's my father. Oh God!" Mai Zinni strangled on the words and had to fight to keep from vomiting again. John knelt beside her. His mouth gaped open in disbelief. Time suspended itself, like the moments after a man's been shot and remains on his knees, stunned, for a brief eternity, before the bullet registers with his heart.

John's grandmother had joined her husband on the porch. As ignorant and hateful as they were, it didn't take much for them to figure out what was going on. One look at John's dark bride and the girl child and the remarkable resemblance between the both of them to the man in the picture and they knew it all and they were disgusted. They'd been bitter and now they were also outraged and didn't want anything to do with John or his family. Their rotten seed of a daughter had started something in motion that was vile and malignant. Who knew where it would stop, but the Preacher wouldn't have any part of it. He wanted these people gone. These people who had nothing to do with him. Nothing. He wished he had said no all those years ago when his wife had begged him for a child. Nothing good comes of giving in to a woman's demands.

Waving the beat up black Bible, John's grandfather buffeted the little family with his obscene words.

Stumbling to their feet, John and Mai Zinni gathered their daughter and drove away as fast as they could, throwing up a mushroom cloud of dust as they went.

They had continued to live together feeling it was best for their daughter, but the knowledge of the true nature of their relationship tormented them and would not leave them be, and finally tore them apart. John left without a word in the middle of the night when Little Star was not quite six years old, devastating his wife and child again.

Ten years later, when he returned, haunted and broken, he found that Mai Zinni had dissolved the marriage, thinking him dead, and she and Little Star had moved on as best they could. Little Star was angry about his desertion. She had a vague memory, of course, of the old man screaming on the porch and her parents bundling her into their truck and driving away in a shocked cloud of dust, but she had been too young to understand what the mean man was yelling about. In the subsequent absence of her father and her mother's silence on the matter, she did the only thing a young girl could do, she blamed her mother for everything. John hadn't been back in town long when Little Star began acting out in ways both frightening and predictable. And then, pregnant at seventeen, she emulated her father and left in the middle of the night, without a word, devastating her parents. Like the fabled Lost Cherokee, they never heard from her or her child again.

"Oh Mai!" The two women had been sitting in silence, except for the incongruous twittering of birds, for many moments since Mai Zinni had ceased her talking and hung her tired head in remembrance of her long buried shame.

"Mai." Tears streamed down Jane's face as the full force of the story hit her, and she tried, and failed, to find words that would comfort her friend.

Mai Zinni cut her off. "Hush Dear One. The tellin' heals." She rolled her shoulders and shook her head slightly, drawing in a breath, "Yep. The tellin' heals. It's been a long time needing to be told and I thank you for being a vessel today. This story's been weighing me down most of my life and it's killed my Johnny, and lost me my daughter and my grandchild, and I'm ready to put it down now. Come on, Child, let's go."

Mai Zinni rose and it seemed that her rising was a little easier than it had been lately. Less creaky, not quite so much resistance from her joints. She wasn't smiling, but a peacefulness had come across her face, and at a certain angle, when the sun came through the thick canopy of leaves in just the right way, for a split second, she looked young and beautiful, and Jane

May's breath caught, but before she could register the thought, the beloved old woman's lined face had returned. Jane May rose now and followed her friend through the deep woods, back to the old woman's cottage.

Chapter 34

Some days later after Mai Zinni had told Jane her story, the two women walked for what seemed like hours, deeper and deeper into the forest. Mai seemed more peaceful than she had been since John's death. The trail had wound around and back on itself and the canopy was so thick that there was no way to tell where the sun was in the sky. The forest was beautiful here, lush and fragrant. Jane May was certain that she'd never been on this trail.

After a long while, they stopped and sat on a fallen log, which was covered with moss. Some sort of lichen ran up one side of the old tree, looking like whorled ears. Jane May had the thought that the forest was alive and listening. From a deep pocket in her skirt, Mai Zinni pulled a bundle wrapped in a linen cloth and tied with twine. She laid it on the log between them and opened it. There were little cakes with violet sweets on top, a chunk of hard, cream-colored cheese, which released a sharp fragrance that made Jane's mouth water at once, and a small cellophane bag of almonds. She reached again into the seemingly bottomless pocket and pulled out a small thermos and two collapsible tin cups. Into each cup she poured a measure of amber-colored tea and, lifting one cup toward Jane, she said something in a language that Jane did not understand. Jane wanted to ask the meaning, but unable to form the words, she drank. She was so happy to be back in the forest with Mai Zinni again. But something was different today.

Swimming up from somewhere deep, the sound of falling water grew louder and louder. Her eyes remained shut, but her vision expanded slowly. She'd been in the water. She was underwater for a long time, longer than she should have been able to hold her breath. She remembered stars exploding everywhere and the feeling that her chest would break open, but it didn't, it just expanded and expanded outward, until finally her body broke the surface of the water and with a gasp she took a breath and it felt like her first.

She opened her eyes slowly. She was lying on something soft with hard rock underneath. She reached out and touched the rock and it was smooth and cold. She saw a small fire burning and it gave off a welcome warmth. Beyond the fire, the source of the thundering, a huge waterfall. Plummeting straight down from a height of maybe fifty feet. She was under some sort of rocky overhang. Green vines tumbled over the outcropping and hung down like a curtain.

Rise, she heard with the ears of her heart. And she felt strong and alive and glad.

"Jane, you're awake. Good." The voice, familiar and gentle, came from behind her. Rolling over, she found herself looking into the crinkled eyes of her friend and teacher, Mai Zinni.

"What is this place?"

"Remember."

Jane May closed her eyes again.

"It's time to go, Jane. We can't stay here now."

When Jane next opened her eyes, she was lying on the sofa in her own little stone cottage by the creek at the inn. Someone was in the kitchen, fussing about.

Mai Zinni poked her head around the corner and smiled. "Good, you're awake. How about tea?"

When they were settled in with their tea and a little plate of fresh fruit and cookies, Jane May took a deep breath and asked, "Mai, what's going on?"

"What do you mean, Dear?"

"I think you know what I mean. I don't understand what's happening and I need to. Don't be coy."

The old woman sighed. "You're trying to put words where they don't belong. Listen. You understand perfectly. Listen."

With that, Mai Zinni rose and like a breath, she was gone.

Jane May felt protest rising in her and then she felt it fall away and she lay back on the sofa and fell into a deep sleep.

Sparks arose from a huge fire. They seemed to fly up like fireflies and then bzzz-pop, they exploded in mid-air. One at a time at first, and then many at once, and after a time they all seemed to synch up with each other and fly in one great swarm from the fire and BZZZ-POP! they exploded like giant pyrotechnics, lighting up the whole sky. Then, all was quiet, save for the slow, soft beating of a drum. Or was it a heartbeat? Another sound came to the forefront—breath. The breath of the world, breathing in and out, in and out, and the drumbeat became fainter and the dreamer became aware of herself and as she did, she noticed that her own neck was in the jaws of a giant fawn-colored cat. The dreamer lay suspended between life and death, knowing that death was at hand and not minding, only noticing. Feeling the hot breath of the animal upon her neck, the soft, thick fur against her face, the weight of the teeth on veins and skin, the moment just before penetration. Sliding effortlessly into the mind of the mountain lion, and looking out through its eyes, the dreamer simultaneously saw herself prepared to die, and felt her own cougar teeth sink in, popping through the jugular vein and tasting salty blood. She tore at her own neck, suddenly desperate to get to the bottom of things, to devour her former self, she snarled and gnashed and shook her head from side to side, tearing flesh from bone and swallowing as blood matted the fur of her chest. And then the word *Rise* was all around and the panther woman ceased her devouring and raised her head. She felt the wind ruffle her fur, she leapt to her feet and began to run faster and faster and faster until her feet left the ground and she felt her shoulders twisting and her arms morphed into wings and her eyes grew smaller and able to focus keenly and she soared over the earth and saw the dead and mangled body of a woman below and next to it a ghost cat, sleeping the sleep of one who has feasted on one's own demons.

Leaving all that behind, she flew higher and higher, the sun hot and bright on her feathers, until she was over water and there was nothing but water as far as her eyes could see. Resting, she let her body be carried on the wind, only shifting her wings this way and that to catch the updrafts. She moved on the wind in swoops and spirals and looked down on the vast water and felt a joy and a peace that she could not remember ever not knowing.

With a jolt, the dreamer was catapulted out of the body of the bird and sent plummeting to the sea far below. Terror. Fear. Her heart seized as she anticipated hitting the water, which would be like concrete from that height. Faster and faster the water rose up to smash her body, but instead she became a dolphin and sliced the water with grace and precision. Diving down deep, she saw that there were others. All around her, swimming, diving, playing. Her kin. They called to each other and three or four of them surrounded her and began to push her up and up and they were all calling and laughing and she was too, and then she was a tiny spark, shooting up through the watery world, with millions of other sparks all around her. Buoyed up by an unseen force, the sparks rose as one until they burst through the surface and into the air, the word Rise shimmering all around them, the far off sound of a beating drum calling them to shore.

Jane May began to be aware of first her body and then, slowly, her surroundings. She was lying on a blanket in Mai Zinni's yard. The air was soft and warm, but Mai Zinni was standing a few feet away tending a fire in the iron cauldron. By her side was her old hide drum and a drumstick, adorned with feathers, fur, beads, and strange fetishes, and a rattle made of a gourd with seeds inside, mounted on a willow twig. Jane May had only seen this drum and stick and rattle once before, in a cupboard in Mai's house. When she'd asked about them, the old woman had been vague, saying only that they were *from a long time ago*. How strange to see them lying on a cloth in the grass today.

Jane May sat up slowly and shook her head a little.

Mai Zinni turned from the fire and said with a curious smile, "you are not the one I've been waiting for."

"What are you talking about Mai?"

"It's not you."

"What's not me?"

"I was so sure." Mai Zinni laughed and shook her head from side to side, as she stared into the fire. "Crazy old woman seeing what she wants to see."

Jane May was no longer in the mood for riddles and her exasperation quickly reached a fever pitch. Rising, she stood across the fiery cauldron from Mai Zinni.

"Look at me, Mai."

"Hmmm?" The old woman seemed positively dazed and it was beginning to niggle at the edges of Jane's mind. Was her mentor losing it? Had she had some kind of stroke? Or was she herself losing her mind?

"What is going on? What are you talking about, and what has been happening to me. First I'm in the forest and then I'm lying beside some huge waterfall, and then I'm in the cottage, and now I wake up here in your yard and . . . . "

"Settle down, Little Seashell, now's not the time for you to get yourself in a tizzy. You need to be quiet and listen." As she spoke, Mai Zinni returned from whatever nether lands she had wandered off to, and Jane was relieved by that, but growing angrier by the minute.

"Dammit, Mai. All I want to listen to is you explaining what is going on here. Now!" Slowly a thought began to bloom in Jane May's brain. She tried to push it down, but it would not stop whispering. "Oh my God! Did you? Did you . . . . " If she finished her sentence and let the question see the light of day, she knew there would be no going back, but she could not keep the words contained.

"Did you drug me, Mai?"

Night had fallen while the two women sat and talked. Mai Zinni had much to explain and Jane May forced herself to listen patiently.

At first, of course, she'd been horrified to learn that the tea she had innocently ingested in the forest had contained powerful herbs known to induce vivid dreams and visions.

"Not a drug, Dear, an ally. You needed help to see some things. And so did I."

"For the love of God! You don't get to drug me! What were you thinking?"

"Simmer down, Child. It wasn't anything that will hurt you. I know what I'm doing."

"Good God! I don't even know what to say." Jane May rose from her seat and began to pace back and forth.

"Maybe now would be a good time to give it a rest, then?" Mai Zinni was smiling up at Jane.

"Do you think this is funny?" Stopping in front of the old woman, she was shouting now. "Do you?"

The old woman spoke softly and in measured tones. "Maybe I made a mistake."

"Maybe you did." Jane dropped into the chair next to Mai Zinni and tried to regain control of herself. She resisted the urge to run away in anger or to throttle the old woman. In resisting, it was as if she sat in the middle of a fire, but wasn't burned by it. As the fire raged around her, she could feel her indignation, her self-righteousness, burning away.

Finally, realizing that she felt fine and in fact had seen some things, powerful things, Jane May began to calm down, and she realized that those things were far more interesting to her than the fact that the tea she had been offered was perhaps not sufficiently explained.

"Mai, why did you say I was not the one? What did you mean?"

"Well, Dear, while you were traveling and having your visions, I was having my own. I was seeing more clearly than I have in a very long time. The drum can do that."

"The drum?"

"Yes. The steady beat of the drum clears the mind. This one belonged to my grandmother. She got it from her grandmother. Who knows where it was before that."

"And?"

"And, it's been made clear to me that while you were most certainly led to me, you are not the one I've been waiting for. There is another yet to come."

"Who?"

"Well now, if I knew that, I wouldn't have thought it was you, would I?"

"Mai," Jane paused, wanting to speak truthfully. "I think I knew it wasn't me all along." She was surprised at the mix of feelings that arose in her as she spoke the words. Grief, deep and sudden, but also relief, freedom, liberation. Her story wasn't written. She felt giddy with possibility.

Mai reached out her hand, firm and warm, and covered Jane May's cooler one with it. And there they sat until the moon rose over the shoulder of the mountain and shone a silvery blessing upon them.

"Now what?" Jane May sighed as she turned to her friend, wondering where they would go from here. Knowing that she was not the long awaited *One*, there was a lot to think about.

"Now we sleep. It's been a long day." Mai Zinni rose with an agility that belied her age and headed for the house. Jane rose as well and began to gather their belongings. The drum and drum beater, the rattle, her own purse, which had somehow miraculously materialized in the yard. "Leave it," the old woman said over her shoulder. "We're sleeping out here tonight. Help me get blankets, please."

That night may have been the deepest sleep Jane May Gideon had ever had in her life. If she dreamed, and she did, she didn't remember any of it. If strange goings-on occurred in the forest while she slept, and they did, she knew nothing of them.

When she awoke at first light feeling refreshed and rested in spite of having slept on a thin pad on the ground, covered only by an old quilt, she was alone except for a rather large fawn-colored cat lying some distance away and watching her. Morning, still being coy, gave nothing more than a rosy blush to light the fading darkness, so maybe her eyes were playing tricks on her.

But no, the beast arose and began a slow pace toward her. Jane May's first instinct was, of course, to scream and run, but she didn't. She remained right there where she awoke, only sitting up to meet the mountain lion's gaze. She searched her mind for alarm and found only curiosity and awe. The animal did not seem to mean her any harm. Its yellow eyes held hers as it approached slowly. Suddenly she remembered the lion in her vision from yesterday, biting down, snarling, bloody. And still she remained calm.

"I mean you no harm," the panther spoke inside her mind. "I am your friend. Your ally. You've listened well and received my gifts in the between realm. You have dug deep inside yourself to find your own courage. Family is central in your world. You haven't lost your family, only your notion of what it looked like. Your daughter is your heart. You will build a new vision of family. It's time to embrace what you've learned. It's time to own your ferocity, your loyalty, your patient, loving, gentleness. This is your power. This is your effectiveness. Seek the council of the Great Mother to help you on your path, just as a cub does. You must find the balance between freedom and boundaries. You must travel your path alone, for a time, until you've fully integrated all these gifts."

Jane May watched in wonder as the cougar padded away and disappeared into the forest.

The sound of drumming was insistent, vibrating the tiny bones deep inside her ears, spreading like waves throughout her skeletal system and into her organs and bloodstream. Her whole body thrummed at an astonishing frequency and she could barely stand it. She remained quivering there for a time, on the cusp of intense sensation. Just as she thought her cells would explode, the drumming slowed and she began to move forward, toward the sound. One foot and then the other, moving deliberately in the soft springy grass, closing the gap between the darkness and the glow of firelight. She felt a need to be in the midst of the glow, and yet she proceeded with a measured pace, as if there were no reason at all to hurry.

Topping the hill, she stopped and took in the scene below, which was so strange and yet so familiar. A large bonfire, the logs laid teepee style, sparks, flying out of it and exploding in the air, flames leaping and dancing, a beautiful woman dipping, stomping and swaying to the drumbeat. Around the periphery of the fire behind the woman were panthers. Yellow eyes glinting, standing, like sentinels to the dance. There were seven of them.

She stood for an eternity at the top of the hill, taking in the details of the scene, memorizing them and then effortlessly, as if it were the easiest thing in the world, she awoke in the dream. "I am dreaming," she said out loud to no one but herself.

She breathed deeply and breathed the scent of woodsmoke, grass, and something musky and animal in nature. As she reveled in this dream awareness she became more and more cognizant of sounds and smells. Gardenias, faint and far off in the distance. Her mother had loved gardenias. Saltwater, leaf mould, baking sugar, ion charged air after a rainstorm, the smell of her newborn daughter's neck nestled in with all of this and suddenly a door opened in her heart, hinges creaking and light pouring out. She looked down at this door and saw that honey was dripping from her flung open heart and catching the firelight from below. She touched her chest and scooped up a finger full of the nectar and lifted it to her mouth, sighing as the elemental sweetness melted on her tongue.

The drumming became insistent and instinctively her feet began to carry her once again toward the fire and the sparking and the dancing and the seven sets of yellow eyes. She remembered that she'd been in this dream before and knew that this time she would remember it when she woke up.

As she approached the fire, the drumming slowed and so did the dancer, who came to rest with feet apart and arms akimbo, facing the dreamer.

"At last. You've come."

Jane was aware of the silvery moon overhead and the yellow eyes watching and the strong and ageless beauty of the woman who stood before her.

"Who are you?" she asked the dancer.

"You know who I am. You've always known. Time to wake up now. Watch for the Chickadee."

"What?" But her question was drowned out as the drumming intensified again and the big cats began to growl and snarl. First one and then another, until all seven joined in, raising their voices to the moon, and sang the songs that were written before they were born, the songs that sang them into being.

Once again Jane May woke in Mai Zinni's yard. The old woman was stirring the fire and tending a kettle hanging over it from an iron spider.

"How about some cowboy coffee, Chickadee?"

PART 4

THE MAIDEN

Mama! No!"

The cycles of life and death repeat endlessly. There is no escaping.

Little Owl came upon the lifeless body of her mother deep in the forest, where she had gone the day before to gather mushrooms. It was already almost dark and the young woman hadn't eaten all day in her frenzy to find her mother, who hadn't come home the night before. "No, Mama, you can't leave me," the young one cried, throwing herself on the body and recoiling at its stiffness. It was spring, but the nights were still frightfully cold. She quickly wrapped the rough woven shawl she was wearing around her mother and began to croon to her, "There, there now, everything is all right. I'm here now. You'll be fine, Mama, as soon as I can get you home and get you something to eat. You're just cold and hungry."

Little Owl's voice became a keening, as she went on in desperation. Her mama had been tired lately, and a little shaky, having to stop and think about things she shouldn't have needed to stop and think about. The proportions of herbs to alcohol in her tinctures, for instance. Or how to lay a fire . . . things that were second nature to her. Little Owl had noticed, but not understood.

Once she had laughed at her mother and made her cry. She remembered that now and was stabbed with a blade of regret. "I'm so sorry, Mama. I didn't mean to laugh. Everything's all right now." But even as she spoke, she knew that nothing would ever be the same. The spark had left her mother's strange and beautiful eyes. She was alone now and would have to step into her mother's shoes, as her mother had done before her, and her mother and hers, all the way back to the dawn of time. That's the story Little Owl had been raised with and the only one she knew.

Long ago, in the time before time, a girl came alone, on the back of a wild white pony named Gruffyn, to this forest, and made her home in this little root house. She lived among and came to know the plants and the trees and the animals here better than she knew any human being. Eventually she had a daughter who was called Little Owl and that daughter received her mother's knowledge and also her name when the mother died. The mother had been called Owl Feather, and so the daughter called herself that too, when it was her turn to step into the role. She ministered to the people of the village as her mother had done and eventually she had a daughter to whom she passed down all the knowledge and also the name and so it has been and so it would always be. And one day, Little Owl becomes Owl Feather and steps into her power and is the guardian of the knowledge for all of those to come.

That day had come before Little Owl was ready, but ready or not, she knew what she had to do. She had been preparing for this all her life. And so she burned her mother's body and with it her own childhood and from the ashes and the dance rose Owl Feather once again.

The new Owl Feather stepped into her power as all the women before her had. She continued to hunt and to gather and to minister, when asked, to the villagers. She delivered babies and sewed up wounds and prepared tonics and potions. She knew that one day she would give birth to a daughter. The only thing she didn't understand was how she would get that daughter. Oh, she understood the mechanics of it. After all, she had been raised in such a natural state that from as far back as she could remember, she'd seen babies conceived and brought forth by watching the animals. But she was alone in the forest. The only time she saw other humans was the rare visit into town when the people avoided her as if she were contagious, and the ones who came to her in the forest were sick or in need of her help. How in the world, she wondered, would she ever get with child?

Only three moons after the death of her mother, Owl Feather found out.

She returned to the clearing late one morning, two rabbits slung over her shoulder and a basket of mushrooms and bark and medicinal leaves on her arm. She had a slingshot, but it was tucked into the bag she wore across her chest, so she was defenseless and off guard when someone grabbed her roughly from behind. She screamed and was thrown to the ground, where she hit her head hard on a rock. Reeling, she tried to bring her knee up, but missed the target and only made her assailant more determined. He laughed a violent, angry laugh as he shoved his way into her. Calling her vile names and spitting in her face, he pumped his seed, unbidden and unwanted, into her sacred inner sanctum.

Owl Feather left her body, once it was apparent that she could not stop the attack, and traveled to the realms where her mother had taken her so many times. She was safe there and the old ones met her and wrapped her in skins and cared for her gently. They were saddened, but there were limits to their protection and they could not intervene in the heinous act that was occurring. All they could do was to hold her spirit and gather round her.

When she came back to herself, the monster was gone and she was bruised and broken and violated to her core. She dragged herself to the stream downhill from the clearing and scrubbed her skin and soaked her sore bones until she felt that she had washed the vestiges of him off herself. But in two moons time, there was no denying that the monster had left something of himself with her.

Now Owl Feather, wise in the old ways, knew how to rid herself of this child and felt justified in doing so. In fact, she prepared for it, but somehow she couldn't do it in the end. She'd had a dream in which she was impregnated by a bolt of lightning, and when she woke she thought that maybe the monster had been an instrument of destiny. Maybe, as cruel as this was, it was meant to be. She would know if a daughter was born to her, that she had been right to keep her, and if it was a son . . . well, then she'd have to wonder some more about the ways of the all knowing, allloving Holy One that she'd been taught to trust and love.

The girl child was born on the winter solstice. As the world hung for those few hours in a state of suspended animation, poised and rocking on the edge between the light and the dark, Owl Feather labored alone in the warmth of the root house. The baby was early, but Owl Feather was ready, having read the signs for days before. She'd brought in plenty of wood, and set a large pot of stew simmering in the fire. The birth was easy, but Owl Feather missed her mother as she never had before and, as she looked into the face of her daughter for the first time illumined by firelight, she felt her mother was there with her. She was. She stood, just behind, looking over her daughter's shoulder at her granddaughter, and she whispered in Owl Feather's ear, "Call her Melle, for she came from far away, by lightning."

Owl Feather put her daughter to her breast and sang a little song to her.

> Ayla, Bayla, Melle, all new in the world
> Ayla, Bayla, Melle, her own precious girl.

Something fundamental in the universe had shifted with the birth of this one and Owl Feather could sense it. The long unbroken chain of knowledge and secrets handed down from mother to daughter would go on, but in a different way. The daughters would no longer take on their mother's personas or their names. Each new woman would stand alone, unique and sovereign in her power, bringing her own gifts. She would pass those gifts on, but each new one would bring her own, and so on and so on down the line, adding with each birth to the complex tapestry that was their lineage. And the line would begin to branch out, to curl and twine, splitting here and there and winding ever outward, to all the ends of the Earth. Melle would give birth to two children, one a son who had the strange eyes, one blue and one brown. And her son would father twins, two girls, one of whom would give birth to a single girl and one to three boys. They moved away from the little root house, which had become a shrine, a holy place, where the descendants came from time to time, to make offerings and do ceremony. They moved into the world, for the time had come. They moved into villages and towns and lived among the people there, sometimes seamlessly, and sometimes not. Melle's son and daughter were the first to do this, to renounce the forest. Melle understood and did not attempt to hold them back with her words or her tears. She knew that the time had come and that the change was part of the plan. The world was ready for and in need of the Knowledge. Although it would have to be held close and protected so that it would never be lost, it was time to begin to share it and she was proud that her children would be part of that, taking the old ways into the world.

Chapter 35

Several weeks had passed since Mai Zinni's revelation that Jane May wasn't the one she'd anticipated passing her knowledge down to. That threw a bit of a kink into the embryonic plans Jane May had been making. She had not been entirely sure about purchasing the inn and now she was filled with doubt. Jane felt as if she'd entered a thick fog and couldn't find her way out. Hadn't she been led here? What of all that had transpired? She knew herself to be a completely different woman than the one who had arrived at the inn on an early spring morning all those months ago. She couldn't go back where she'd come from, but staying here didn't seem to be her path anymore either. A season of great confusion had arrived. A time of walking a groove into the floor with her late-night pacing. She felt a sense of waiting. Awaiting further instructions.

She had continued to spend a lot of time with Mai Zinni at the older woman's insistence, and to her own everlasting relief and confusion.

"Why are you wasting time on me?" She'd asked one day as they sat around Mai's fire pit in front of the little cottage.

"Honey, no way is time spent with you a waste. Why would you say that?"

"Well, I mean, if I'm not the one, you're going to have to start over with somebody else, right?"

"Now listen to me," Mai Zinni said. "We are kinswomen, you and me, there's no doubt about that. I never said we wasn't kin."

"What do you mean, Mai? We're not related."

"Dear One, kin means something much more than blood relation. Kin means our hearts recognize each other. Kin means we don't have to blabber all the time, we can be in silence together and be happy there. Kin means we chose each other. We know each other. Like the green things in the forest know each other. We been together before. Understand?" Jane nodded and tears welled up in her eyes. The old woman reached over and patted her hand.

"I don't know what I'm supposed to do, Mai!" Jane wailed. "I thought I knew and now I don't know anything. I pray and pray and God doesn't speak to me anymore. I feel so lost!"

"That's good, Child. That's a juicy place to be, ain't it? Let that bubble for a while." With that Mai Zinni got up from the chair she'd had herself planted in and hobbled toward the house. Today she was a little stiff and looked her age.

Jane May threw another log on the fire and settled down in the weathered Adirondack chair. With a sigh, she closed her eyes. A calm came over her as she breathed slowly, in and out, in and out. Her body began to feel lighter, as if a weight had been lifted from her. The fog had begun to clear. Jane still didn't know what she was to do with her life from this point forward, but somehow she was content to be sitting right here in this comfortable old chair on the edge of a beautiful and possibly enchanted forest, listening to the song that the breeze made in the trees. She had no idea what would happen next but, at least for this moment, she was content to wait and see.

After a time, the old woman reemerged from the house carrying a bundle under her arm. Jane shook off her musing and smiled at her friend in her old boots and raggedy blue skirt. Mai Zinni's approach was slow, giving Jane a chance to really see her. It was peculiar how changeable she was, appearing one time as a strong woman in her prime, and again the next time, like today, as a crone from a child's fairy tale. She had a faded red cloth tied around her head, partially hiding her abundant greying hair, and a man's plaid shirt cinched up with a thin piece of rope, from which dangled various objects: a wishbone, a smooth rock with a large irregular shaped hole, a key, and a small leather pouch with fringe and a bluejay feather hanging from its flap.

How Jane May had come to love this old woman! She was stabbed by a pang of sadness at the thought of leaving her and this place where she had found refuge. Thoughts crowded into her brain, jostling for her attention. *I lose everyone I love. I'm not good enough to be the one that she waited for. I will never have a home again. No one will want me.* Suddenly, Jane stood and banished the thoughts like a swarm of mosquitos. "Leave me!"

she spoke forcefully, but under her breath. She caught Mai Zinni's smile in her peripheral vision and knew that she'd been seen. Mai Zinni had taught her carefully to be ever watchful of the mind demons who would steal her power and destroy her peace. Mai Zinni wanted her to be healed, to be whole. There is power in knowing that another human being cares about our well-being. A measure of protection comes with that knowledge, small but mighty.

Jane rose and approached the older woman, taking her arm. Together they walked back toward the fire and Jane helped Mai settle into her chair, the bundle on her lap. Sitting down herself, she waited, anxious to know what the bundle contained, but content to abide in the old woman's presence until she was ready to reveal the contents.

The bundle was a neat square. Wrapped in coarse linen and tied up with a length of knotted jute twine with red beads dangling from the bow. It looked like a present and anticipation rose in Jane May's body against her will. *Ah, how sweet!* she thought. Mai Zinni had gotten her a present. A booby prize. You are not the one, but here is a little gift to help you feel better. On and on, Jane May's thoughts went, tumbling about in her head, until the older woman spoke.

"It ain't a present."

"Oh, well, no, I wasn't thinking that." It was very disconcerting to feel that Mai was reading her mind, although it happened so frequently, she should be getting used to it by now.

"Sure you were. That's okay. Just let me catch my breath for a minute and I'll show you what it is." Mai Zinni sat panting lightly, the bundle in her lap.

Jane became fixated on the contrast of coarse, natural linen against the faded blue of the old woman's skirt and the bright red beads like flowers scattered on the surface of deep water. Her conscious mind wandered and she sunk down into the visual sensations until she was floating in a light linen-colored wooden boat, trailing her hand in the deep blue water, as red flowers floated on the surface. She felt a breeze on her face and heard birdsong in the trees surrounding the lake upon which she floated. The water was cold. The sky was an intense azure without a cloud in sight. She felt heavy and laid her head down on the edge of the boat. From here, her face was very close to the water and as she gazed into it, the surface rippled and rolled and then gathered into a scene: two women sitting around a fire, one old, the other, well, less old, flames contained in an iron cauldron licked the air in front of them as they sat together gazing into it. Surrounding them, at some remove from the circle of fire and women, was a fog, thick and swirling. As she watched the scene, a young girl walked out of the mist, wearing a red dress. On her shoulder sat a small bird with a black cap. A chickadee.

"Okay. Can you help me please." Jane was lifted from her daydreaming by Mai's voice. She rose to give her friend a hand. "Lay the bundle on the ground, carefully," Jane did so and then slowly untied the twine as Mai asked, laying the cloth back and exposing the contents. A smallish wooden bowl, a smaller bundle wrapped in black cotton, a thick twig with a tight bud at one end. She unwrapped the smaller bundle and found a collection of pebbles, smoothed and polished over millennia by water.

"Sit down on the ground cross-legged. Now put the stones in the bowl and stand the twig up in the middle."

When Jane May was situated, Mai Zinni told her to hold the bowl in her left hand and place her right hand over the top, not quite touching the twig.

"Now close your eyes and breathe three deep breaths."

Jane May felt the familiar grounding that deep breathing always brought her. She felt her spine sending roots into the ground, felt herself becoming part of the Earth, and then Mai Zinni said and Jane obliged, "Repeat after me: To reach within me, to take a side, to use this knowledge and to decide."

The sounds of the words seemed to hold some power of their own, beyond the surface meaning. Jane felt a vibration in her hands, both the one holding the bowl and the one hovering over. She waited. She breathed. A light breeze rustled the leaves on the trees and blew away the fog in Jane's mind.

"I can't stay." She was surprised to hear these words come out of her own mouth. "I've been trying to make it work in my mind, but it was never quite right was it? I love it here in Gideon. I love you. I've felt safe here, but I'm not done yet. I have more to do. Mai, when you realized I was not the one, I didn't want to admit it, but I felt so... free. Liberated, you know? I've no idea what I'm to do or where I'm to go, but the weird thing is, right now at least, I feel fine about that. I know that I'll be led, as I always have been, just as I was led here, to Gideon, to you. And I know that when the time is right, I'll know."

The two women sat for a little while, letting this new knowing settle over them. Soon, though, doubt began to creep in to Jane's May's mind, and then, having gained a foothold, to burst in like a gang of rowdy, ill-mannered school children.

"Banish the thoughts, Child!" Mai Zinni could tell from the furrowing of Jane's brow what was going on in her mind. "Banish them quickly and grab a hold of the knowing. Be still. Let it sift down into your bones. You spoke truth. You spoke your deepest desire and now your task is to guard that knowing with all your might. Protect it like a tiny flame.

"I was starting to feel at home in Gideon. Like maybe I belonged here."

"Child. You don't even know what Home is yet. You think that you have lost your home, but you haven't. You cannot. Your home is within you. You're like old Turtle who never goes anywhere without her home." She mussed Jane May's hair as she said this, in a gesture so affectionate, so intimate, that for just a moment, Jane thought maybe she did catch a glimpse of the true meaning of Home.

Chapter 36

The mountains were in the last throes of summer one afternoon in late August when Jane May's phone rang. She jumped at the sound, weeks having passed since she'd heard it. Her Isabelle had not returned any of her calls and Mai Zinni preferred to show up unannounced or send Charlie with a message when she wanted to talk. Jane went to Mai Zinni's cottage in the woods most days anyway, so there was little use for the phone. But ring it did on this beautiful day.

"Mama?"

"Issy!" After all this time, here was her lost daughter, separated from her only by air. "Where are you? Are you okay?"

"Yes Mama! I'm fine. I'm in New Mexico." Issy paused and Jane held her breath. "Mama, I'm sorry."

"Me too, Baby," Jane interrupted her daughter, "I'm sorry, too. I'm just so glad you called! Oh Issy, I've missed you so much." Jane May's voice caught in her throat and she couldn't go on.

What emerged from the breathless jumble of words that tumbled forth from Issy was that she and Ben (Jane, not willing to jeopardize this tenuous reconnection, held her tongue on that issue), were leaving New Mexico where they'd been all this time and coming to Gideon.

"What a coincidence!" Isabelle had said, although it had been lost in the jumble. Only later did Jane remember, or thought she remembered hearing these words, and she wondered at them.

It would be a while, maybe a month or six weeks, before they arrived. They had to put some things in order first, Isabelle said.

Jane May had gone immediately to Mai Zinni's house with her news of a reconciliation with Isabelle and her impending arrival. Mai was thrilled for her and the two embraced for a long moment.

"It's not time for me to go yet. But after Issy's visit . . . ."

"You'll know, Child. Trust yourself to know."

The two women's relationship had continued as if nothing had changed after Mai's announcement that Jane was not the one. Mai Zinni continued to impart her knowledge of the edible and medicinal uses of the plant life all around them. They continued to go out into the forest and into the mountains to find and harvest the plants and then, coming back to Mai's little house, they prepared them so that they could be used for healing a wide variety of ailments. Some were hung from the rafters of the old smoke house, which sat behind the cottage and had been converted just for this use, with racks and hooks hanging from the ceiling. They were left to dry, while others were used fresh and made into tinctures, decoctions, or used in cooking.

The two women had also continued to journey together, and separately, into the realms, as Mai called the dreamlike meditations, facilitated by drumming or rattling. Sometimes strong herbal concoctions were used as well, but always now with Jane's knowledge and consent. Jane had become more and more comfortable in this alternate reality as time went on. She met guides there who helped her and encouraged her healing. She dreamed more vividly than she had since she was a child. And while it was sometimes difficult to tease meaning from her dreams, she felt that they worked on her somehow. Like a person undergoing surgery while in the blank state of anesthesia, she often woke and felt as if she'd been stitched up while she slept.

On this day, they were looking for Squaw Root in the forest. The strange orange pinecone shapes sprang up in a cluster on the ground. Mai Zinni said they were a woman's best friend in pregnancy and labor and explained that the term *squaw* originally meant *powerful woman*.

"My great-grandma labored with my granny for forty-two hours. The mid-wife thought she might die. Nothing would open her up so my granny could make her passage. And that would mean that I wouldn't be talking to you right now. And then, my great-grandma's ma, a powerful medicine woman who lived next door, knocked. She had heard the screaming and got tired of not being called to help and just came on up uninvited. My great-grandma was ruled by pride and she wouldn't listen to anything her ma had to say. She'd hired the mid-wife, refusing to be administered to by her own ma and her witchcraft, as she called it. In my great-great grandma's bundle, she had a jar of dark liquid. An infusion made from the dried root of the plant called squaw root. She shooed the up to then useless mid-wife over, and she held my great-grandma's head and had her drink all of the bitter stuff. Pretty soon, my granny decided to go ahead and come on without any more trouble. My great-great grandma, the old medicine woman, caught Granny Street, 'cause the mid-wife was, by then, properly respectful of her knowledge and had moved out of the way and was just watching from the corner and standing by to see what she could learn and if she could be of any help.

After my granny was up and toddling on her own in a year or so, my great-grandma took herself on over to her ma's house and said, 'Here I am. Teach me.' Which is what happened and is how I come to be teaching you today."

"Wow. That is a great story. And so your great-grandmother and her mother made peace then?"

"Well . . . ." Mai Zinni laughed and said, "I don't know about peace. The women in my family don't seem to live so much in peace as in respect for each other's powers."

"It's such a shame that old knowledge has been mostly lost."

"It ain't lost. We're here doing it right now. I'm teaching you, ain't I?"

"Well, yes, but I don't think I'll be delivering any babies with what I've learned."

"Well, child, you just never know, do you?"

That evening, as the two women stood, washing up from the day's work and the little dinner they'd prepared at the end of it, Jane May asked, "Mai, do you think the person you're waiting on will come?"

"What do you mean, Child? I *know* that one will come."

"But you were sure it was me, right?"

"The Knowing ain't wrong, Dear One, just the timing."

"Well, I hope you don't have to wait long."

"Don't reckon it'll be much of a wait at all." The older woman snickered happily. "Don't you worry yourself, now."

Jane May smiled along with her friend and teacher. She was so fond of Mai Zinni and often felt indulgent of Mai's flights of fancy, as she sometimes thought of the strong intuition that guided the woman.

Chapter 37

Isabelle was relieved to have made contact with her mother. She had missed her terribly since she and Ben had been gone. So much had happened. And so much still to be done before they could wrap things up here in New Mexico and head back east, to Gideon. Wasn't it strange? That they were being pulled to Gideon and her mother had also made her way there. Issy couldn't wait to find out the details of how that had happened.

"Issy! Come on, we're going to be late for the ceremony." Ben loped into the room. He was so handsome in his borrowed suit. It hung a little loosely on his slender frame and made him look even thinner. Isabelle was astonished again at how she loved him.

"Where's your head, Chica?" He put his arm around Issy and pulled her to him, kissing her lightly on the mouth.

She laughed. "I don't know. Far away, I guess. But I'm back now and you sure do look handsome."

"And you are beautiful, as always. I'm so happy today, Isabelle."

"Me too, my love. Are you ready for this?"

"I am so ready." He grinned and she grinned and he lifted her and spun her in a wide circle and they walked out into the bright summer sunshine.

Ben had insisted that they get married before they left New Mexico for Gideon. "We're a family now, Issy. This is important."

"You're just trying to butter my mother up." She laughed, but she worried that his motivation was too wrapped up in what her mother might think.

"I do think that it will get me some points, with the Dragon Mama, but I want to marry you because I want the world to know that we are a family. I'm all in, Issy. I'm all in. And I want you all in with me. What do you say?"

What could she have said? Her mother had been so wrong about Ben from the start, projecting her own fears and hurts onto him. Here was a good man. And gentle and funny and smart. Isabelle Gideon was not about to let him get away.

"I say, yes. Of course. You make me want to say yes, Ben. You make me believe in yes."

Some memorably good loving had followed that conversation and now here they were, one week later, proving that weddings did not need to be hard to plan. Or expensive.

She was sad that her mother wouldn't be here. And also Nina.

Nina Trew, was a single mother to Sophie when she met Issy and Ben. Nina served up tofu salads and raw juices in a vegetarian cafe on the square in the small, tight-knit community in New Mexico that Issy and Ben had called home since their arrival. They came in almost every day, and gradually a friendship developed between the three of them. In a short time, Issy and Ben had come to love Nina and her precocious daughter. They had no idea that Issy's estranged mother, Jane May, had arrived in Gideon, North Carolina, the birthplace of Nina's mother, Little Star Trew, until Isabelle had called Jane to say that they wanted to come wherever she was now, for a visit.

After the conversation, Issy had shared with Nina. Excited to have reestablished contact with her mother, she told Nina about it over coffee on Nina's day off.

"What did you say the name of the town in North Carolina was?"

"Gideon. Isn't that weird? The same as our last name."

"It's really weird," Nina said, "That's the very town that my mother came from. I've always wanted to go there and take Sophie. Mama wouldn't even talk about it. 'There's nothing there for us,' was all she would say about it. After she died, though, I began to think of going there to see for myself. And also to show Sophie where our people come from."

"What a marvelous coincidence. You and Sophie have to come with us, Nina. It'll be a grand adventure!"

"Yes. You know Issy, I've never felt like I had a real home in the world. I don't want Sophie to grow up that way. Who knows what we'll find there, but I say yes!"

Isabelle and Ben were devastated when Nina died, suddenly and with no warning, just a few days later. They were baby-sitting Sophie at their house and hadn't planned to return her to her mother until morning, so they didn't realize that Nina hadn't made it home. No one did. That was part of the story of Nina Trew's life and of many of the lives in her lineage of women alone. No one to know, no one to notice, no one to care if she made it home or not.

The next morning a delivery truck noticed Nina's small car overturned in a ditch off the road and by then it was too late to help her.

Issy and Ben had been granted guardianship of Sophie and the child had agreed to honor her mother's wishes by traveling to Gideon, the birthplace of her grandmother.

Issy and Ben began to pack their meager belongings in preparation for leaving the desert Southwest.

While the landscape that they had sojourned in was grand and beautiful, it had never felt like home to either of them. They were southerners and needed moisture to thrive. Both anticipated the return to a lush green world with a mixture of joy, relief, and trepidation.

Chapter 38

After John's death Jane May and Nanette had brokered a tenuous peace. Nanette also lived on the property, with Charlie, in a cottage similar to Jane's but downstream from it. On this night, however, she and Charlie were not home. They'd gone to spend a few days with Nanette's mother, a sad woman who lived in the next county.

Jane May was alone.

She awoke, as she had done many times over the last months, in the tiny, but comfortable bed across from the window in the stone cottage behind an old ramshackle inn just outside the small town of Gideon, tucked into the Smoky Mountains. It was still dark and the room was filled with shadows. She had the feeling that something had awakened her, but she couldn't grasp what it might have been.

The tender spring in which she had arrived, blown into town on the airborne seeds of southern dandelions, had given way to the full green lush of summer, with its beebuzz and bird-song and lingeringly long days. That season too, had begun its inevitable golden magenta slide into autumn, but it was still fairly warm, and Jane, of a certain age, was prone to hot, so her windows were open on this night. Moonlight glinted on the tiny Sheela Na Gig figure on the windowsill, and yawning, Jane May recalled the day she'd bought it. That first day when she'd stumbled upon *The Light Within*. She chuckled to think of herself then, carrying heaviness of every kind: physical, mental, emotional. She had been fat with sorrow and worry and regret and somewhere along the way, she'd put that down, most of it anyway. Relieved to be coming out from under the heavy burden of self-recrimination, not to mention anger, she had barely even noticed the actual pounds melting away. Jane May touched her hip bones and smiled. She rolled over to go back to sleep, hoping for peaceful dreams when the shadows were split open by a zigzag of lightning so close that there was no waiting for the furious and simultaneous crash of thunder that sent her diving under the covers. As if there could be any protection in that soft cave.

Jane peeked out and, clutching the bedclothes and clinching her teeth, she waited for the next crash, but was met with only eerie silence.

Gradually, her eyes readjusted in the post lightning darkness, and she was startled to make out shapes in the gloom. Many of them. A crowd, a host, of people gathered around her bed in the darkness. *I'm not afraid*, she reassured herself.

Before she could tell if this was true, one of the people stepped closer and spoke.

"Don't be afraid, Jane," she said, for it was clearly a woman. "We're here to help you."

Jane May sat up in bed and shook her head and rubbed her eyes. Neither action did anything to dislodge the apparition standing before her. It had to be an apparition.

"It is time for healing to begin," said the woman, who seemed solid enough, except that Jane noticed that if she squinted a little and held her head just so, she could make out leaf shadows on the wall behind the woman and she realized she was seeing right through her.

" I don't understand. Who are you? Who are all these people?"

"We are the ancestors of your ancestors. The old ones. And we are here because the time is now. Enough of the sins of the fathers and mothers being visited upon the children. Enough of the cycles of pain and suffering being continuously repeated. Enough of the so-called genetic predispositions. We are here to help you break all of this apart and free yourself and your descendants."

"How?" Jane squeaked.

"Rise now, and come with us, Dear." The hazy woman extended a hand toward Jane, and Jane took it as much out of curiosity as anything. She needed to know if that hand would be solid or if her fingers would grasp at thin air. It was solid. And warm. And the second Jane's fingers made contact it was as if she, too, were made of stardust. Effervescent and light, she was part of the air around her.

Chapter 39

"Mai, my family has been broken for so long. Eons, it seems. I never understood this until now. Poor Issy. She hasn't a hope in the world of having a decent, healthy relationship. She's got it from both sides, her father's and mine." Jane had arrived, agitated, on Mai Zinni's doorstep, the afternoon following the strange visitation.

"Honey Child, everybody's family is broken. You sure ain't telling me nothing about broken families. It's nothing to be ashamed of, but it is something that needs healing in everybody. And that healing can be done, 'spite what anybody thinks about the past being past and all that. The past ain't exactly what we think, as in done and gone."

"I don't know what you mean, Mai!" Jane was querulous in her pain. The visitors she'd had the night before had taken her to a place made of crystal and stone and showed her something like a movie. It had contained a phantasmagorical mishmash of scenes of people from antiquity to modern day. She'd recognized the more modern ones, some of them at least. Her grandparents and great-grandparents, whom she'd never met, but knew from family photos, her parents and herself as a child and a teenager, all hurting each other and themselves in ways both great and small and largely, but not always, unintentional. She saw herself misusing her sexuality on bare mattresses in dirty apartments and the backseats of cars with boys she barely knew because she didn't understand the power or the sacred quality of her femininity. As she had watched, mesmerized, patterns had begun to emerge. Patterns of betrayal and abandonment, of shame and anger. She'd watched a man dressed in skins beat a woman almost to death, with a child huddled and screaming nearby. She'd been shown scenes of lonely women, staring out of windows and wondering how they would feed their hungry children. She'd seen her own grandfather, beloved as he had been to her, in bed with a strange woman, and her grandmother crying, the two of them in a heated argument, and then her father in a similar aspect and later, her mother pleading and crying and then scenes of her own marriage, so eerily similar as she and Lenny had begun to fly apart. She had felt the abandonment and rage of all those women, and the hapless wonderment of defeat and shame in the men, and the fear of the children, as if she actually inhabited all of them, body and soul. She had been flayed open and overwhelmed and now she felt hopeless, helpless, impotent, in the face of generations of misery.

"I don't know what you mean. How can anything be done about all these lifetimes of pain and sorrow? How in the world can this cycle be broken? Mai, I don't want Issy's life to be like this. I don't want her granddaughter or hers to one day be shown this movie. I don't know what to do about it. And I feel like I've failed completely as a wife, a mother, and a woman." Jane crumpled in the shame of regret.

Yes, it was regret. Not death, not pain, but the hollow, empty, twisting of regret that was at the bottom of her fear. She was beginning to understand this clearly now. The fear of the bitter poison of regret, pure and simple. Regret for all that had been done and left undone, said and unsaid. For not watering her mother's roses as she lay dying. Impatience with her precious child. Dear God, what had ever been more important than being with her, holding her, teaching her, listening to her? And her marriage. For her part in that, and yes, she knew that the blame could not be laid solely on Lenny's shoulders. She knew that she had carefully constructed a world in which he could not breathe, and they had all paid the price for that. She wanted to spit, to vomit, to rinse her mouth, her soul, with something clean. She longed for the minty flavor of redemption. "Honey, there're lots worse things than death," her grandmother had told her as she lay on her death bed. Yes indeed. Regret, unlike death, could kill you. Your soul would surely survive death, but regret? She was not so sure about that.

"Come now, Little One," Mai Zinni crooned, as she patted Jane's head and gently rubbed her shoulder. "Seeing it is the first part of healing it."

"The first part?"

"There's things you can do now, Child. You'll see, the Old Ones came because they need you. They're asking for your help."

"How can I help, Mai? It's all done. I can try to do better, I won't marry again. I won't make that mistake. I can try to talk to Issy about it."

"Come back in a few days and we'll see what we can do, but for now, it's getting on supper time and this old woman's got an aching in her bones tonight. Rise and come inside and let's have us a little supper."

At the word *Rise*, something rose in Jane. Something like a memory, but fainter than that, more like wingbeats against her heart. She rose and went in, comforted, at least for the moment, to be with her mentor and friend.

After a light meal of wild-gathered mushrooms and rice, Jane May had returned to her own cottage and dropped into bed, exhausted and without a bath. She slipped quickly under the spell of sleep. Her dreams that night were fitful. Images flitted across a screen, not to be captured in the morning. But somehow when dusty blades of sunlight struck the floor of her bedroom and inched their way up onto the bed, nudging her awake, she felt better. That old optimism had its way with her again in the night and the world looked cleaner and brighter. Although she still felt the weight of her past, she knew now that she had the strength to bear it. And Mai Zinni had given her a glimmer of hope that maybe somehow, some of it could be set right, even now.

She bathed in the old claw foot tub. In the green, leafy light, which bore the first, golden traces of autumn, she washed herself clean of the remnants of despair. Afterward, she breakfasted on fresh eggs and toast with blackberry jam that she and Mai had put up in the peak of summer. She got dressed in a clean skirt and a soft old tee, then threw a worn green cardigan over her shoulders. She faced the mirror and admired her body. She had missed it, having been out of touch for so long now. It was older and softer, saggy in some places and wrinkled in some, but still it was hers and it had served her well. It was a strong body. After all, she came from a long line of sturdy people. In spite of her not always taking the best care of it, it was a healthy body, quick to brush off colds and flu, healing itself from minor irritations. She allowed herself to feel immense gratitude to this body and the weathered vessel that it had become. It was the temple of her soul. This temple was built on joy and sorrow in equal measures. Maybe it was even beautiful.

Her mother's body had betrayed her completely, manifesting every emotional and spiritual wound as a disease, and finally succumbing too early to death. Or maybe it was her mother who had betrayed herself by not attending to those wounds before they became physical. Jane vowed not to let this happen to her own body, to break that cycle, if she could. She had discovered, since her first overnight walk to Shining Rock, the joyful pleasure of taking her body outside into the wilderness. There had been other walks up to the top of that mountain and some of its sister mountains as well, as she'd learned to love rambling around on the forest trails in this paradise. And she had begun, under Mai Zinni's tutelage, to eat more seasonal and simpler food and it had resulted in this slimmer, stronger body that stood reflected in the bathroom mirror. Yes, lightness. Jane May found that she had begun to crave lightness. Letting go. She ruthlessly tossed or recycled everything non-essential that came into her life. She wanted to travel light from now on, like a wild animal roving stealthily through the forest, undetected in her passage. She was becoming a feral woman. Reclaiming her wild nature.

Acting on a suggestion from Mai Zinni to turn bad memories into birds, she had cut up some of her old journals—the angrier ones—snipping the hate-filled pages into bird shapes. She'd spent several days immersed in the project. She'd applied a blue watercolor wash to all of the birds which had first been stiffened with cardboard. Several she'd strung into a mobile along with crystals and found feathers. It gave her so much pleasure to see the happy little birds made of her old anger turning easily in the breeze by her kitchen window. The rest of the birds she'd burned ceremonially, watching her transformed rage go up in smoke and drift away.

Upon arriving at Mai's cottage, Jane found the old woman already outside and stirring a fire in the pit. On the ground near the cauldron was her old quilt, her ancient drum, the small rattle and a thermos. *Oh Lord,* thought Jane, *I wonder what she's brewed up.* It would be too much to hope for just coffee.

"Well, good mornin', Sunshine!" Mai Zinni was ebullient. "Ready to get started?"

"Um, sure, I guess so. Yes, and I'm sorry I lost it yesterday."

"No apologizin' now, Young'un. Ain't nothing to apologize for. You feel what you feel. It's all part of learning to live."

"Thank you, Mai. No really," she interjected as Mai started to protest, "you can't know how comforting it is to be with you and to not have to apologize for anything. Honestly, Mai, I like myself so much better when

I'm alone or with you. When I see myself reflected back by most people, I don't like what I see. I seem like a boor and a bore, an overly nervous, talkative, neurotic boring boor. Uncool, awkward and unattractive. But when I'm alone, or when I'm with you, I feel like myself. My real self. The self that I love. I thank you for that, for being a mirror guide for me. I love you, Mai."

"I love you, too, Janie, and you will learn to love yourself. Now let's get to work."

Chapter 40

Nanette was worn out from her own anger. Exhausted by years and years of resentment and envy gnawing away at her. A lifetime, really, when she thought about it. She had been angry her whole life. Was she born angry? No one had ever lived up to her expectations of them, from the very beginning. Her father, an absent alcoholic, her mother, a doormat, who seemed to think she deserved him. Nanette watched her skulking around, trying to appease him whenever he deigned to come home. The way she would cower even as she served him, setting a plate of food in front of him, or a drink, or herself. As often as not, he would fling whatever the offering was away, whether he'd asked for it or not, declaring it inadequate, or overcooked, or undercooked. Her mother would crawl around on the floor, cleaning up the mess and apologizing and little Nanette saw this and hated her for it, vowing never to allow a man to treat her this way and yet, what had she done? Picked the same damn man.

When John came along and helped her out of that mess, it seemed that her life had turned around. She felt whole and strong. Capable. And then he had gone and offed himself and now what was she to do? Alone again. Poor. And with Charlie to take care of. Damn him!

And Jane. That was another thing. Just who did she think she was, ingratiating herself to Charlie and bringing treats to the house. Her kindnesses grated on Nanette. And she suspected that Jane's motives were not pure either. She wanted everybody to see what a kind and lovely person she was. *Look at me, in spite of the fact that Nanette is so mean, here I am continually trying to befriend her and her poor little boy.* Why couldn't she just mind her own business and leave them alone? Nanette didn't need any friends. Hell she had her hands full trying to keep a roof over herself and Charlie. Friends just took up time and energy and she had neither to spare.

Ricky had kept her from her old friends with threats and trickery. He liked to lie and say, "I saw your friend, so-and-so in the grocery and overheard her telling somebody else such-and-such about you." Nanette hadn't believed him at first, but eventually his words would wind their way into her self-loathing heart and masquerade there as truth. She would make excuses when her friends called and gradually they'd all wandered out of her life. It had been just as well, it was too hard to keep the truth and the bruises from them anyway. And John had been a good friend to her and Mai had as well. They were all the friends Nanette needed, even though she still felt a sting of rejection from the older woman. Mai Zinni had never been anything but kind and motherly, but still there was a distance. Maybe it was self-imposed by Nanette herself. She supposed she was willing to entertain the possibility.

As angry as she was, Nanette felt herself leaning toward Jane May as if toward a mother or a mentor. And this leaning in angered her too. *No! She told herself. Don't make that mistake again. Don't let yourself be rejected.*

But was it possible that Jane May simply needed a friend herself? After that first time she had brought the soup and cornbread something had shifted in Nanette, but she was afraid to let her guard down. *I don't have time for this,* she told herself. *I've got to find a job and figure out how I'm going to take care of this boy of mine.* But Jane kept coming around. Charlie loved her and the two of them had a rapport.

And then there had been Mai's big revelation that Jane wasn't the one she'd been waiting to pass the knowledge down to. That must have stung and Nanette could sure understand it. And now here was Jane May, skulking around, looking like her dog had died.

As angry as Nanette was at John for leaving them, she couldn't help but remember that he had predicted that Jane would eventually be a friend to her. It seemed, in retrospect, that he was trying to tell them that everyone would be okay without him. She had never understood the origins of John's torment, although she had a few theories, which she'd always kept to herself. He had been a hero and a savior and a friend to her and to Charlie, but she always knew there was a sadness, a despair that underlay John's strength. She hoped that he was at peace now and thought the best thing she could do for him was just to be all right. Just to calm down and let go of her anger and accept what he had always told her.

"Girl," he had said on more than one occasion, "you make things harder than they need to be. You're getting in your own way. Let go of some of it.

Just put it down and let folks step in closer." Maybe he'd been right, after all. Maybe he had.

Early the next morning, Nanette stood on Jane's doorstep with a basket filled with a glass mason jar full of homemade soup and a plate of brownies, covered in foil. She'd been standing there for quite awhile actually, deciding to knock and then reconsidering several times, before she finally gave in and rapped on the door.

Jane May opened up, looked at the younger woman, and then beyond her.

"Nanette, slowly turn around," Jane whispered.

"Well damn," Nanette immediately went on the defensive and bowed up, but Jane shushed her, keeping her eyes on the cat that stood across the creek.

"Hush now, and turn around very slowly."

Nanette turned and gasped. "What the hell?" Both women stood, not daring to move, until the animal ambled off and disappeared into the woods. "My God!" Nanette had turned back to Jane, "What was that?"

"I'm not sure. You saw it too, right?"

"Yes I saw it," Nanette assured her. "It was big! Was that a mountain lion? It couldn't be, right?" Jane invited her in, and over coffee and brownies, a rare sighting of an animal widely thought to be extinct here, and their mutual rejection by a crotchety old woman, the two put down some of their antagonism, their defensiveness, and realized that they actually had quite a bit in common besides their mutual love of Charlie.

They spent the morning in decadence, deciding that they deserved it, after all they'd been through. They drank coffee and ate the warm brownies that Nanette had just taken out of the oven and they laughed and they even cried a little bit. About John, about the time they'd wasted on jealousy.

Jane May told Nanette about Issy and about her visit from the ancestors and that she was going to do some work on that with Mai Zinni, and this time Nanette wasn't envious. Well maybe just a little. When Nanette rose to leave, Jane asked her to wait. She ducked into the kitchen and took the blue bird mobile down from its hook. Returning to the living room, she said, "I want you to have this."

"Oh! It's beautiful!"

"Thank you. A wise woman once told me that we each have the power to turn our painful emotions into something else."

The two women embraced on the front porch of the stone cottage.

"Jane?" Nanette turned halfway down the steps.

"Yes?"

"Almost from the moment you arrived in Gideon, John said that we would be friends one day. I never believed him, although I secretly wished for it to be true."

"I know. He told me the same thing.".

Chapter 41

Charlie sat rocking back and forth underneath an ancient apple tree. He sat at the edge of the Safe Range. He'd meant to breach the barrier. What did it matter now, anyway? Uncle John was gone. His mama had been madder than ever and hardly paid any attention to him at all and when she did, it was to smother him with questions and food, til he thought he'd scream. So he'd come into the forest this morning, thinking that maybe he'd disappear too, just like Uncle John had, beyond the Safe Range. Probably no one would even notice.

But when he'd gotten to the edge, the new edge that John had negotiated for him with his mama, and he knew he was forbidden to go farther, he couldn't let himself go beyond it so he'd sat down and hugged his knees under the old tree.

Tears began to fall and this was upsetting to him. What if they never stopped? Could that happen? His mama had said, after they'd buried Uncle John, "You're my little man, now." He didn't feel like a man, even a little one. He felt like a big old snotty baby. How could Uncle John have left him like that? He didn't even say goodbye. Charlie must have been wrong about everything. They weren't friends. Uncle John didn't love him. He just wished he had.

What would they do now? Old Mai Zinni, his mama, Miss Jane, who'd been so nice to him, who had seemed like a friend, even Mr. Mac, who was always happy, always ready to listen to Charlie's stories or tell him some— they were all so sad now. Charlie had never felt so lonely. At night he lay in his little bed, listening to his mama cry or pace the floor. Once, when he was supposed to be asleep, he'd heard her cry to someone on the phone, "How will I feed my boy now?"

The next morning he had retrieved a beat up old coffee can from its hiding place under the porch of their house. In it were all the crumpled dollars that he'd gotten from the guests at the inn. He knew his mama was mad about him taking those dollars, so he'd hidden them from her and that was wrong, but now he thought maybe this was why. He left the little pile of dollars and some spare change in the bowl they used for fruit. It was empty now anyway. It seemed like they couldn't afford fruit anymore. Or maybe Nanette had just forgotten. She barely remembered to fix supper anymore. He left the money there and let the screen door slam behind him as he headed out for parts unknown. His mama had left the house an hour ago, the slamming was for his own benefit. He didn't leave her a note. He knew that John hadn't left much of a note because the grown-ups talked over his head, as if they'd forgotten he was alive. He'd left a *cryptic* one, whatever that meant, just for Mai Zinni. It was very short. Charlie didn't know what cryptic meant and he couldn't think of what he would say except goodbye, so he just left.

He thought he'd walk and walk until he came to someplace else. That was all he had in his head. Well, maybe a vague notion of comfort and the good smell of cookies baking . . . a smiling mama . . . but then he'd gotten to the edge of the Safe Range and he couldn't go any farther. He remembered Uncle John talking to him about what the Safe Range was for and how it supposedly meant that his mama loved him, and though he was curious, he became frightened of what might be beyond. So he sat down. And he started to cry. A squirrel swung down from its perch in the apple tree and peered at him, tail twitching. Charlie wiped his nose on the sleeve of his tee shirt and said, "Hi." Crows began calling and first one and then another swooped down to sit in the tree above his head, until the tree was full of black wings, caw, caw, cawing. Soon they settled down and began to preen, fluffing and arranging their glossy feathers, as if they had nothing else to do. A rabbit sat twitching its nose nearby. He felt a little better in the company of these animal friends.

There was a rustling in the trees. Fall had arrived while everyone was grieving and now the boy noticed the sun-kissed gold and red leaves dancing in the breeze. As he watched, some of them let go and fell. Twirling in the wind, riding the air currents to the ground, they took their last bow. He closed his eyes and lifted his tear-streaked face to the wind and the wind dried his tears and he heard someone say, "Little Brother."

Charlie opened his eyes and then opened them wider, for there in the clearing before him stood his Uncle John.

"Hey Buddy," he said, as if nothing had changed.

Charlie scrambled to his feet, but John lifted a hand and said, "You're okay there, Bud. I just wanted to talk to you for a minute." So the boy settled back into his seat, although his mouth was hanging open. John laughed. "You seem surprised to see me."

"You're dead."

"And do you know what that means, Charlie?"

"Gone. For good."

The old man laughed, but it was tender. "No," he said, "not even close. I'm right here, Charlie. You see me, don't ya?" When Charlie nodded, John continued. "Death is nothing. I can hardly believe it myself, but it's true. I ain't gone, I'm just someplace else. Do you understand?"

"Uhn uh." Charlie shook his head.

John laughed again. "Yeah, it's kind of hard to explain, I guess, but what I want you to know is that I'm near. You're not alone. Ever'thing's okay. You may not be able to see me like this, but you can talk to me whenever you want and I'll hear. I gotta go now. You're a good boy. Ever'thing's going to be okay. Do you hear me?" Charlie nodded and a fat tear slid down his cheek. "I love you, Charlie."

"I love you too. I wish you could stay."

"I know, son. I know." John's form was getting hazy. It shimmered around the edges and Charlie could see through it. Tears were falling now and John said, "Oh, and Kiddo?"

"Yes, Uncle John?"

"The cat you saw? It was a lion. A mountain lion. It was real!"

"I knew it! I knew you believed me!" Charlie jumped up now and moved toward John, but his image became even more amorphous.

"You'll see her again one day. I promise." And with those words, John's shape dissolved completely and Charlie stood still and time stopped.

And then, because it always does, the world began to spin again, the crows cawed, the squirrels scampered off, rabbits ducked back into their holes, and a little boy turned toward home.

When he was almost there, something caught his eye up ahead in the path and running to it, he bent down and smiled at the large paw print in the mud. He put his pudgy boy's hand that would one day be a man's hand down next to the print and whistled softly and said out loud, "That's a big 'un."

Chapter 42

Jane May Gideon had done much healing here in these mountains, but every time she peeled off a layer of herself, she found another layer underneath it. She understood that she'd never be the way she had been. She was becoming something new. Again. And there was no going back. Like a snake, she thought, constantly shedding its skin. So much shedding, so much letting go. She was continually morphing into something that's never been before, again and again and again. She thought that it was not a coincidence that our actual skin sloughs off constantly and we become completely new creatures every seven years, every single bit of us having been shed and created anew.

The moon had waxed and waned and waxed to full again since that night when Jane was jolted awake by the visitors. She and Mai Zinni were sitting around the fire pit, basking in the silvery, selene light. The time of Issy's return was drawing near and Jane was feeling anxious. During this time of healing with the ancestors, Jane and Mai Zinni had insulated themselves in a cocoon of sorts. She was feeling strong, but she knew that her newfound strength would be put to the test when Issy arrived.

A few days into their work, the two women were sitting in the darkling evening around the fire.

"Mai," Jane's voice was so low that the old woman had to lean in to hear her, "Mai, how can we go on living in a world like this? How can I ever feel okay about my daughter being in this world? About any woman, any person, being alive and so vulnerable to all the violence, all the hate in this awful world. I can't seem to find any hopefulness. Any joy." Jane's voice caught in her throat.

Mai Zinni sat while Jane's grief fully manifested itself. She'd been expecting this and she knew that there was no way for Jane to go except through it. She had all the time in the world. She had brought blankets out and she reached for one now to make this dear one more comfortable. And the moon arced its silent curve across the velvety sky.

Mai Zinni dozed in her chair, but her ears were alert.

The moon had set and the night was at its darkest, the stars blazing overhead. The two women sat beside each other for some time, as the cool night breeze ruffled their hair. Mai Zinni kept the fire fed and it burned low and steady on its bed of coals, warming their feet.

"Look." The old woman pointed to the sky and Jane lifted her head to see a meteor streaking, leaving faint fiery trails in its wake. In spite of herself, Jane gasped with wonder and brought her hands together in front of her mouth as if in prayer. Mai Zinni smiled and patted her friend's hand. "It will be okay." They sat together for a long time, meteors shooting this way and that from a central point overhead. Each one punctuated Jane May's pain and at the same time, cauterized it.

"Dear One, I want to tell you a story. The ancients tell us that the Earth is a living, breathing being. She's our mother. Pachamama. Long, long ago, before time began—it's hard to imagine, I know, just let your mind float free. Long ago, when the whole world was merely an idea inside the mind of God, the Earth a tiny marble in that hand, God put the Earth into God's own mouth and rolled it around, savoring the fine and complex flavor of this new creation and a thought was born. And thoughts, you know, are the energy of the world, the foundation. In the beginning was the Word, the Thought. And God's thought was this: that the Earth, this beautiful, beloved creation, would be the fertile training ground for all of us. School, in other words. The Earth agreed to this. To be in service to us, to be the place where we come down, from God, which is our true home, to learn.

We know this, 'course we do, but we forget, and we think that this Earth and this life of ours is all there is. And those of us who've been here many times nobly think that we must strive hard and ever harder to make this Earth a paradise. We have a vision and we believe that we can will it into being, this vision where everyone's awake and safe and whole and we all live in harmony together."

"Ha!" Jane May snorted.

"But listen, my sweet, if you had gone off to college and you'd earned a big old fancy degree, would you look back and expect everyone behind you, all the way to kindergarten, nursery school even, to just wake up and suddenly possess the hardwon knowledge that you've earned? Of course not. This is school. There will always be young ones coming up and those will always have free will to choose and some will choose badly. This is school. We are here to learn and to grow, not to create paradise. Paradise already exists and we'll be there one day. And all of us will be there, not just some, all of us. Some take longer, some fail and have to repeat, some drop out and waste time and come back to it later, some move forward, quickly at first, and then begin to lag, some are slow starters. You get the point?"

Jane May stared into the fire, as if she hadn't heard anything Mai had said.

"Listen, Beloved, there ain't no guarantees in this life. That ain't what this is about. There is pain. There is suffering. There is cruelty and meanness that can't even be spoke. And there is beauty and light and joy. It's a heady brew. And it can crush the weak of mind or spirit. It's our job to wake up. To be strong. To study. And to jump in. We ain't meant to sit on the sidelines. We have to go to class. We'll get dirty. We'll get hurt. Things will get messy from time to time. We have to give with our whole hearts. We can't hold nothing back."

"Stop. Please stop. I haven't anything else to give, Mai, can't you see that?"

"No!" Mai Zinni rose from her chair and stood between Jane and the fire. She pulled her shoulders back and puffed out her chest, making herself seem taller and bigger than she was. "No! You listen to me, girl. Will you give your power away, again? Will you? Will you just throw up your hands and let fear come and take your power from you?"

"Mai, you don't understand."

"Like hell I don't!" the old woman thundered. "What do you know? Do not make the mistake of thinking that you've got it harder or worse than anyone else. Do you understand me? You are responsible for yourself and no one else in this life. Love the ones you can and leave everyone to their own path. You can't know what it's like for another. You can't know!"

Jane cowered under Mai's fury. "I'm sorry, Mai. You're right. I'm sorry."

Mai Zinni took her seat again and they sat in silence as dawn crept over the mountains and washed the sky in ashy grey. The old woman threw another log on the fire. It had been a long night, and soon they would need to eat and rest, but it wasn't over quite yet.

Bzzz-pop! Sparks flew from the fire and Jane May's mind soon became entrained with their synchronistic rhythm. The boundaries between herself and the fire began to blur and she felt herself move into the red hot flames, danced there as if she'd always been flame, always been heat. She had no desire except to burn, giving off light and warmth.

She felt herself lifting up, up, up. She was lifted on the wind and the wind was a word and the word was *Rise* and she rose up until she looked down on herself and her friend, sitting before a fire in a clearing in the woods. She liked floating there, above herself. It was quiet and she felt as if strong arms held her aloft. She felt herself swaying in these strong arms, above the Earth.

She was jolted by a snarling sound, and looked down just in time to see a large creature come crashing through the forest. The beast—was it a mountain lion—leapt and for a moment it was flying through the air and then it was upon her, and she was again sitting by the fire and the animal was tearing flesh and growling and snarling and a bright red stain of blood flowered on her clothing and she noted, with some surprise, her lack of fear or anxiety, and then the lion and the Jane May below and the Jane May above all came crashing together into the Adirondack chair with a thud and Jane cried out, but didn't make a sound, and then she was alone in the chair.

Panting, she looked over at Mai Zinni only to find the older woman snoring softly in a light sleep.

Jane May breathed and sat, her eyes squeezed shut, until her heart slowed. Then she rose and gathered up the blankets that were strewn about the lawn. Hearing her, Mai Zinni awoke and rose also, and the two women moved without a word toward the cottage.

For the span of one full moon cycle, it went like this. Jane and Mai Zinni established a rhythm of cooking, walking in the forest, talking and journeying. Every night Mai drummed or rattled and Jane journeyed to the realms that are not visible except to those with eyes to see and ears to hear. Jane's eyes and ears were developing rapidly. And she traveled further and deeper on each journey.

Mai traveled too, but she did it by herself, without the aid of the drum, as she had taught herself many, many years ago when she lost her grandmother and the drums went silent. She journeyed for her friend. She met with Jane's Old Ones and did ceremony on Jane's behalf. She was well acquainted, by now, with these ancestors and she knew what they wanted from Jane, but she had stores of patience that would chagrin an ancient monk. She would wait for Jane to come to this knowledge on her own.

"Mai," Jane began one crisp and lovely morning toward the end of their work together, "I've had the visitors again, the Old Ones. They're coming to me in my sleep almost every night."

Mai Zinni nodded. The two women were sitting at the kitchen table and Mai Zinni was knitting something the color of deep forest moss.

"They want me to do something." She waited to see if Mai knew what that was. But if Mai did know, she wouldn't own up to it.

"And what do they want you to do, My Dear?" Mai's eyes remained on the green yarn in her lap, her fingers flying as the needles click-clacked on each other, but Jane could see that she knew perfectly well what the answer was and, not for the first time, she wondered just how her friend knew the things that she seemed to know.

"They want me to write a letter to Lenny, telling him that I don't blame him for the breakdown of our marriage."

"Yes. And how do you feel about these instructions?"

"Well, the letter is something I've thought about before, but didn't think I was ready to do. I think they will help me write it, though, and I can trust them." The two women sat in companionable silence.

Presently, Jane stood, stretched and said, "I think I'll get started on that letter. It might take me awhile to finish it." She patted Mai's shoulder and turned toward the house.

There was a room in Mai's cottage, it was a closet really, just barely big enough for a single bed, an iron chair and a tiny desk. Mai had given Jane the use of it for the duration. It was a place to journal her experiences and her thoughts about them. A quiet room to meditate or regroup or nap. The little room suited Jane just fine. It felt like a nun's cell and she felt safe and sequestered inside. And the dreams she'd dreamt in here, on the nights when she'd stayed over, after a particularly intense session around the fire. The tiny space seemed infused with her dreams. It was as if the walls had absorbed the smell of countless bonfires and fireflies had become entrapped in the lace panel that draped loosely over the one tiny window. When she looked up at the ceiling, she almost expected to see a Milky Way strewn indigo sky. And the Old Ones. Their presence seemed to have meshed with the atmosphere. It wasn't like they were in there, crowding the space. No, it was more that the air was made of their essences, infused, somehow with their nature. Jane often thought that she'd like to plaster over the door. A voluntary immurement. To die in this room would be heaven, she thought.

She didn't start on the letter that day. It could wait. Instead she stood in the room, reflecting on the work that she and Mai Zinni had done, with the help of her ancestors. They had had conversations and cut energetic cords that had entangled them all for generations. Once Mai invited beings in who she said were psychic surgeons. They removed blockages and injuries from Jane's energy field. Last night the ancestors had come to her again in a dream and taken her to the place of the first night. The hall of crystal and stone. She'd been shown another movie and in this one she saw babies and children and young people, treating each other with love and respect, caring for each other, laughing with each other.

She felt ready now, for whatever came and especially ready to reconnect with her daughter.

Chapter 43

The day had come, at last, for Isabelle to arrive in Gideon. Jane May was so happy and excited to see her girl. To get her hands on her. To lay her eyes on her. God, she had missed Issy! She hadn't even fully realized the ferocity with which her heart had ached for her daughter during her long absence. It was as if all the hurt of her life had crystallized in this abandonment. She had been bereft in her separation from Issy.

At the same time, she was nervous and felt awkward about seeing her only child after all this time. So much had happened in the interim. So much about her had changed and she could only imagine how true that must be for Isabelle too. The phone calls that had passed between them had seemed warm and sweet, but Jane knew that it might be different when they found themselves face to face. Mightn't the old animosities, the old issues, rise up again? Jane May knew now that she could take whatever came. But all she wanted to do was to hug Issy and sit with her and listen to her talk and gaze at her beautiful face. She would, had already, forgiven everything, including herself. But would Issy forgive her? Would she ever be able to understand any of it? Why the marriage had ended, why Jane had struggled so to accept it, and why she had to leave soon.

All this anxiety had her pacing and ready to jump out of her skin.

"Goodness, Child! You 'bout to make me a nervous wreck. What do you call yourself doing? Stop that round and round and sit down. Come on, now. Sit down and drink this cup of tea." Mai Zinni had taken Jane by the arm and led her to a chair near the open kitchen doorway, looking out on the trail that ambled down from the pull-off on the main road. Handing her a steaming cup of chamomile tea, she said, "You can see 'em soon's they come round that bend in the path up there. Give you time to jump up and run around in a circle like a chicken with your head cut off. For now, please sit and give this tired old woman some peace!"

"I'm sorry, Mai. I'm sorry. I'm just so nervous."

Mai Zinni put a leathery hand on Jane's shoulder, which had an instantly calming effect on her, and the two women gazed out toward the trees.

"I understand, Dear One. Everything's gone be all right."

"Umm," said Jane as she leaned into Mai's soft breast. For the thousandth time, she felt a pang of regret that she had to leave. Part of her so wanted to stay here forever. To be home here. But even as she watched the thoughts go by, like clouds scudding along in the sky, she knew that it could not be. Something was calling her back out into the world. In the last few months, Jane's inner voice, the voice of her heart, the part of her that did know, had come back so strongly, and she was listening and would listen now for the rest of her life. She would not doubt again, that voice. She would not let her heart close. The voice resonated so deeply within her, thrumming with truth, beckoning with authenticity, she could no more consider not heeding it now, than she could think of not breathing.

A steady rain had fallen all day in the little clearing where Mai Zinni's cottage hunkered down. The rain had slowed an hour ago and then finally stopped, leaving the trees and the grass bejeweled with raindrops, and a heavy mist had begun to descend. As the two women watched the path expectantly, the fog wraiths swirled and gathered and finally settled in among the trees, filling all the spaces between leaves and tree trunks with their ghost breath.

"The Old Ones called these mountains Shaconage. Land of blue smoke," Mai Zinni spoke as if from a dream, pronouncing the word *shah-co-nah-hey*.

"I can see why." Jane May had forgotten her anxiety and gazed, mesmerized, into the mist.

Mac had agreed to meet Issy and Ben at the airport in Asheville. After taking them by the inn to drop off their luggage, he would bring them to Mai Zinni's house.

Maternal instincts kicked in and Jane was pulled out of her chair by a knot of fear twisting in her belly.

"I hate for them to be driving in this soup!"

"There, there, Honey. Everything will be fine. They're probably at the inn already. Mac's taking care of them. Don't you worry none. They'll be here soon." That soft but strong old hand on the shoulder again did its trick, restoring Jane to equanimity. With a long, slow exhale, she turned and walked to the front of the house and stepped onto the porch, looking out at the forest. She remembered the first day that she'd stumbled upon this place. Nothing about that day seemed coincidental from the vantage point that she now held. Her coming upon *The Light Within* and finding Mac there. His telling her about the waterfall and giving directions, which she didn't feel that she really understood, but finding the place nonetheless. And then the wonderful and impossibly long hike through the enchanted forest, dressed in velvet moss, shot through with sunlight, and her baptism in the water and the deep sleep that followed. Her first glimpse of her beloved Mai Zinni, a blue flash in the forest, which she had been compelled to follow.

"Mai," she turned then and said to the old woman's back, "you know I would follow you anywhere."

"Yes, Child," said Mai without turning, "but you got to follow your own self now."

Jane May stood a little straighter and smiled as she answered, "I know, Mai." And she did. She did know. When she was quiet and she listened, she knew. After the reunion with Issy, which she assumed would last for a few days before they'd be on their way back out west, she would make her plans to leave.

But listening and allowing one's inner voice to be the guide was a far cry from knowing the future.

Chapter 44

"Here they come." Mai Zinni was half way down the steps, the words streaming out behind her. Jane May followed so quickly that she collided with the old woman's words, scattering them to the winds like chattering chickadees.

"Issy!" The word pushed itself forward and dragged Jane May with it into the arms of this grown woman who had swum under her heart so many years ago and left a part of herself there. "Issy." This time it came on a tear-choked breath.

"Mama." Isabelle's laughter tumbled out as her mother squeezed the breath from her.

Jane May became aware, through a scrim of joy, that Ben was standing awkwardly to the side. She moved to embrace him. She might as well. It would appear that he was here to stay and if he loved her girl, she would love him for that. His embrace was strong and warm and she sensed a release of tension in it. He'd been waiting for this all along. It was she who had been resistant. As the embrace ended and Jane and Ben simultaneously stepped away from each other, she saw that Mai was gazing at something on the path.

In the heavy, swirling mist had appeared a young girl. She was maybe six or seven years old. She wore a red dress and had long dark hair, which was braided into two thick plaits, each tied at the end with a wide red ribbon. Her skin was creamy with a spoonful or two of coffee swirled in and her eyes were captivating. Like John's! One a soft, velvety brown and the other as blue as a Carolina sky. As Jane May gaped at the girl, a small bird flew out of the mist and came to rest on the child's left shoulder. A chickadee, its jaunty black cap and bib setting off its sweet little white face. As all of the adults turned to the child, the bird spun out a four-note song which hung in the air like glitter. The girl had stopped on the path and was watching the adults. There was a shyness about her, but also a sureness. A grace that suggested the strength and confidence that would come with age and experience.

Jane was mystified. She had no idea who this strange child might be, or why she should be looking out of John's eyes, but Mai Zinni stood, mesmerized, recognition filling her beautiful old tear-streaked face.

"I knew you would come home," she whispered.

Issy broke the silence that followed. "Mama, Mai Zinni, this is Sophie."

Mai Zinni stepped forward and bent over to address the girl on her level. "Welcome, Child. I've been waiting for you." Sophie stepped forward into the old woman's arms as the chickadee fluttered off and perched on a branch overhead, its little head cocked curiously to the side. Jane May was rooted where she stood, as her brain tried to sort through all the new information. *Had Issy and Ben adopted this child. Were they married? Why did Mai Zinni seem to know what was going on?*

All her questions were temporarily quieted when the girl stepped around Mai Zinni and held out her thin arms to Jane, who buried her face in the dark hair and breathed in the scent that is as old and as fresh as time. Youth. Sunshine, lemons and something else . . . cinnamon.

I've been waiting, Mai Zinni had said. Was this child the one? The one that Mai had mistaken Jane for? *Watch for the chickadee*, floated up in Jane's mind. "I have so many questions."

"Yes," Mai Zinni took charge. "We all have a lot of talking to do. Let's have something to eat. Mac, you stay." She saw him on the periphery, turning to slip away, in that quiet way he had of leaving. "This concerns you, too."

And so the little party began to move up the steps and into the small cottage where Mai Zinni and Jane May had prepared a welcoming feast. Issy helped the women lay out the salads and pastries and fresh breads and bring a pot of soup to the table, while Mac and Ben stood on the front porch, looking into the forest over the head of Sophie, who was talking to Period. The crotchety old feline purred and arched her back under the child's tender overtures as the two men talked like old friends.

Mac had, like the true southern gentleman that he was, managed to establish a connection with Ben very quickly. Mac had a way of putting people at ease, and it was evident with Ben. The two men, one grey-haired, short and round, the other tall and young and angular with a mop of floppy brown hair, were so comfortable with each other that an outsider might have thought they had known each other for years. Mac told jokes and Ben responded with an easy, deep laugh. Their voices rose and fell and echoed around the misty clearing. The clearing itself and the forest beyond seemed to welcome this male energy that had been long absent from the place. The mist began to dissipate, and Sophie chased Period around the sun-latticed yard, laughing with delight.

And then, "Soup's on!" Issy's voice rang out, calling them all together to the feast.

Chapter 45

The child at Mai Zinni's feet had wriggled quickly into the old woman's heart and settled there.

Mai Zinni had suspected, ever since Jane had told her that Issy and Ben would be delayed because of the death of their friend, Nina, that something big was afoot. Even if the name, Nina, had been a coincidence (that was what she and John had called Little Star), still, it felt like a sign. The sign that had been missing with Jane. Mai Zinni had a strong knowing about this. And when she'd seen the girl in the clearing, she'd known. The child was the spitting image of Little Star. It had thrown her, at first. She lost track of time and thought it was her own baby for a minute, but then it had all clicked in her mind. *Oh, Spirit surely works in mysterious ways!*

"Twist that last one around widdershins, Lovebug."

"What's widdershins?"

"That means, the other way."

Sophie giggled. "Granny! You're funny!"

Mai Zinni clucked with fondness as she watched her great-granddaughter fashioning a corn dolly out of lavender stalks.

"Tell me again, Granny, about the corn dolly," the little one never tired of hearing Mai Zinni's stories. She'd taken to calling her Granny from the first day they'd met, knowing nothing of their relationship.

"A long, long time ago, First People planted crops and sometimes they grew and all the people were fat and well and sometimes they didn't grow, and the people were hungry and sick. One year, after the crops grew good, someone thought to trap the corn spirit until spring, hoping that she could be put back in the fields, and the same thing would happen the next year, the crops would grow and the people would be strong. So, from the leavings after the harvest, corn dollies were made and kept in the houses until spring. When it was time to plant again, the people brought the corn dollies to the field and buried them, so the corn spirit could be returned to the ground."

"Did it work, Granny? Did the crops grow again?"

"Well, sometimes it worked and sometimes it didn't. But the people had faith and they kept trying. And that's how come we still make corn dollies today. But now I want to tell you another story. One you haven't heard yet."

Sophie sat up straighter and even her fingers paused in anticipation of hearing a new story.

"Keep twistin' or you'll lose what you've got. You're doing good. That's a fine looking dolly." Mai Zinni settled herself deeper into the soft cushion of the old wicker rocker and searched for the beginning of the story.

"I want to stop working on the dolly, Granny. I want to sit in your lap to hear the story." Mai Zinni smiled and reached for the doll that was taking a rough but pleasing shape under the direction of Sophie's nimble young fingers. Quickly tying off the twine that had been left hanging to secure the lavender wands, she then splayed the longer stalks out to form a skirt. Plucking another short piece of twine from the table next to her, she laid it on her lap and put the doll face up on top.

"Okay, but first go pick three big fat fuzzy leaves off that lamb's ear in the kitchen garden and bring 'em to me. Careful not to crush 'em." Sophie scrambled to her feet and skipped off to retrieve the leaves. She knew the plant. Mai Zinni was delighted with how fast she learned. Her curious mind picking up the names, properties, and characteristics of the kindred with lightning speed. It was in the child's blood, after all. When Sophie returned, Mai Zinni had her position the leaves vertically just so at the doll's waist and she pulled the ends of the twine forward and gently tied a knot holding the velvety apron in place. She lifted the doll and danced her side to side while saying in a sing-song voice, "Hi Sophie! Can I be your winter friend?"

"Yes you can! And be my summer friend too. I like you. Don't ever leave me, Dolly, please." The child's delight was contagious, but Mai Zinni was solemn as she spoke for the corn dolly.

"I'm sorry, Sophie, I can only stay with you for the winter. In the spring I have to go back to the Earth, my home. I have a job to do. I have to make the crops grow so that you and all the people can eat. But I will never forget you."

"Oh Granny, that part of the story makes me sad." Sophie's head hung down and she clutched her new friend to her heart.

"I know, Child. Most stories have sad parts." Mai Zinni patted her lap as she spoke and Sophie climbed up and settled in, laying her sweet head on the old woman's cozy breast.

"Why?" A little whine crept into her voice.

"Shh, hush, Little One, and let me tell you this story."

"Does this one have sad parts?"

"Yes, I'm afraid so. But it also has wonderful parts. It's a good mix. Are you ready?"

"Yes, Granny."

Sophia Louisa Trew, was the daughter of Nina Trew, and the soon-to-be adopted daughter of Isabelle and Ben Davis. She was the granddaughter of Little Star Trew, (who had once been called Nina Magena by her mother and father). Sophie's great-grandmother was Mai Zinni Trew, named after a rangy wild thing (Mai means coyote) and a happy flower, by her own mother who was also called Sophie.

Little Sophie smiled and shifted her body until it conformed to the shape of the old woman and listened for the very first time, but by no means the last, to the true creation story of her own life. It was all true, but not all of it was told, not yet. That would come when Sophie was older. There would be no more secrets in this family.

"So you see," Mai Zinni murmured into her great-granddaughter's soft black hair, "I really am your Granny."

"I knew that, you silly," Sophie kept her head buried in that soft breast as she spoke, "but why did my mama's mama leave you?" These words were spoken softly, shyly, as if the child could have some idea of the pain they were capable of inflicting.

"I don't know, Sweet Pea. She was young. She wanted to be someplace else. I guess she was mad at me."

"But why? I could never be mad at you." Sophie's thin arms by now had a death grip on Mai Zinni's neck, and the old woman began to realize that the abandonment the child had suffered was far greater than any she herself had had to deal with. Or at least it was so immediate that decades of grief and regret fell away there and then and all Mai Zinni wanted was to hold this sweet child in her lap and rock her until she knew that she was safe and loved and no one would ever leave her again. If only she could make that promise.

"Granny?"

"Yes, my dear one?"

"Will I ever see my mama again?" Sophie had sat up in Mai Zinni's lap in order to search the old woman's eyes. Mai Zinni could see the hopefulness there and it broke her heart all over again.

"Yes, Honey Bee, you will, one day, but not for a long, long time. And not only your mama, but your mama's mama and my mama and her mama. They are all there in the Land of Beyond. But in a way they are with you all the time."

"Where is that, Granny? I want to see them! I want to go to Beyond." Sophie's plaintive cry broke Mai Zinni's heart.

"You can't see them, but they can see you. They are standing all around us right now. If you're very, very quiet, and you listen with the ears of your heart, you will hear them and you will know that they are near."

One fat tear rolled down Sophie's cheek now and she said, "But I don't have ears on my heart." Mai Zinni pulled the child closer.

"Shhh. Hush now. Be very, very quiet and just listen." The two sat that way in the silence for a long time. So long that Sophie fell asleep in the old woman's arms. Mai Zinni rocked and listened to the birds chirping outside and watched a sunbeam move across the dusty wooden floor.

Soon it would be time for Isabelle and Ben to pick Sophie up. They dropped her off at the head of the path to the cottage every day after school. Mai Zinni met her on the path and Issy and Ben picked her up again before supper time. They had accepted that their Sophie was the one chosen to receive the old woman's ancient knowledge, and agreed to nurture the gift in her in any way they could. After all, she was a direct descendant of the Old Ones who had passed the knowledge down from mother to daughter and father to son in an almost unbroken line. Sophie's grandmother, Little Star, had been raised with the knowledge. She knew it like she knew her own heartbeat. The rhythm of the old words passed orally from woman to woman for untold generations had coursed through her blood and echoed in her heartbeat. But long ago, in anger at her father's abandonment, and fear at what she suspected of her parents' relationship, she had rejected the knowledge, her parents, and her entire heritage, and run away, thinking she could escape who she was.

Little Star's daughter, Nina, whose name was a nod to Mai Zinni and her affectionate nickname for her daughter, hadn't known a thing about her lineage, only the name of the place her people had come from. Little Star had probably felt that she gave her daughter a great gift by raising her wholly unfettered by the past. She never knew of her grandmother or of her own birthright and she never saw Gideon, North Carolina.

But her daughter would know. For Spirit had plans for the Trew women and those plans involved so much more than abandonment and loneliness. The line would continue, almost unbroken. As long as the people had breath, and as long as the mountains stood, proud, ancient, enshrouded in mist, the old ways would always live on in that magical place, called by the ancestors, Shaconage. Land of Blue Smoke.

The End

Epilogue

Jane May Gideon had completed her jubilee year, and what a stellar year it was.

She had stayed in Gideon for four more months after the arrival of Isabelle and her new little family. They had all, including Mac, Charlie, and Nanette, celebrated Christmas in Mai Zinni's tiny cottage in the woods. Everyone brought food and small gifts for each other, mostly found treasures or something home-made. The wee house had been festooned by the women, with help from Sophie and Charlie, with cedar, pine, holly, and galax from the forest and the yard. A small tree had been cut and dragged inside two days before Christmas. Sophie had made it her solitary mission to create the most beautiful, iconic Christmas tree anyone had ever seen. A tree worthy of the pages of the most beloved of the classic Christmas tales. Sophie and Charlie worked for days leading up to the celebration, stringing cranberries and popcorn, gluing construction paper chains and making ornaments of dough, which were baked to porcelain hardness in the old oven. And there were real candles in little brass holders that Mai Zinni found in a musty, long neglected box in her attic. Atop all this splendor, the corn dolly perched, arms out-stretched in joy.

The ragtag group had feasted, sung, danced and toasted each other until the grownups were giddy and Sophie and Charlie had both curled up under the glittering tree and fallen asleep like kittens. The elders had covered the young ones in blankets and tiptoed out into the sidereal splendor of the night and continued their revelry until they just couldn't anymore and then Mai Zinni had invited them all to look up at Orion's Belt, the bridge to home, as it climbed the sky over the mountain. Afterwards, they had collected the sleeping children and taken their leave, muttering sounds of contentment, as they trudged up the trail, flashlights bobbing in the dark.

As for Jane May and Isabelle, after the initial joyful reunion, they found that many of the things that had vexed them about each other, were still in play. The difference was that, in the interim, both had become better acquainted with themselves, and so approached the other with more respect, more patience. Their relationship was and probably always would be a work in progress. Isabelle, in separating, for a time, from her mother, had found in herself a confidence that allowed her to have more faith in her own judgement. Also, in forging a family with Ben and Sophie, she found authority and autonomy, apart from her mother. But she still felt as if a part of her had been ripped away with the divorce of her parents and that caused confusion, which bubbled up from time to time as snappish anger directed, usually, at her mother.

Jane May, for her part, had learned to recognize in herself, her own wounded places, and to react, at least with less ferocity, when those places were triggered by some needy word or dismissive look from Issy. She saw herself as a vessel, deep and wide and capable of holding Issy's emotions, her pain. A friendship between the women, that had not been possible before now, was developing and both of them cherished it. Issy, thrust suddenly and unexpectedly, into the role of mother to a motherless child, came, frequently, to Jane May for advice and affirmation that she was not doing it all wrong. Those occasions were balm to Jane May's heart and probably did more than anything else to heal the old hurts that both had inflicted on each other.

As instructed by the Old Ones, Jane May had written a long letter to Lenny, owning her part in the unraveling of their marriage and the pain surrounding it and thanking him for releasing her. And then she burned it. Just as they told her to. She'd built a fire in a rusty bucket down by the creek in front of her cottage. She had sat by herself as the Milky Way flung itself across the sky like some royal road, holding the letter for a long time in her hands, as she let her mind drift in and out of memories. After a while, an owl called three times and she dropped the letter in the last of the embers. How beautiful and brief the flame that arose from it.

Issy and Ben had decided to stay in Gideon and buy the inn. Jane co-signed on the loan, banking on the success she knew they would make of it. After they'd closed, they'd moved in to the laundry house with Sophie while work began on the main building. Ben's carpentry skills and the artistic vision shared by both promised a warm and beautiful update to the tired old inn.

On a crisp winter morning, Mai Zinni and Jane met on the porch of Jane's cottage by the creek and performed an ancient ritual for cleansing. They burned sage and Mai Zinni shook her small gourd rattle. She placed crystals in each room and then clapped her hands three times in every corner. They sprinkled water from a spring sacred to Mai Zinni's ancestors and lit white candles and chanted incantations of clearing and protection. At the end of the ritual, just before Jane May followed Mai Zinni out onto the porch of the little cottage, she turned in what had been her bedroom and slowly, reverently, removed from her pocket a small statue of a funny little goddess, grinning and fecund, and placed it on the windowsill. "Bless and protect this place and all who enter here," she whispered.

    Cleansed and empowered, Jane May Gideon stood in the clear bracing air beside her friend on the little porch overlooking the creek. "Mai," she said, as she embraced the old woman, who was looking young and soft this morning, "You've changed my life."

    "No, Child, I ain't done nothing. You just let Spirit take your hand and lift you. That was your choice."

    "Umm," she mused, "still I owe you. You've given me so much and I wish I could give you something in return."

    "Sweetling, I'm an old woman and I don't need nothing no more. Just you being your own beautiful self is gift enough for me. Besides, don't you see? You gave me back my lost girl, in a way. I never thought I'd see her again and now to have her very own granddaughter here. My great-granddaughter! No, I don't need no present. What I need from you is for you to go out in this old world and shine. Go and see what you can see. And come back home every now and then."

    Jane May laughed and embraced her friend and mentor again. She knew that she would be back, maybe for good, after she'd rambled enough in the world. The blue mist, like ghost's breath, had wound its stealthy way around her heart, and the kindred were an umbilical cord binding her forever to this place. Arm in arm the two women walked the path back up to the main building, where Issy and Ben and a handful of painters were making the place new again.

"Hey you two, come in for a tour," Ben yelled down from the roof where he was repairing shingles. "Hang on, I'm coming down." He scrambled backwards down the ladder that was leaning again the building and jumped the last few steps. Spinning around in midair, he landed directly in front of the women and snatched them both up in a burly bear hug.

Damn, thought Jane, *I'm going to have to love him after all.* The childlike exuberance that Issy loved in him shone this morning.

They entered the main building and clucked and chattered at the new paint and the newly raised wood-beamed ceiling, which lent a spaciousness that John would have approved of. Jane walked to the stone mantle, which was the centerpiece of the room, across from the heavy oak check-in desk. Someone had, on this chilly day, laid a fire and it warmed the room with its glow as much as its heat. Jane stood in front of the fire with her hands out and then she saw it—a small carved figure on the mantle.

"Where did you find this?" She didn't turn around.

"Oh, it was in a cabinet in the kitchen," Ben said, coming toward her. "Just pushed up behind some cans and stuff, like it was nothing. Can you imagine? The craftsmanship is fantastic. Do you think the old man made it?"

"Yes," Jane said. "John carved it. It's a mountain lion. A lioness actually. It's made from lightning wood. Wood from a tree that was struck by lightning. The Old Ones believe that such wood is infused with great power. It's sacred to them."

"You should take it, Jane." Ben reached around her and lifted the little carving and held it out to her.

"Oh no. No. It belongs here," she said with certainty. "Right here on this mantle." Issy and Mai Zinni had joined them as they talked and Issy embraced both women now.

"I'm sorry I didn't know John. He sounds very special. I'm forever grateful to him and to you, Mai, for taking such good care of my mama."

"Look at you three beautiful goddesses," Ben said, reaching for a camera. "I am the luckiest man on Earth. Stand there, right there in front of the mantel just like that. I want to take your picture. I want to remember this day forever. Jane, hold the carving."

"Damnation!" Mai Zinni sputtered, wiping her eyes with her sleeve, "Boy, you are nothing but a vexation to this old woman."

Ben shined his big toothy grin on Mai Zinni and winked at her just before he snapped the picture.

That photo of three women, all in their prime in different ways, one holding a little carved cougar, one gazing lovingly at the camera, and one laughing full out with crinkly, sparkling eyes, hangs on the wall behind the check-in desk. It hangs right next to a glossy black and white picture of a younger Sophie, and her own mama, Nina, in the New Mexico desert. The picture was taken at sunrise. Nina is kneeling beside Sophie and smiling at the camera, dark hair blowing in the wind, while Sophie is caught in a turn, twisting away from the camera, gazing to the East, her long dark hair, her birthright, the mark of her line, mimicking her mother's.

In a swirl of anticipation, nerves, and a bit of melancholy, Jane had packed an old green duffle bag with a notebook, books, sturdy boots and clothing. Placed carefully into the pages of the notebook was a photo of a family, somewhat awkwardly posed, but all smiling, around a Christmas tree.

In the morning she would leave Gideon and head west. That was all she knew for now, but she trusted that she was on track and the next step would be revealed, and then the next. She'd be back. She knew that much. Her people were here. Her heart was here.

She sat, on this last night, alone by the creek and looked up. There in the vast raven-dark nightfall, spangling the sky, three stars in a row, the belt of Orion the Hunter, the Bridge to Home.

WITH HUMILITY AND GRATITUDE . . .

First, in the mentors I've never met category, I have to thank the author, Sue Monk Kidd. It was her book, *Traveling With Pomegranates*, that gave me the idea to ask for a story. To ask the Universe for inspiration. Strange I'd never thought of it myself, but I hadn't and when I read it in her marvelous book, I made supplication to the gods of fiction, and immediately, I was visited in my dreams by Mai Zinni. I had meant that I wanted a story when I'd finished the memoir that I was working on at the time, but I didn't specify, and the gods saw fit to give me what I asked for right away. It came fast and furious at first, and then in fits and starts over the next few years. This story wanted to be born, to see the light of day so badly, that it would never let me rest for long.

Also Tom Robbins. Reading his books is like taking a little hit of acid and not having to wait eight hours to be able to leave the house—my doors of perception are blown wide open every time I inhabit one of his books for a little while. Reading him has given me encouragement, even a mandate, to raise the level of my writing out of the box and into the wild ether. And in fact, every writer I've read in my life has led me to this point. If you want to be a writer—read!

I'm thankful to the muse and to the characters themselves, all of whom I love. A big debt of gratitude is felt for all my helpers, incarnated and not. Among them Kathryn Magendie, editor and author extraordinaire. She gave me encouragement, advice and a few stern talking-tos, most of which I took to heart and followed. And for finding all those comma splices and split infinitives that we'd missed, I am most grateful. Nancy Carman Flowers, the gypsy queen, sister of my heart, always encouraged me and I am forever grateful.

Beth D'lap, thank you for the artistic inspiration. Deb Lloyd, your contribution through the gift of Reiki, along with your powerful insight, cannot be overstated. Bloom Post, Alison Colberg, Faith Grieger, and Hannah Kim, thank you for holding space for me to do my own healing. I don't think the book could ever have been written without your lovely presences. Stella Osorojos, manifested near the end and offered the suggestion of an *elegant solution*. I hope I've found it.

My three daughters, Kate Folkins, Jenni Roselle and Anna Stout, are the joy of my life. They inspire me always to be the best human that I can be. My sons-in-law, Brian Landis Folkins and Ryan Stout, enrich my life with their talent, their humor, and their love. And they are marvelous fathers to my grandchildren. I had no experience with sons and have been surprised and delighted by these two strong and gentle men chosen by my daughters.

And to Kreszenz, Charlotte, Henry and Sam, the guides who led me into the strange new role of Gigi and made me feel so welcome there, I am forever indebted to you all and my hope is that you will always listen to the voice inside who knows that everything you need is already there. And that you will rise and be beacons of light in the world.

I am grateful always to and for my beloved Bobby, who supports me and loves me, and is my true companion on this strange and beautiful journey. This book would not be what it is now, without his encouragement, his suggestions for how to make things flow better and work more smoothly, and his grammatical and punctuational expertise.

To everyone at Astute Communications in Nashville, who brought this book into being, navigating the murky waters of publishing, marketing, and social media. Especially to Anna Stout for the beautiful cover design. You listened. You heard me. You got it.

And to Lois Inez Weeks, who has known Mai Zinni since time before time and who always believed in me, I am most humbly grateful.

Spirit, the Infinite, God, is always calling us to rise. To rise above our circumstances, our limitations as spiritual beings in physical bodies, to rise up in love and to light the way for each other. My hope is that this story will inspire someone to that. It is my offering.

About A.F. Jordan

A.F. Jordan came late to writing. After a good life in the Deep South, raising three strong, amazing daughters, she stumbled into another good life in the Appalachian Mountains, where she lives with her husband and an aloof and self-contained feline, Smidgeon Bastet Pontouf.

Jordan took notes in the form of journaling for nearly half a century, preparing herself to answer the call of the Muse when it came. She writes in a sweet spot with a mountain view.

Jordan is also the author of We End in Joy; Memoirs of a First Daughter, published by University Press of Mississippi in 2012.